A Scandalous Passion

THE SINS & SCANDALS SERIES

KELLY BOYCE

The Sins & Scandals Series

While there are those who spend their time in modest pursuits, upholding propriety befitting the lords and ladies of the ton, it would seem that for others, scandal is just a sin away...

AN INVITATION TO SCANDAL
A SCANDALOUS PASSION
A SINFUL TEMPTATION
THE LADY'S SINFUL SECRET
SURRENDER TO SCANDAL
A SINNER NO MORE
THE SWEETEST SIN
A MOST SCANDALOUS CHRISTMAS
A HINT OF SCANDAL

*A big thank you to all the readers who enjoyed **AN INVITATION TO SCANDAL**. It was my first stab at self-publishing and your support meant the world. I hope you enjoy Caelie and Spence's story as much as you did Nicholas and Abigail's.*

And, as always, for John – because real life heroes never go out of style.

Chapter One

L ady Caelie Laytham stepped off the busy dock and onto the gangway leading up to the deck of the *Windswept*. The narrow stretch of wood wobbled beneath her feet and she froze.

"Come along." Her mother shot a swift glance over her shoulder, her gaze and purposeful stride filled with impatience. Caelie looked down at the dank, dark waters beneath her and opened her mouth to question once again whether leaving London was truly the best course of action. Then she closed it just as quickly. What was the point? Mother had made her decision and Caelie had already received an earful from her first two attempts to change her mind.

There was no turning back.

Behind her, the noise from the dock rose up and pushed against her. Wagons and carts with their iron wheels clanged against the cobbled streets and echoed in her ears only to be over-powered by raised voices and the stench of fish mingled with salt air and a bevy of other aromas she could not pinpoint nor wished to.

She had spent her entire life in London, yet at three and twenty this was the first time she had ever seen this section of the city. To think her last vision of home was to be a jungle of spars and masts jutting upward into the grey morning sky did not seem right.

Caelie let out a breath and forced one foot in front of the other. The damp wood made for a slippery surface. Beneath her, the Thames churned and splashed between the ship and the narrow wharf. Her stomach roiled at the thought of falling into the disgusting waters below.

Then again, perhaps that would be a much more tolerable fate than the one that awaited her in Italy.

Her mother had informed her a month ago of the journey. Caelie had possessed no notion her mother corresponded with a distant cousin, Mr. Beechum. Not that Mother was in the habit of sharing personal information with her. Still, it had come as a shock when she announced they were to leave London for Italy, as Mr. Beechum had proposed and she had accepted. She claimed the union was their only chance at getting out from under the embarrassment and scandal they had suffered these past two years.

A feat, she made a regular point of mentioning, Caelie had failed to accomplish by securing a proper marriage herself.

She could not fault Mother's accounting of the situation. Society had all but turned their backs on them after Father's scandalous death. Her heart panged at the memory, a wound that was slow to heal.

"Caelie!"

She started at Mother's harsh tone and reached out a hand to grab the rope strung alongside the gangway. "Coming, Mother."

Mr. Beechum would be sorely disappointed if he expected a gracious companion to enjoy his later years with. Edythe, the

Countess of Glenmor, was not known for either warmth or a genial manner.

Caelie cast one last look at the water below then stepped onto the ship's deck. A bevy of activity surrounded them. Men of all shapes and sizes moved along the deck with purpose, heavy loads hoisted onto their shoulders. Profanity peppered their rough-hewn speech, enough to turn Mother's normally sallow skin an almost pretty pink.

Caelie forced back a smile. Something she had grown accustomed to doing around her mother. Amusement belonged to the lower classes, she often said. A lady comported herself in a much more sedate and dignified manner.

Beneath her, the strong sway of the ship did nothing to settle the anxiety tossing around inside of her. She did her best to ignore it. Nothing could be done about their departure. Mother had made her decree and Caelie, as was her duty, followed it. Her cousins had begged her to stay, but pride was a funny thing. She loved Benedict and Abigail dearly, but she would not be a burden to them.

Water lapped against the side of the *Windswept* hard enough to be heard over the chaos on board. Her stomach rolled as each wave mocked her decision.

Caelie glanced about the deck in search of Mr. Marcus Bowen. The ship belonged to a fleet owned by the Marquess of Ellesmere. Mr. Bowen, his man of business, had agreed to ferry them to Italy, though the ship's final destination lay somewhere well south of that.

The ship wasn't generally meant for passengers, but Mother had no intention of backing down from her plans to leave England. Caelie's new cousin, the Earl of Blackbourne, had therefore spoken on their behalf and ensured their passage. He wanted them to travel with someone he trusted, and Mr. Bowen was a close friend.

Unfortunately, Mr. Bowen was nowhere to be found.

"This is indefensible." Mother's sharp eyes searched the deck. Caelie glanced down at the small bag her mother held in her hands. Her gloves creased where she gripped the handles as if her life depended on it. A marvel the wood didn't snap from the pressure. Mother did not tolerate tardiness.

"I'm sure Mr. Bowen will be along promptly." Mother would take a strip off the gentleman if Caelie didn't intervene. It would not get their trip off on the right foot.

Always the peacemaker. Abigail's voice sounded in her head and a lonely pang pierced her heart. She blinked back the tears that pricked her eyes. Her cousins were the closest things to siblings she'd ever had. Her own brother, her twin, had not survived their birth. A fact Mother never failed to remind her of, as if she were somehow responsible.

Being an only child, and not a son, had proven a very lonely existence until her aunt and cousins arrived to live with them a decade ago. They'd brought a welcomed warmth into an otherwise cold home. She would miss them fiercely. But Abigail had married, and Benedict had his hands full as the new Earl of Glenmor upon her father's passing. They had their own lives and, as Mother reminded her, there was nothing left for her there. Her father's suicide following his scandalous affair with the famed courtesan Madame St. Augustine and her own broken engagement to Lord Billingsworth had ensured that.

Abigail's marriage to Lord Blackbourne had improved the situation somewhat, but it hadn't been enough. Though she could show her face in public once again, no one went out of their way to repair old friendships or court new ones.

She remained a pariah amongst the ton. The dream she harbored of finding a husband to love, children to care for, a place to belong—remained well out of reach.

"You there!" Mother barked at a burly man with a large sack of something resting on his shoulder. The man stopped and shifted the burlap sack as if it contained nothing more than a load of feathers.

"Ma'am?" He looked her up and down and Mother's beady eyes widened in revulsion. She recoiled and held her gloved hand to her nose in an apparent effort to ward off the stink of sweat wafting off the large bear of a man.

"I demand you take us to Mr. Bowen this instant."

The large, bushy, black moustache above the man's upper lip twitched. "Might be 'ard t'do, seein' as he ain't har." His voice rolled with the thickness of an accent Caelie couldn't place. Northern perhaps?

"I beg your pardon?"

"He isn't here," Caelie translated. She smiled as she addressed the man in front of her, an attempt to soften the effect of Mother's strident tone. "Has he not arrived as yet?"

"Nah. Won't be either, lassie."

Caelie swallowed the rush of hope, afraid to let it bloom. Had she been granted a reprieve from Mother's forced exile? "Mr. Bowen will not be sailing today?"

"No' accordin' to 'is majesty." He jerked his head toward the opposite end of the ship then continued on his way without so much as a by your leave. Mother let out a huff filled with self-righteous indignation. She did not care to consort with the lower classes, but Caelie did not see how she could avoid it on this voyage. It appeared they were the only ones of high birth on board.

Caelie shifted her gaze to where the man had nodded and quickly realized the error of her assumption. She recognized the identity of the man referred to as *'is majesty.*

"Oh dear."

"We 'adn't expected you, m'lord."

Spencer Kingsley, Earl of Huntsleigh, smiled as he took the two steps leading up to the helm in one leap. His black Hessian boots smacked against the deck and slipped a little where the spray from the water below had dampened the wooden planks. Under foot, he could feel the familiar swell and roll as the waves pushed against *Windswept*. Of all of Grandfather's fleet, he favored this one. It reminded him of freedom. Even the name evoked the sense of being swept away from it all—which is exactly what he planned to be.

"Captain Moresley, my good man." He clapped the old sailor on his shoulder and grinned. "I am afraid Mr. Bowen has been detained. I will be taking his place. Are we set to pull anchor?"

The thinly built shipmaster nodded slowly, one eye narrowing. How a man so lightly built had not blown away on rough seas and wind remained a mystery, but the captain had been at sea for longer than Spence had been alive, first with the Navy and now as shipmaster of the *Windswept*. Time and again, the old man had proven to be the most adept sailor. And not once had he been swept off the deck. Spence suspected the old sea captain glared into the wind and scared it off, much as he glared at Spence now. Suspicion riddled his weathered expression.

"And should I bother askin' on the whereabouts of our Mr. Bowen?"

Spence offered the man his most charming smile but the old goat wasn't fooled for a minute. "Mr. Bowen is occupied with other business." He didn't bother explaining he'd been the one to send his good friend off on a fool's errand; a tactic meant to delay him long enough for the ship to launch and be well on its way before Bowen could arrive and summarily eject him.

Grandfather had given his former ward and now man of business strict instructions that Spence was not to set foot on the *Windswept*. His grandfather had other plans for him. Hideous plans such as marriage and procurement of an heir.

Spence shuddered involuntarily.

"Might I hazard a guess as to who sent Mr. Bowen on this *other business*?"

"You may hazard and guess as much as you wish, Captain Moresley, but I do outrank my grandfather's man of business, do I not?"

He tilted his head to one side. "Aye. I 'spose as Earl and heir that would be the right of it. But I am master of this ship, laddie."

Spence's shoulders drooped. Neither pulling rank nor charm would help him in this instance. Which left him a little out of his depth, as charm was how he attained most of the things he wanted. He would have to apply to Captain Moresley's sympathies, if the old salt hound had any.

"You know as well as I do, Mr. Bowen despises sea travel."

"Aye, he's a land lover, I'll give you that."

"And you do not *need* him for this trip, truly. Do you?"

"No," the captain allowed. "Not me personally."

"And it is imperative that you sail on time to meet the tides and Mr. Bowen's delay could potentially endanger this."

"I'm certain we can manage."

Spence sighed. He was wasting time. Bowen possessed a quick mind, too quick in Spence's estimation. It would not take long before he figured out the supposed errand for the Marquess of Ellesmere was in truth nothing but a ruse.

"Captain Moresley, would it not be better for Mr. Bowen to stay behind? Why the man lost nearly a stone the last trip and was green around the gills for weeks. I am willing and able to take his place. I concede that it is fully up to you who comes aboard your ship, but I am pleading—begging, even—that you allow me to replace Mr. Bowen in this instance."

The captain stared at him for a long moment with eyes an even paler blue than Spence's own—as if the salt air had leeched the color right out of them. Finally, he gave a curt nod. "Fine then, but make yourself useful."

"Useful?" Did the man expect him to haul crates or sacks? Swab the decks?

"See to our guests. They'll be stayin' in Mr. Bowen's cabins. You'll be bunkin' with me."

"Guests?" When had the *Windswept* become a passenger vessel?

Captain Moresley lifted his chin toward mid-ship where two well-dressed ladies who had no business being in such surroundings stood frozen in one spot.

He recognized one of them instantly. The fiery red hair was hard to disguise even with the bonnet tied securely beneath her chin. A few thick strands had escaped and wafted in the air with the wind. "Is that—?"

"Indeed, it is, m'lord. Lady Glenmor and her daughter will be sailin' with us as far as Italy. Mr. Bowen made the arrangements at the behest of your dear friend, Lord Blackbourne."

Spence turned back to the captain. "This is Nick's doing? He said nothing to me about it." Damn Nick. What foolish notion led him to putting two gently bred women on a cargo ship?

"Still want to usurp Mr. Bowen's position on the ship, m'lord?"

This was a most unwelcome turn of events. One to be remedied immediately.

"Not at all." Spence straightened and turned. "I will see to our guests."

Spence set his most charming smile in place, the one that had ladies of all ages bending over backward to do his bidding. He only brought it out on special occasions where his usual charm did not suffice. He'd heard stories from Nick about Lady Glenmor's frigid demeanor. He would need all the ammunition at his disposal if he intended to get her and her daughter back on dry land.

Lady Caelie had recently been jilted by her former fiancé, and given the scandal around her family, her prospects at finding another were dismal, at best. He would be an all too attractive—not to mention captive—target on board the ship. No matter what arrangements had been made between Bowen and Nick, neither lady was making this trip.

Spence crossed the length of the ship and stopped in front of Lady Caelie and her mother, greeting them with a curt bow. "Ladies. Good day. May I escort you from the ship?" He waved a hand in the direction of the gangway. Perhaps not the courtliest way of dismissing them, but he did not have the time for such niceties. By now, Bowen had likely caught wind of his ruse and was on his way to the dock.

Lady Glenmor's gaze slithered down her straight nose and landed on him with all the warmth of a winter's wind blowing off the Channel. Lady Caelie, on the other hand, let hers drop to the deck, her hands clasped in front of her.

Such a shame a lady so lovely to look at lacked even the smallest hint of spirit. She reminded him a little of a damp rag, really. It had been his experience that red hair often coupled itself with a feisty personality, but, if so, Lady Caelie had not been informed. A pity, really.

"What you may do," Lady Glenmor said, "is show us to our quarters." Her voice did little to soften her hard countenance, which Spence suspected had been chiseled from stone by an unskilled hand. Not that she was necessarily ugly, but it did beg the question if the lovely Lady Caelie had been a foundling passed off as blood.

"I am afraid there has been a mistake. We cannot convey you to Italy. Much too dangerous and far too...far. Now, if you would be so kind as to follow me." He held out an arm to Lady Caelie. For a brief second, she glanced up at him with a mixture of relief and hope in her eyes before she bowed her head once more.

But in those few seconds he'd had the loveliest view of eyes so green they rivaled any emerald. Good heavens. He had danced with her on occasion at the behest of Nick; how had he not noticed such eyes? Likely because she kept her gaze averted, much as she did now.

He gave himself a mental shake. Bloody hell, man. What did the color of her eyes matter?

It didn't. The only thing that mattered was getting them off the *Windswept* so the ship could set sail before Bowen arrived. Friend or no, as Grandfather's man of business, Bowen would brook no interference in the Marquess's plans. It mattered not that he loathed being onboard a ship or did not want to leave England. Bowen never considered his own wants and needs, but forever put others' first. In that sense, Spence was doing Bowen a great favor.

That his own interests were served as well only sweetened the pot.

But said interests would not be met if a certain unmarried miss decided to set her cap for him. When women with nothing to lose grew desperate, anything could happen.

Besides, the trip to Italy took weeks and he had never been very good at avoiding temptation. Despite her lacklustre disposition, Lady Caelie possessed an enticing countenance. Too enticing. One did not wave a red cape in front of a bull and not expect it to charge.

Spence avoided innocents as a rule, but it was a long trip and—

The wind hurled itself over the side and buffeted Lady Caelie's skirts and cloak. The strong gust pushed the material against her lithe form to reveal more curves than Spence would have suspected. Blast!

No, it would not do. She must leave and take her battle axe of a mother with her.

"Lady Glenmor, I am afraid we cannot accommodate you. I'm sure my grandfather will recompense you for whatever fare you paid him—"

"I most certainly did not pay him!" She spit the words at him as if the idea of paying for a service left a foul taste in her mouth.

"My cousin, Lord Blackbourne, arranged the transportation for us," Lady Caelie said. Her voice, though quiet, had a clear quality to it. Like bells on a still morning.

"As I have come to understand," he said. He would be sure to have a long talk with Nick when he returned to London, but that would have to wait. Until his grandfather came to his senses and stopped harping on Spence's need to marry, he had no intention of coming back.

"We apologize for the inconvenience. Did Lord Blackbourne not inform you of our plans?" Her crystal voice proved a complete contrast to the strident tones of her mother. Spence questioned her parentage yet again. Granted, her father, the late Lord Glenmor, had been quite the affable type of fellow. At least until he lost his wits.

"He did not. Unfortunately, I cannot allow you passage on the ship. So, if you'll follow me, I will escort you—"

"We are not leaving."

Spence glanced at Lady Glenmor, though not too closely in case he turned to stone. "Beg your pardon?"

"We are not leaving." Lady Glenmor's tone afforded no room for argument. "As I understand, it is the shipmaster who has discretion on such matters and he has not indicated we are to go anywhere. You may show us to our rooms now, if you please."

If he pleased? He did not please at all. Well, he did please, quite well in fact if his last mistress was to be believed, but not under these circumstances and certainly not with the likes of Lady Glenmor, who had all the personality of a scorpion ready to strike.

Lady Caelie's shoulders slumped and she cast a forlorn glance at the dock. For a moment, Spence wondered if she were contemplating hopping over the side of the ship into the churning waters below, but Lady Caelie did not strike him as the type prone to bold behaviours.

The first mate's voice called out over the din for the anchors to be pulled.

Spence spun on his heel and held up his hands as if he could hold back the wind and stop Captain Moresley from doing exactly what he'd asked him to do in the first place—leave port with all due haste.

"No!" He waved his arms, but the melee on deck drowned him out. He rushed forward, dodging burly men who reeked of sweat and fish. He sprinted toward Captain Moresley. The old salt hound's feet were planted firmly on the deck next to the helmsman. When Spence reached him, the captain smiled beneath the neatly trimmed, white beard covering the lower half of his face. "You must stop this instant!"

"Thought ye wanted to leave—with all due haste, wasn't that your wish, m'lord?"

"Yes, but—" He motioned back toward Lady Glenmor and her dull yet delectable daughter. They were no longer where he'd left them. He scanned the deck until he caught sight of the spring green of Lady Caelie's cloak, a perfect complement to her mesmerizing eyes. "Where are they going?"

"I asked Garron to show them to Mr. Bowen's quarters, seein' as you weren't gettin' the job done. Best they get settled and get their sea legs under 'em, m'lord."

The echo of chains pulling the anchors taunted him.

He turned back to Captain Moresley. "No. No sea legs are required. I can't have them here. Lady Caelie is an innocent. This is no place for her."

The captain's whiskers twitched as he smirked. "Don't recall you ever being concerned about a lady's virtue before, all due respect, m'lord."

Spence glared at Moresley but really had little to say in his own defense. Though, truth be told, he preferred widows or wives. He steered clear of innocents. He had no desire to find himself marched to the altar from one slight misstep. But it was a long trip, and Lady Caelie, while lacking in spirit, was a very beautiful woman—

No! She was Nick's cousin. No way in hell could Spence even entertain such a thought. Forget being marched to the altar. Nick would simply drown him in the Channel after beating him within an inch of his life. Which, in his mind, would be a better alternative than marriage. But given that escaping the marriage noose was his reason for being on the *Windswept* to begin with, he had no other alternative but to set the two ladies off the ship, pronto. Truly, it was in everyone's best interest.

"Captain Moresley, I demand you not leave this dock."

The captain locked his hands behind his back and rocked on his heels. "M'lord, as we established earlier, I am the highest authority on this ship. And as such, I am not inclined to stay. As you said earlier, we must stay on time with the tides. And so, we shall."

"But—"

"And were you not adamant we leave to prevent Mr. Bowen from coming on board?"

"Yes of course, but—"

"Then you might want to take a look." The captain inclined his head toward the docks. Spence followed his gaze.

Bowen, always the calmest of men, ran along the cobbled street that lined the dock. His arms gesticulated like a mad man. Spence could see he shouted, but the words were lost to the sounds of the sea, the dock and the ship.

Just as well. Bowen did not appear pleased. Spence would have much to atone for when he finally did return.

"Still want me to drop anchor, m'lord?"

Spence ignored the hint of humor in the captain's tone. He cleared his throat and straightened. "Well, it appears we are underway now, so I suppose there is nothing to be done about it."

"Suppose you have the right of it. Though I might add, the ladies are under my care, m'lord. I won't brook any mischiefs where they're concerned."

Spence fixed his jaw. "I will assume you are referring specifically to Lady Caelie."

Moresley shrugged and grinned. "I've 'eard your tastes run to wives and widows, so I'll be sure and keep my eye on both the ladies, m'lord."

Spence shuddered. As if he would ever entertain the thought of sharing a bed with a cold fish like Lady Glenmor. He'd rather turn celibate. The pretty Lady Caelie was more to his liking, but he kept clear of innocents. They were nothing more than a quick trip to the altar.

Spence had seen firsthand what kind of wreckage marriage wrought.

He would have no part in it.

"I will be on my best behavior."

"Ye best be, m'lord. I'm not opposed to marryin' you at sea, if the lady's virtue is in any way compromised."

The captain's warning sent a slice of icy fear deep into Spence's belly. He would throw himself into the Channel before he ever let it come to that.

Chapter Two

✦

Caelie closed the door to their room and set her satchel on the floor next to her. The neatly appointed room reminded her of Mr. Bowen. Lord Ellesmere's man of business had struck her as a quiet and capable man on the few occasions she had spoken with him. She'd imagined he would be agreeable company, and as he had traveled to Italy in the past, she'd hoped he could ease her worry over the strange world she was being thrust into. If she could do nothing to change Mother's mind, then making the best of a bad situation remained her only recourse.

But alas, Mr. Bowen had not arrived. Lord Huntsleigh had. And, rumor had it, the only company Lord Huntsleigh kept was that of women who had tired of, or buried, their husbands and found the future marquess's charms and handsome face irresistible.

The change did not sit well with Caelie. She had been charmed once before and paid the price for such folly.

She would have to be on her guard. Not that Lord Huntsleigh had the smallest interest in her. When he'd danced with her at Lady Blackbourne's annual party she'd known it had been as a favor to Nicholas. When the set had ended, Lord Huntsleigh made a quick departure. Oh, he did nothing to offend, but neither did he do anything to strike up further conversation. She didn't blame him. In her first foray back into society since Father's death, her nerves had gotten the best of her and rendered her tongue-tied. No doubt Lord Huntsleigh thought her intolerably dull.

She sighed and looked around. A cot had been wedged into a small space adjacent to a three-quarter bed. Their trunks took up residence against the wall next to Mr. Bowen's desk. Set in a small alcove was a tiny sitting area and off of that another room which housed a table that sat eight.

With the extra cot in the sleeping area, their quarters were cramped. It left little room to maneuver and even less hope of temporary escape from Mother, save to venture above deck, which Mother had already strictly forbidden. An order reinforced once again when she realized Lord Huntsleigh would be on board.

The man did have a reputation, after all.

As much as she preferred fresh air and open space, the sight of churning water left her stomach in a state of flux. Perhaps if she hid below deck, she could convince herself she was on dry land, though the sway of the ship beneath her feet did little to encourage this.

"You may take the cot." Mother waved a hand in the direction of the narrow bed without looking her way. Hardly surprising. She often spoke to her in much the same manner she did the servants. Caelie could not remember a time when Mother went out of her way to be friendly to anyone. She treated everyone she met as if they were beneath her contempt, though she had saved the worst of it for Caelie and her father. Was it any surprise that Father had taken a mistress? She could not blame Papa for seeking out warmth and affection elsewhere, not when she had done the same thing after his death.

She shook the memory from her mind and sat down on the cot to take in her surroundings. Two small porthole windows let in a modest amount of light and overhead a small barred window offered a view of the gray sky. It provided enough light to chase the shadows into the corners. The warm, honeyed wood kept the room from appearing too dark and dismal, but not enough to invite a sense of hominess. Though, perhaps that had more to do with the company than the décor.

"Are you certain marrying Mr. Beechum is the right thing, Mother?" Even if Mother was determined to leave London, marriage to a man she had not seen for nearly four decades was a drastic step.

Mother pinned her with a harsh look. "Did you leave us any choice?"

"Me?" But of course, her. Was she not to blame for every folly that befell their family beginning with the death of her twin brother?

"Had you managed to keep Lord Billingsworth's attention, perhaps it would not have come to this, but you failed in that respect, and you failed to capture the attention of a husband after he jilted you. What other recourse did you leave me?"

Caelie dropped her gaze. What choice did she have? Should she have begged Billingsworth not to break off their betrothal? Pleaded with him for mercy? The man had not even had the decency to give her the news personally.

And even if he had, Caelie had not sunk so low as to prostate herself for the likes of Billingsworth. The man had no honor. If only she'd known that sooner, she would have saved herself a world of hurt.

Caelie didn't bother lodging any further protest with her mother. The ship had set sail and begun its journey through the Channel. Not even Lord Huntsleigh's attempt to set them on shore had proven successful.

"I'm sorry I have been a disappointment to you, Mother."

Mother huffed and walked to the porthole. Her uncommon height allowed her to see out of it and she stared toward the horizon in silence for a moment before addressing Caelie once more.

"You still have a small purpose."

Something in Caelie's stomach twisted, though whether that was from the dip of the ship or Mother's words, it was difficult to say. "Purpose?"

"Mr. Beechum has a stepson, Ellis, of whom he is quite fond."

The twist became a knot.

"I see."

"He has indicated there is a dearth of proper English ladies he deems suitable for Ellis to marry. I told him you would be amenable to having him court you, seeing as no one else finds you remotely palatable as a potential wife."

The words cut Caelie to the quick. "You mean to marry me off to him?"

Mother turned away from the window. "Mr. Beechum made it a condition of his proposal that I consider it. I see no fault in his reasoning. It is high time you stopped being my burden. I have done all I can by you and you have failed me at every turn. It is time you begin to do for yourself. It is not as if you have any other prospects."

Caelie had no argument to give. Mother's words were true. She didn't have any other prospects. But that did not mean she wanted to be bartered off as part and parcel of a betrothal agreement made without her consent.

"What if we are not suited?" What if he was horrid or dull or lacked even the smallest amount of wit or imagination? What if he despised her and treated her with contempt? What if they were ill-suited as friends and had nothing tenable to even begin to build a relationship on?

"You will do as you are told. This is the best you can hope for and you will be happy for the opportunity."

Caelie sat on the cot, stunned. Any hope of making the best out of a bad situation flew from her mind, chased out by unpleasant images of her newly decreed future.

Oh, why hadn't Lord Huntsleigh tried harder to toss them back onto the dock!

A short knock on the door interrupted her thoughts. Mother had turned her back once again to stare out the porthole, leaving Caelie to sidle between the two beds to answer the door. The roughhewn sailor they'd first met on deck stood on the other side. He pulled his cap off and revealed a mop of black curls peppered with strands of white. His arms were the width of tree trunks and his chest the size of a barrel. She wasn't sure she'd ever seen a man quite so large or thickly built.

"Cap'n and Lord Huntsleigh wished to convey their invitation to join 'em for sup' this evenin', m'lady. Someone can come and fetch ye when the time comes, if it suits you?"

"That is most kind, Mr.—"

"Garron, ma'am. Just Garron."

"Garron, then. It would be most appreciated. Thank you." Any reprieve from her mother's company was a welcomed one.

The seaman nodded and slapped his hat back on to his thick mop of hair then headed back up the narrow staircase. Each step echoed his departure.

She glanced over her shoulder at her mother. "Captain Moresley and Lord Huntsleigh have invited us to dine with them this evening."

Mother's shoulders stiffened. "I suppose we have no choice in the matter. It would be impolite to decline." She turned. "But do not think for a moment of prostituting yourself to Lord Huntsleigh thinking he will offer a proposal."

"I...prostituting myself?" Fear rippled up her spine.

Mother glared. "You are nothing like me and therefore I can only assume you have more of your father in you. His reckless, hedonistic ways were his downfall, and by proxy, ours. I will not lose the one opportunity we have left by allowing you to squander it on misplaced passion you lack the ability to control."

"I would never!" She swallowed. What did Mother know?

"See that you don't. If I have to sell you spoiled to Ellis Dornam, I will. And do not for a moment believe Lord Huntsleigh will object. His reprobate behavior is well known. He will think nothing of foisting you off on another unsuspecting gentleman if it means he does not have to take you for himself."

Caelie sat back down on the bed and stared at the wall in front of her. Her insides rolled and her head buzzed. Her skin had turned cold and clammy.

Mother directed her not to prostitute herself to Lord Huntsleigh, yet she thought nothing of selling her like a whore to the highest bidder when it suited her own purposes.

She closed her eyes to keep the tears from spilling over.

It was going to be a very long voyage. Though nowhere near long enough when she thought of what waited at the other end.

Dinner proved a dismal affair. Spence had to stop himself from repeatedly checking his timepiece every few minutes, not because it was rude—which it was—but because he could not bear the disappointment when he realized only three minutes had passed since the last time he looked, and not three hours like it felt.

He had done his best to engage his guests in polite conversation, but Lady Glenmor appeared disinclined to utter more than one-word answers in a tone that clearly indicated she did not care to converse further, and Lady Caelie did little more than stare down at her plate and push her food around.

Granted, they were likely unaccustomed to such rudimentary fare as salt pork and root vegetables, but the ship was not equipped for fancy dining, nor should it be given its purpose as a cargo vessel, not a vehicle for passenger transport. Still, the hearty meal did not deserve the tepid response it received from the ladies present.

Spence decided to make one more stab at polite conversation before he gave up, submitted to rudeness, and abandoned the ladies to Moresley's capable hands. Penance, he decided, for the man agreeing to Bowen and Nick's decision to transport the two of them to Italy in the first place.

"And what is it that takes you to Italy? A grand tour?" He wouldn't blame them for trying to escape the scandal that still hung about the Laytham name. Perhaps Lady Caelie could find herself a nice Count to marry. Heavens knew she'd had no luck in London after her father's death. Still, banishing the poor girl from the only home she'd ever known seemed a rather harsh punishment for a scandal she had no part in.

"Indeed, no," Lady Glenmor said. Her words came out clipped and cold.

"I see." He glanced at Lady Caelie in the hope she would add to the conversation. He noted she looked rather drawn, paler than when she'd first arrived on deck.

She cleared her throat yet her words lacked the clarity her voice had possessed above deck earlier in the day. "A wedding, my lord."

"Ah, a happy occasion then." Though in his estimation

weddings were anything but happy. Rather they were the beginning of the end. But saying so would be impolite. Had the Laythams found an Italian match for Lady Caelie?

"And who is the lucky gentleman who has proposed to make you his wife?"

"Oh no." She shook her head and her skin turned even paler. At this rate, she would be translucent in no time. "It is not I. It is Mother. She has accepted a proposal from Sir Bernard Beechum, a distant cousin."

The news surprised him, though not more so than the strange relief he experienced knowing it was not Lady Caelie being bartered off like unwanted baggage. Not that it improved her situation any. She had still been forced to leave her home and remaining family to follow her mother to a place unknown to her.

Sympathy settled in his belly. He knew the agony of being subjected to the decisions of others.

"I see. Well, felicitations on your upcoming nuptials, Lady Glenmor. I wish you happy." He tried not to choke on the word. He wasn't sure happy existed within Lady Glenmor's scope of emotions. In fact, he was quite certain it did not.

She inclined her head, the only acknowledgement his good wishes were received. "You may wish my daughter the same. She will be courted by Ellis Dornam, my cousin's stepson."

"Oh, then two marriages are in the offing?" While he felt sympathy for Lady Caelie, at least with her already spoken for, the chances of him being trapped into a situation he wished to avoid lessened considerably.

She glanced up at him and the anguish he saw in her bright green eyes stopped him cold. She did not want this. She did not want this at all. But as quickly as she looked at him, she looked away.

"Lord Huntsleigh, Captain Moresley," Lady Caelie said, lifting the linen napkin to her lips. "I'm afraid I am feeling quite exhausted by the day's events. Would you please excuse me? I believe I will retire to my room."

Captain Moresley beat Spence to his feet. "By all means, m'lady. Shall I escort you to your rooms?"

Lady Glenmor stood as Moresley made his way to the door. "That will not be necessary, Captain Moresley. Thank you."

"I insist," he said. "The sway of the ship can sometimes make a body a bit unstable if you're not used to the motion. Lord Huntsleigh and I shall ensure you both reach your room unharmed."

Spence came around the table and held out an arm to Lady Caelie. If forced into escort duty, he would take the lesser of two evils. Not that Lady Caelie had an evil bone in her body. Clearly, she took after her father, which made her impending fate all the sadder. So far, he had managed to evade the marital noose. The same could not be said for his companion.

He smiled down at her in a show of sympathy, but with her head bowed, she did not see.

Bowen's rooms were at the far end of the hallway from Captain Moresley's. The narrow span of the hallway made for tight quarters and Spence had to tuck Lady Caelie close to fit them both through side by side.

Her quiet voice floated up over the sound of their footfalls. "Forgive me, my lord. I did not mean to cut the meal short."

"It is of no matter. Do not trouble yourself." He could not remember a time in recent history where he had been so happy to see a meal end.

"I'm afraid I have yet to find my sea legs. Every time the ship moves one way, my stomach goes the other. It's rather disconcerting. I'm sure a good night's sleep will put me to rights. I promise I will not be a burden for the duration of the trip."

Spence glanced down at her. Her red hair appeared darker in the shadows of the hallway and reminded him of low burning embers. She lifted her chin to meet his gaze. The lantern the captain carried swayed a few feet ahead of them and a beam reached back and lit her eyes. It rendered Spence speechless as he stared down at the brilliant emeralds. They really were quite captivating.

A jolt of heat cut through his body and he bit down until it passed.

"Perhaps a little fresh air will help as well. Mr. Bowen claims it does." Spence had no idea on the veracity of such a claim. He'd been born with sea legs and the currents and waves did not affect him.

"Does being on the water bother him as well?"

"Very much, though he will never say so." He likely shouldn't rat Bowen out in such a way, but part of him wanted to keep her talking, to gaze upon those pretty green eyes of hers and listen to her sweet voice. Such a stark contrast to her mother's unkind utterances. How had Lady Caelie survived an entire life under that type of tyrannical rule and yet still maintained a sweet nature? For she did, which surprised him. He'd thought her dull and timid, and though he remained on the fence about her timidity, he was no longer certain he would call her dull. Quiet, perhaps. And sweet. The voice alone—

"Do you worry about him then?"

Her question surprised him. She had cut to the quick of the matter. "I suppose I do. Mr. Bowen is far too stoic to complain or let my grandfather down. That is why I thought I would save him from his stubbornness this one time and make the trip in his stead."

"How very kind of you, my lord. You are a good friend."

His kept his smile in place, though the statement made him a bit of a fraud. He had wanted to save Bowen the torment of another sea voyage, yes, but he'd also come aboard for selfish reasons, to avoid being forced into marrying some tepid miss and making them both miserable.

Spence let out a sigh of relief when they reached the door to Bowen's quarters. These newfound revelations of Lady Caelie's true nature left him unsettled. The image he'd had of her had begun to crumble and beneath its thin layer a picture, far lovelier than he had originally anticipated, evolved. The dichotomy intrigued him. And it was never good for him to be intrigued. He would do well to remember his purpose here—to avoid marriage.

Lady Caelie was an innocent and bound for a new life with the promise of a husband at the end of it, not a treasure awaiting his discovery. He had no right to rob her of her future or to saddle himself with something he did not want.

He must avoid Lady Caelie as if she carried the plague, otherwise he may find Captain Moresley making good on his promise to marry him at sea.

C aelie sat atop a crate half covered with a coiled rope thicker than her arm. She could not imagine the strength it would take to lift such a thing. Thankfully, a small corner of the crate remained uncovered and she did not have to find out.

Though several men milled about, tending to duties or standing watch, the deck remained quiet. At the far end of the ship a man stood at the wheel, and above, higher up, men sat in what appeared to be a large bucket built around the mast.

The murmur of their voices, however, could not rival Mother's snoring as it echoed off the walls. Between the snoring, and her roiling stomach, sleep had evaded her. Resting had done her no good as far as acclimating to the sway of the ship. What little she had eaten at dinner swam around until she feared it would reappear if she did not act. With no other recourse, she had pulled her wool pelisse over her night dress and crept above stairs in the hope Lord Huntsleigh's suggestion of fresh air would find her some relief.

Caelie's shoulders hunched against the cold air. Dampness clung to her skin and hair until one refused to warm and the other began to frizz. Still, she favored it over her confinement to the tiny room and Mother's snoring.

She pulled in a lungful of salty sea air. Water and blackness stretched out before her as far as the eye could see. Even the moon and stars had trouble lighting much beyond the ship's prow, giving her the sense that they travelled into nothingness. The image left her disconcerted and a little frightened. Everything familiar had been stripped away and she was left adrift with nothing recognizable to cling to.

Save for Lord Huntsleigh, she supposed. Though his demeanor made it obvious he was not happy about their being aboard. She did not blame him. If anything, she shared his unhappiness. In fact, when he had yelled at Captain Moresley to keep the ship from leaving port, hope had surged within her. But, like every other hope and dream she'd harbored over the past two years, this one too came to naught.

She pressed her hand against her stomach through the thick wool of her coat. A chill had settled deep into her bones. Would she ever be warm again?

It was horribly inappropriate for her to be up on deck alone and dressed in such a way, but she hadn't dared try to dress herself before she slipped out of the room. Mother had insisted they did not require a ladies' maid and could do for themselves for the duration of the voyage. In truth, none of the maids in Benedict's employ had wanted anything to do with a long voyage tending to Lady Glenmor. Caelie wished she'd been given the option to stay or to go.

Except that wasn't true either. She had been given the option. Abigail had all but begged her not to go, as had Benedict and Aunt Lorena. But Abigail was newly married and expecting her own child in the summer, and Benedict would not be far behind. If she stayed, she would only be a burden, a reminder of the scandal that had tainted the Laytham name. Perhaps with her gone, things would go easier for Abigail and Benedict.

Either way, Mother claimed her cousin, Mr. Beechum, would provide them with what they needed. Whether Mr. Beechum's claims of fortune were true or exaggerated, Caelie could not say. Nor could Mother for that matter, though she insisted the older gentleman, the third son of a respectable viscount, could be trusted. How his family connections translated to a stellar character, Caelie did not know. She'd met plenty of gentlemen born to high rank who lacked both character and depth. She'd almost married one of them.

The spray from a wave as it hit the side of the ship interrupted her thoughts before she could travel again down that particular path. Just as well. She had no desire to relive the end of her relationship with Lord Billingsworth, nor the fateful day he broke off their engagement only a fortnight after Father's death.

"Oh, Papa. I do miss you." Despite the final year of his life when his obsession for the famed courtesan, Madame St. Augustine, had caused him to lose his mind and take his life, he had been a good man. A kind one with a gentle heart. It had been Papa who had fostered her love for books when Mother insisted she did not need to fill her head with such nonsense and learning to be a proper lady.

And it had been Papa who had insisted they give Abigail's family shelter after his estranged brother's death, despite

Mother's strict objections. For that, she would be forever grateful. Abigail and her family, their love for each other and for her, showed Caelie what a true family could be. Papa had tried his best to soften Mother's dislike toward her. He had made a point of reminding her she was loved, that she was beautiful and that she deserved a happy life. She had believed him. The alternative had been too ugly to contemplate.

Until the ugliness came home to roost and she'd had no alternative.

Losing Papa in such a public and scandalous way had been hard to bear. Caelie had crawled inside herself for the better part of the year. Easier to hide than to face the censure in Society's gazes and the whispers behind their fans. And as it turned out, the ton appeared just as happy to have her gone. Abigail, Benedict and Aunt Lorena had done their best to shield her from the gossip, but it did not change the truth.

And the truth was, she had been all but exiled.

Tears sprouted in the corner of her eyes. She had not allowed herself to cry once since they'd buried her father. Mother would not countenance such messy emotions. She considered it undignified and, in her estimation, Papa didn't deserve it.

But now, alone for the most part, Caelie let them come. She did not have the energy to hold them in any longer. She closed her eyes and let the salt and spray from the sea brush against her skin and mingle with the tears until another wave of nausea rolled through her. Her fingers dug into the edge of the crate as she waited it out. When she opened her eyes again, it took a moment for her vision to adjust to the blackness the meager light of her lantern could not penetrate.

"Lady Caelie?"

Caelie jumped at the unexpected voice and turned in her seat. The motion sent her stomach into a tailspin and she pressed her hand against it as a the dark figure approach. She had recognized the voice instantly and was not surprised when the bobbing light drew close enough to reveal Lord Huntsleigh's lean, athletic figure.

She closed her eyes again. Dear Lord. She swiped at the tears on her cheeks then fisted her hand around the neck of her pelisse. What a sight she must present—boots, coat and a nightdress, her hair in a long, thick braid with frizzy pieces poking out and wafting about her head in the stiff breeze. Not to mention a swollen nose and tear stained cheeks.

This would not do. She could not be caught on deck alone with him. And certainly not in such a state. There might not be much left of her reputation after Papa's scandal, but she'd like to retain what little did remain.

She swallowed. "Lord Huntsleigh."

He drew closer and stopped a few feet away. The golden light from the lanterns bathed him in an angelic aura, though in truth, he looked much more like a fallen angel than one that might be found plucking the harpsichord and singing a godly tune. His coat, despite the cold night air, hung open, as did his waistcoat, to reveal the stark white of his shirt. The cravat he'd worn at dinner had been removed. Concern lit his pale eyes as he held the lantern aloft.

"Are you crying?"

Humiliation set her face aflame and she swiped at her face once again. "I'm fine, thank you."

He made a face. "I don't believe that for a minute."

She tried to look indignant but the ship chose that moment to dip and it was all she could do to contain her supper.

Lord Huntsleigh motioned toward her. "Push over, then. I'll keep you company."

She shook her head which only made her dizzy. Oh heavens, would this ship never stay still? "No, really. That would be wholly inappropriate."

A smirk lit his handsome face and the light from the lantern made his blue eyes dance. "Lady Caelie, you are sitting on the deck of a ship well after midnight dressed only in your nightclothes and coat. I believe you passed inappropriate several leagues ago."

Had her legs not felt so wobbly and useless, she would have jumped off the crate and run below deck, taking her humiliation with her. As it was, her legs refused to cooperate and the notion of moving at anything beyond a snail's pace sent her belly into turmoil.

She acquiesced to his earlier request and moved over. He sat and gazed down at her.

"Pray tell, what brings you up here to cry your eyes out at such a late hour?"

Caelie lifted her chin. "I was hardly crying my eyes out. I feel ill, that is all. I thought your advice about taking in the fresh air might help calm my stomach."

"And has it?"

"No. I'm afraid it hasn't." Her stomach, as if to verify the veracity of her claim, chose that moment to lurch. She clasped her belly with both hands as if she could hold everything in place.

"And that is why you were crying? I thought perhaps it had something to do with not wanting to leave London. Or what awaited you in Italy with your intended courtship."

"I did not intend a courtship at all," she bit out. Her anger flared but she quickly tamped it down as she always did, though this time it went with more reluctance and left behind a bitter taste.

"I see. I suspected as much."

"How?"

He tilted his head and gave her a long look before he spoke. "You did not seem happy with the news."

Happy. She did not recall the last time she had been truly happy.

"I should go," she said. His presence made her far too aware of her state of dishabille and his estimation of her feelings came far too close to the mark to make her comfortable. "It is not proper for us to be alone together."

Lord Huntsleigh's mouth quirked to one side and a strange tingle overrode the churning in her belly if only for a few seconds. "Have you never done anything improper?"

Caelie did not know how to answer that. She lacked the quick wit of a practiced liar, but she could hardly confess her sins to a rake such as Lord Huntsleigh. With his reputation, he might take it as an invitation, or worse, think less of her.

He chuckled. "I guess we all have our secrets, do we not?"

"And what are yours?" She had not meant to say the words aloud, but they popped out before she could think better.

Darkness invaded his eyes. Or was that only the way the shadow dipped and swayed? "I do not wish to marry. At all."

Caelie twisted her lips to one side. "I do not believe that is any secret, my lord." Even she, who had been in exile for the better part of two years, knew the future Marquess of Ellesmere was a consummate bachelor who avoided the altar with the same fervor a fox did the hound.

He shrugged and laughed. "True enough."

She studied his sharp profile as he stared out into the darkness. He truly was a remarkable specimen. Both rugged and yet refined, he maintained a devil-may-care aura about him that made you wonder if he took anything seriously. His charm was legendary amongst the ladies of the ton, nevertheless Caelie detected a warmth lurking beneath the smooth exterior he presented. In fact, once he had sat next to her on the crate, the cold in her bones had disappeared and been replaced with a—

She cleared her throat. She really must go back to her

cabin. "Lord Huntsleigh, as I said, we really must not be up here together. I should—"

He waved her off. "I promise I will tell no one of this rendezvous if you don't. Besides, what if I left and you were swept overboard by a rogue wave?"

"I am not sure that is the rogue I need to worry about," she muttered.

"I am wounded." He placed a hand to his chest but the grin he wore told her otherwise.

His smiled left her tongue-tied. If he had a mind to seducing the ladies of the ton, that was the smile he should use, not the practiced smirk of a charmer he produced at the drop of a hat.

"I suppose I have a rather unsavory reputation, but I assure you, Lady Caelie, it is lies. All lies."

She knew well the power of rumor. "Is it?"

He smiled. "Gullible little thing, aren't you?"

Her insides reeled and she swallowed, rushing the words out of her in the hope further conversation would make her forget her roiling belly. "I try to see the good in people, my lord."

"Ah. And has that been a successful endeavor for you?"

"No. Not particularly."

Her stomach pitched. She floundered for another topic of conversation to distract herself. "If you do not marry, what will happen to the Ellesmere title? Are you not the last of your line? I would think providing an heir would be of utmost importance."

"You sound very much like my grandfather when you say that." He squinted and leaned in close. His shoulder brushed against hers and he smelled of salt air and sandalwood. "Are you my grandfather in disguise? I would not put it past him to hide out here and try to thwart my escape."

His closeness rattled her as much as the undulating waves. "Is that what you are doing? Escaping?"

He pulled away and shot her a guilty glance. "Perhaps."

"No wonder you were so upset to find two women on board."

The ship dipped and rocked suddenly. The motion tossed her against Lord Huntsleigh's side and sent her stomach in several different directions. She winced and tried to calm it, with little success. She pulled in a breath through clenched teeth.

"Lady Caelie, do not take this the wrong way, but you look positively ghastly."

She nodded as another wave of nausea hit. Her stomach heaved upward. Propriety forgotten, she jumped from the crate and rushed to the side of the ship where she promptly christened the waters with the meager contents of her supper. Only when she finished did she realize Lord Huntsleigh stood at her side, holding back her hair with one hand, his arm the only support keeping her upright as her knees wobbled and her strength gave out. If he let go, she would crumple to the deck in a pile of wool, linen and misery.

Lord Huntsleigh bent and lifted her into his arms. "I believe this would be the optimal time to see you back to your room, my lady."

Chapter Three

S trange, how Spence had believed the *Windswept* to be the safest place in the world to avoid the marriage trap. Yet, here he was, with a beautiful innocent in his arms and he on the way to her bedchamber.

Fate surely had a vendetta against him.

Despite Lady Glenmor's original plan to foist her daughter off on her cousin's stepson, Spence was a far better catch. Likely the Countess would jump on the opportunity to attach her daughter to a man of means and title. A feat she had been unable to accomplish in London, where the late Lord Glenmor's kin were still trying to shuck off the indelicacy of his scandalous end. Marriage to someone of Spence's rank would be considered quite a coup and, given her cousin's recent marriage to Blackbourne, wipe the stain of scandal off for good.

He shifted Lady Caelie's weight in his arms. The curve of her hip pressed uncomfortably near his groin. He tried not to think about it, but his mind continued to stray there without shame.

Bloody hell.

He had approached her with only the most altruistic of intentions when he saw her sitting topside, alone and in the dark. Why did every good turn he tried to do of late spin topsy-turvy on him?

"Mother is a heavy sleeper," his little piece of baggage mumbled.

"I beg your pardon?" He kept his voice low, though it hardly mattered. He might as well shout at the top of his lungs. His fate was sealed and short of throwing himself overboard, he saw no escape from it.

"Mother is a heavy sleeper."

He stopped walking.

She continued, her voice barely more than a whisper. "If you are quiet, you should be able to assist me to my bed and slip out without anyone the wiser."

Had she just offered him a reprieve? Most women he knew —in fact all who were not already married—would be more likely to cut off their own arm than pass up the opportunity to drag him to the altar. Obviously whatever illness plagued Lady Caelie had skewed her judgment. Still, he was not one to pass up a sudden boon of good fortune.

After all, nothing untoward had happened between them. Should he be unfairly punished when he had only been looking out for the lady's welfare?

"Very well then. Can I count on you to keep our little run-in to yourself?"

She nodded then fell silent.

He did the same. Better not to belabour the point in case she changed her mind.

When they reached her room, he eased the door open and encountered the most ungodly sound he had ever heard.

"Mother snores."

The thin light from the lantern dangling from his fingertips, led him to the empty narrow cot. He set her feet on the floor, but continued to hold her against him so she did not collapse. She was a slight little thing and a sudden surge of protectiveness took hold. He shrugged it off. He did not need such complications.

He eased her down onto the bed. "Your coat, my lady?" He didn't want her mother to wake and find her dressed as if she'd been walking about. Lady Glenmor did not strike him as the type to take such a thing lightly.

He brushed her fumbling hands aside and undid the buttons. He did have a certain amount of experience in this area and he was eager to beat a hasty retreat.

"Thank you," she whispered, as he pulled the coat from her, leaving her in her shift. Once he had her tucked in, it struck him how small she looked beneath her blankets. Vulnerable. Something tugged at his insides but he ignored it. Or tried to.

"You're welcome."

"Lord Huntsleigh?" A sudden urgency filled her voice.

"Yes?"

Whatever she had been about to say was lost as she dropped her head over the edge of the bed and voided her stomach yet again. Spence shifted aside just in time to avoid being hit.

Bloody hell!

Her breaths came in rapid succession and her fingers clawed into the mattress. Other than that, she did not move. In the larger bed next to Lady Caelie, her mother's snoring ceased. Spence's heart thumped in his chest until his ribs vibrated from the force.

He froze and, in a moment, Lady Glenmor's snoring resumed. He tiptoed over to the small chest of drawers and removed the porcelain bowl and linen towel. He dropped the towel on the floor and swiped it over the mess with his boot.

The smell wafted up and turned his own stomach. He kicked the towel aside and put the bowl in its place.

"I have set the bowl beneath you, my lady. I will leave you now."

She nodded, but only barely.

Spence straightened and retraced his steps back to the door. Once on the other side of it, he heard her retch yet again. He hesitated. When the retching stopped, he heard what sounded suspiciously like a sob. Then another retch. He pinched the bridge of his nose.

The vision of her hanging over the edge of the bed, her body trembling, reached out and grabbed at his heart, squeezing until he, too, felt ill. He could not leave her like this. He pressed his forehead into the wall and banged it lightly against the doorframe.

"Bloody, bloody hell."

He clenched his teeth and marched to Captain Moresley's cabin at the end of the hall.

S pence had waited as patiently as he knew how for Doc to make a prognosis, but eventually the need to know got the better of him.

"How is she?"

He was not prepared for the gravity in Doc's tone. "It does not look good."

"She will recover, of course." Spence made the statement with all confidence. Bowen often felt ill on-board ship and he managed to get along.

"There's no tellin' if she'll gain her sea legs. But if she doesn't..." Doc's voice trailed off and he shook his head. The craggy old man had, like Captain Moresley, served in the navy and spent most of his life at sea. Whether he had any true doctoring skills, Spence could not say, but Captain Moresley trusted him, and Spence trusted the captain. "There isn't much to her as is, m'lord. She can't go long like this without its takin' its toll."

Spence drew closer and glanced down at Lady Caelie's slight figure. If she were to lose weight over the length of the trip, there would be nothing left of her but skin and bones. What would he say to Nick—or worse, Abigail—if Lady Caelie did not rally?

"What can be done?" Lady Glenmor's cold tone reached across the room from where she sat at Bowen's desk. She had been angry at being awakened from her slumber, even more so when she realized the reason, as if her daughter's condition was something Lady Caelie had done on purpose to make things more difficult for her mother.

"I think we'll 'ave to set her ashore, m'lord," Doc said.

Lady Glenmor stood. "I beg your pardon? Set her ashore?"

Doc waved a hand at Lady Caelie. "She's not got the stamina to put up with this much longer. Best for her if we dock at the nearest port and set her off."

Captain Moresley nodded his agreement with a grunt. "Portsmouth is closest. We can be there on the morrow. From there, transport can be arranged for her and Lady Glenmor to return to London once Lady Caelie's well enough to travel."

Spence shifted. Setting the two women ashore certainly solved his problem of having them on board, but worry nagged him. What if it was more than sea-sickness? What if they left her and Lady Glenmor in Portsmouth and Caelie took a turn for the worse? Did he not have an obligation to Blackbourne to ensure his family's safety while under his care?

"We will not be set ashore," Lady Glenmor said. Her voice held the quality of iron.

Spence's anger peaked. Did she not care for her daughter's

well-being at all? "I see no other alternative, madam. Lady Caelie is not well enough for sea travel. Look at her, for pity's sake!"

But she didn't. Instead, she glared at him. "*I* will not leave this ship."

Her clarification sent a chill deep into Spence's bones. He must have misunderstood. Perhaps the lady was in shock. Or denial.

"There is no other choice. You must accompany your daughter."

"I will not." She gave the decree with the same feeling as if she were saying she would not go to market. As if the two things were equal.

"Your daughter—"

"My daughter has been a burden since the day she was born. She has brought me nothing but misery and disappointment. I have had to practically barter myself to make a better life for us where she failed to do so, and now she thinks to rob me of even that? I will not have it."

"You will not have it?" Spence repeated the words as if she had spoken to him in a foreign tongue. The woman was mad. "It is not as if she did this on purpose."

Lady Glenmor made a snorting noise. "Doubtful. She did not want to go. She made that much clear. How do I know this isn't some ploy of hers to return to her old life? Well, so be it. I will not be set ashore. Lord Ellesmere promised me safe passage to Italy and I will have it."

Spence blinked. *I. Me.* Not *us* or *we.*

"Do I understand you correctly, madam? You expect us to set your daughter ashore *alone* and leave her behind unprotected?" Disbelief battled with disgust until neither could be claimed a definitive victor.

"If she wants to return to London, fine. Let her see this

ruse to its conclusion and see how well she does fending for herself without my protection. I wash my hands of her."

The audacity. The cold, unmitigated gall of what she suggested staggered Spence and for a moment, he found himself speechless.

"What of her reputation, madam?" He had skirted around his knowledge of Lady Caelie's condition. The lie had slipped easily off his tongue when he told Captain Moresley he had just happened to pass by the cabin door when he heard her being sick. Thankfully, Moresley's concern over his passenger's welfare trumped any further questions he may have had for Spence as to what he'd been doing at that end of the hallway to begin with.

"Her reputation?" She barked out a laugh. Spence had never heard a more mirthless sound. "Thanks to her father, none of us has any reputation left."

"Captain Moresley can order you off the ship, madam."

She stood and pulled herself to her full height. "I will find passage on the next."

"And leave her behind?" Did a colder, viler woman exist than this? He did not think so.

Lady Glenmor's expression hardened further. "I will do what I must."

Before Spence could respond, she strode from the room without a backward glance. He turned to Captain Moresley. "You'll set her off the ship with her daughter, will you not?"

Doc placed a cold compress against Lady Caelie's brow. Her skin had turned a sickly grey-green color and dark smudges appeared beneath her closed eyelids. Had she heard the things her mother had said? Or were those judgments nothing new to her ears?

Tears and perspiration ran down her pale cheeks. She looked like death. How much more could her body withstand before it came to claim her? They had to set ashore.

He realized Moresley had not answered him. "Captain?"

"I'll give the order to set ashore in Portsmouth," Moresley said. "We will figure something out from there."

Caelie had some awareness of the goings on around her, though they faded in and out depending on the endless cycle of heaving the empty contents of her stomach and recovery from that.

Mother's caustic words she remembered.

She has brought me nothing but misery and disappointment.

Those words would scar the surface of her heart for a long time to come, but the sentiment had not surprised her. Caelie had kept her eyes closed and did not try to protest. Not that she'd had the energy to do so. Lord Huntsleigh's vehemence in her defense surprised her. Only Abigail had ever gone toe to toe with Mother in the past on her behalf. Unfortunately, Lord Huntsleigh met with the same amount of success as her cousin had.

If she'd been able, she would have told him to save his breath. Mother's mind, once made up, was an immovable object.

She was on her own.

What would become of her?

The conversation around her had become garbled after that, lost to the heaving of her stomach and the pounding in her head. She had never felt so ill in all her life.

Blackness claimed her and, not until she sensed a movement different from the accursed lolling of the ship, did she pull herself out of it. Salty sea air hit her face with a burst of cold and damp. She welcomed it—a vast improvement from the stale, fetid air of her room. She tried to pry open her eyes. Had they reached port?

Fear tightened its grip. Would they simply set her on the dock and be done with her?

"You've got what you need then, m'lord?" Captain Moresley asked from somewhere near.

A sigh. A hesitation. "Yes. Garron has loaded the carriage."

"Any luck finding a suitable chaperone?"

"None I would consider suitable. Once we are settled, I will make a more in-depth search."

"Safe travels then."

Caelie must be misunderstanding the conversation. Surely, Lord Huntsleigh did not plan to set ashore with her? Without a chaperone? She could not allow it! The sheer disaster of such folly was...was...

"Be careful then. The coach road is still heavily traveled this time o' year. You'll not want to draw attention until you've secured someone."

"Rest assured I shall take every precaution."

While Lord Huntsleigh's promise gave her some relief, it was not enough. If they were caught, it would be the end of her.

She tried to lift her hand to protest, but like her lids, the limb refused to cooperate. The harder she tried, the faster the blackness curled around her and pulled her down into its inky depths.

After that, sensations ran from one into another. A pair of strong arms lifting her. The warmth of a firm body that chased away her chill. The scent of sandalwood and...and...what? Quiet voices murmuring over her. Steady footfalls. Then finally, blessedly, a soft mattress beneath her that did not dip or sway.

She slept again after that and when she awoke her eye lids complied when she tried to open them. Thick quilts covered her and sunlight filtered in through a window where a body held the curtain back to be silhouetted by the light. A gentleman's silhouette.

She was alone in a bedroom with a gentleman?

She swallowed. Her throat had the consistency of sand but her stomach had stopped roiling about. "Lord Huntsleigh?"

The curtain fell back and shadowed the room. Lord Huntsleigh turned around and walked over to the bed. He leaned down, a hand on either side of her shoulders so she had no choice but to peer up into his handsome face.

"You're awake then?"

She nodded. "And Mother?" Just in case, on the slim chance—

Lord Huntsleigh shook his head.

No. Of course not.

"We are at The White Stag in Hampshire. I will be escorting you home to London."

She blinked. He would be? Her gaze swept the room on either side of her. It was relatively large and, save for them, horribly unoccupied.

"Are we...alone?"

"Yes, since you did not bring a lady's maid with you on your travels."

"None of servants wished to make the trip," she said by way of explanation. "Mother had not endeared herself to the staff."

"I find that most shocking." But the twist of his lips told her otherwise. "I will find you a lady's maid. Until then, there has been a bit of a wrinkle."

She did not care for the sound of that. "What kind of wrinkle?"

A cloud darkened his light blue eyes. This close, she could see the flecks of gray in them. It gave them a depth she had not expected.

"It turns out Lord Iber's wedding to his third wife is taking place at his country estate not far from here. The guests have begun to congregate and as such, all the other rooms have been let."

"All of the other rooms?"

"Yes."

"Then you are staying—"

"Here."

Her eyes widened. "But you cannot!" She struggled to sit up but he pushed her back down and she had not the strength to fight him.

"Fear not. I have told them we are married."

"We are m-married?" But how could they be? Was that even legal? What exactly had occurred while she slept? Her head buzzed.

"Not truly!" He held both hands up as if to fend off the notion. "I'm not that much of a martyr. I told the innkeeper we are Lord and Lady Thurston. Newlyweds who had embarked on a grand tour until we discovered you did not take well to sea travel and we were forced to disembark."

"I see." She could not fault his story. It held enough of the truth to be believable and enough of a lie to keep her reputation from being ruined beyond reparation. But that still did not address the sticky issue of where he would sleep. "Then you are staying in here?"

He grinned. He really was almost too beautiful for words, despite the fact his hair was a bit wilder than current fashion dictated and his clothing, while impeccable, made her think he had dressed in a hurry. Still, his physical appeal could not be denied. His lean, muscular body lacked the thickness one often saw in well fed lords with a penchant for overindulgence. The dichotomy of this wild refinement made him too angelic to be the devil, and yet his reputation made him too devilish to be an angel.

Unfortunately, at the moment, neither side looked at all pleased.

"How would it look if I left my new wife to fester in her illness all on her own? Not very gallant, I think."

"No. I suppose not." Still, the idea of being cared for by Lord Huntsleigh did nothing to calm her stomach that had seen its share of woes already.

Her gaze skirted the room once more. There was only one bed.

"But where will you sleep?"

He straightened. "Do not worry over that. I have ordered some broth to be made and sent up. Try to get some sleep and I will awaken you when it arrives. You need to eat to keep your strength up. The sooner you are well, the sooner we leave this place and get you home to London."

Her eyelids drooped as if on command and only as she drifted off did she realize Lord Huntsleigh had not answered the question as to where he would be sleeping.

Chapter Four

S pence paced the hallway outside the door of her—their
—room. The edge he walked on was sharp and thin
indeed. If the crowd of guests attending Lord Iber's
wedding recognized him—or worse, her—the ruse would be
up. She would be ruined and the only way to repair her reputation would be for him to marry her.

The thought left him sickened.

The noise from the common room crept up the stairwell
to taunt him. He stopped and leaned against the wall next to
two of the trunks Garron had already brought up the staircase.
He'd asked Garron to leave them outside of the room to avoid
disturbing Lady Caelie's sleep. The burly sailor had volun-
teered to accompany them to act as a driver and what not,
though likely Captain Moresley had also instructed him to
ensure Spence be on his best behavior.

The captain needn't have worried. He was not so fool-
hardy as to tie a noose around his own neck.

Spence rubbed a hand down his face. How had his plan of
escape gone so awry? It had been foolproof. Send Bowen on a
fool's errand to delay his arrival, race him to the *Windswept*

before Bowen discovered his intent. But from the get-go, things had not gone as planned. He'd had to convince Bowen of the legitimacy of the errand, not an easy task. His friend knew Grandfather's business so well that even after he'd agreed to it, a glint of suspicion remained in his eyes. Why, they'd barely pulled up anchor and begun to leave the dock when Bowen arrived, running toward them, yelling and dodging vendors of all kinds.

He had never seen Bowen so angry. Spence would have much penance to pay when he returned, even though he'd left a letter with his solicitor to be delivered after his departure, explaining to Grandfather the ruse he'd perpetrated and that it was not Bowen's fault.

Not that Grandfather would be angry with Bowen. He treated the man like family, which in Spence's mind, he was. But he did not want Bowen to feel he'd somehow failed in his duties to Grandfather. He knew how much pride he took in carrying them out properly.

He'd taken every step needed to ensure everything went as planned and he could escape London and the disastrous fate that awaited him there—marriage.

He shuddered.

He had witnessed the catastrophic nature of the institution firsthand. His parents' epic battles had left an indelible impression on him as they waged war against each other. By the time he was nine their lives had become a constant contest to see who could cause the other the most hurt. It did not seem to matter that he was caught in the middle.

How many times had he begged them to stop, to be nice to each other?

Be nice to each other.

He'd been such a hopeful child. Not to mention a blind fool. Their deaths had ended that, though. When they died, the truth glared him in the face. There had never been any hope. How could there be? Marriage was nothing more than a prison that held no hope for escape or pardon. Survival could only be found through affairs or vice. Or both.

The bevy of married women Spence had bedded, and their husbands who had mistresses of their own, only reinforced the veracity of that belief.

Yes, marriage was an institution to be avoided at all costs.

Yet, when he tried to do just that—while doing a good turn for Bowen as well—Fate, with its warped sense of humor, decided to throw Lady Caelie and her heinous mother in his way.

The sudden turn of events went beyond absurd.

Heavy footsteps sounded on the wooden steps used by the servants. A few seconds later, Garron's jovial voice joined the footsteps as he hummed an unrecognizable tune. Once he'd reached the door, he swung the trunk in his arms and set it down next to the others.

"How is she?" Garron pushed the trunk against the wall with the others.

"As helpless as a mewling kitten." He'd requested the local doctor and received word the man would be there once a Mrs. Cranston had delivered her baby.

"Can't say as I 'eard her doing much in the way o' mewling, m'lord. She's been a right stalwart type, if you ask me."

"Which I didn't." He didn't need the reminder of Lady Caelie's virtues. He'd had the great misfortune of seeing enough of them when he'd tucked her into bed. Her mother had not seen fit to dress her before they left; leaving her in the same linen shift she'd been wearing when she first fell ill. The lack of care galled him.

"Seen men twice her size cry more over a splinter than she did bangin' at death's door."

The image of Lady Caelie going toe to toe with the Grim Reaper did nothing to improve Spence's mood.

"She is not banging at death's door. She will be fine. I'm sure when the doctor arrives, he'll tell us she'll be ready to travel in a day or two and we can quit this place and be on our way." Not that he was in any rush to return to London, but the longer they were together, the greater the chance they'd be discovered.

Still, he had to admit Garron had the right of it. Lady Caelie had been quite stoic in the face of adversity. Even when he told her they were to share a room she did not faint away from the horror. She was not pleased, of course, but she'd voiced little in the way of objection. Though whether that was because she possessed a sensible nature and understood nothing could be done about their situation, or because her mother had never allowed her to express an opinion, he could not say.

He only hoped her sensible nature extended far enough that she would not expect him to do anything so foolish as marry her for real because of this short-term imposition. He had, after all, been on his best behavior. Well, other than that one peek when he'd tucked her into bed.

He'd regretted it immediately. That one glimpse had hinted at a wonderful treasure, ripe for discovery. Gentle curves, lush skin and—

Hell and damnation! It had been easier when he'd thought her dull and ordinary.

"We need to leave as soon as possible," he said. "Tomorrow perhaps. Or the next day. If we stay too long, we risk being recognized."

He made it a habit not to debauch innocents. He had some morals, questionable though they were. But he was also a man, and the more time he spent in Lady Caelie's company, the more he realized her true beauty.

It was a dangerous combination.

Garron crossed his arms across his barrel-shaped chest.

"We'll leave when she's well enough to travel and no' a moment a'fore. Settle yourself to it, laddie. I gave Captain Moresley my word I would see to her safety and I mean to keep it."

His eyebrows shot upward. "Settle myself to it?" When had he abdicated control?

"Aye. Now go tend to your *wife*. Better you stay out o' sight as well, with all these lord and ladies millin' about. Now, if you'll excuse me, m'lord. Seems the innkeep 'as a bevy of fine-lookin' daughters. Think I'll get m'self some of that stew they offered."

Garron turned and disappeared down the servant's staircase. Spence stared at the man's broad back as he left. It appeared Lady Caelie had captured the loyalty of Garron. The burly ox refused to budge an inch on his proclamation. It wasn't until Garron had disappeared from sight that Spence realized the trunks still needed to be hauled into the room.

"Bloody hell," he muttered.

He opened the door and then grabbed the leather strap on the end of one trunk, hauling it inside. When he finished his task, he quietly walked to the edge of the bed. Lady Caelie remained still. He leaned down close enough to feel her breath against his skin. Her color had picked up somewhat, but when he laid a hand upon her cheek his concern returned.

Was she too warm?

The fear that hovered in the back of his mind rushed to the surface. He could not afford for her to catch a fever. He touched her face once again. Definitely warm.

What did he do now? His particular skill set did not include nursemaid. Mr. Brampton, the innkeeper, had several daughters. Perhaps one of them could assist. He strode out into the hallway but balked as he glanced over the railing to the common room below. It had filled to capacity with the arrival of a group of dandies. Spence returned to their room. He couldn't chance going downstairs and being recognized.

How long until the doctor arrived? Spence knew little about the birthing of babies, but he guessed expelling another human from one's body was not a quick endeavor.

He racked his brain and tried to think back to his own childhood. He'd been uncommonly healthy, rarely catching more than the occasional case of sniffles, but there had been one time as boys that he, Bowen and Nick were climbing trees. His foot had slipped on a weakened branch and he'd tumbled to the ground. Nothing had been broken, but he had managed to bump his head.

He'd been put to bed and the doctor called. He had no recollection of what they had discussed, though he did remember Mother had stopped by briefly, kissed him on his cheek, blamed his father for Spence's fall, then left again. It had been Grandmother who had stayed with him. She'd sat on the edge of his bed and wiped his face with a cool cloth while scolding him for partaking in such a dangerous activity.

"Such a foolish boy. What would I have done if I'd lost you?" Worry had lined her face.

"I'm sorry, Grandmother. I promise I won't climb the tree again." She gave him a dubious look. She was right to do so. He'd loved climbing trees. Oh, he would keep his promise and not climb that particular tree again, but he'd climb all the others and they both knew it.

"I hope you never know the heartbreak of burying a child," she whispered as she pressed the cool cloth against the bump on his forehead. Blood pounded beneath the skin and bone, but the cool cloth and her soothing touch made him feel better somehow.

Perhaps the same would help Lady Caelie. Spence walked over to the chest of drawers and poured cool water from the washstand ewer into the bowl. A small towel hung nearby and he soaked it, then carried both to the night table next to the bed.

The mattress compressed where he sat on its edge. He wrung out the cloth over the bowl and placed it on Lady Caelie's forehead. After a few minutes, he drew it down one cheek then the other. A small sigh escaped her. It must be helping. He dampened the towel again and slowly pulled it down her slim, graceful neck and onto the exposed skin above the dipped neckline of her shift. She'd moved about after he'd settled her and the covers had slipped downward. He forced his gaze to go no lower than her chin.

He did not need that kind of temptation. He had been several weeks without a woman since he'd broken off his affair with the Duchess of Franklyn. The woman had become rather demanding, as if their relationship had some deeper purpose than slaking their lust. The situation had left a bad taste in his mouth and he had not sought out new companionship since. The bulge straining against his trousers after only a few moments of touching Lady Caelie suggested he should have.

He kept his breathing even. If he kept his thoughts pure and his gaze fixed elsewhere, it would be fine. He could do this. Surely, he had not sunk so far into depravity that he could not minister to the needs of a lady—no! No, that was the wrong way to think about it. He was not ministering to her needs. He was...he was...

Lord, she had the most delectable skin.

Sweet Judas! He yanked his hand away from the swell of her bosom where it had inadvertently dipped beneath the shift while he'd kept his gaze averted. It was not averted now, however. Now it had firmly fixed on her breast. The linen shift did not allow much in the way of modesty and he had a perfect view of a softly rounded mound.

His body tightened. The messages his brain sent to his eyes to look away were ignored. Lady Caelie stretched and took a deep breath. Any hope he'd had of averting his gaze lost as her breast pressed more fully against the linen until the budded nipple came perilously close to spilling over her low neckline. God help him but he wanted to lean forward and put his mouth on that eager little bud and know its taste.

Alarm bells clanged loudly in his head until they deafened, and still he sat there like some green boy while unexpected desire strained his groin and good sense until it dangled by a thread.

What was wrong with him? He couldn't be doing this. If Nick ever caught wind of it, he'd drag him to the altar—after beating him within an inch of his life. He considered Lady Caelie a part of his family now. This behavior was unacceptable. He needed to gather his wits and—

"Lord Huntsleigh?" Lady Caelie's quiet voice threaded through the noise in his head. "Might I inquire as to what you are doing?"

"I beg your pardon!" Spence jerked his hand away even though it had been nowhere near the breast his gaze had coveted. "I—I—"

She stared up at him, her eyes widened in expectation.

"Nothing. My mind wandered..." Did a more pathetic excuse exist?

"As did your gaze, apparently." She reached for the recalcitrant quilt and pulled it to her neck.

"You were flushed and I...I thought to cool you down with a damp cloth." Where the devil did the cloth go? He looked around only to realize it had slithered away and hung on the edge of the bed.

"I see."

What had he done? She had bewitched him. What else could explain it? Why, he'd been contemplating taking her breast into his mouth to draw in her sweet taste. What would have happened had she not awakened?

"I meant no disrespect." The words possessed a hollow ring.

"What did you mean?"

He closed his eyes. Her question was not said with accusation but rather...curiosity. If only he had a suitable answer to satisfy it, but the truth was far too scandalous to speak aloud. Here he had feared discovery by the crowd down below, as if they were all that stood between him and the reading of the banns. Instead, *he* had been the enemy, his own desires lying in wait to sabotage his quest for freedom. He'd been trying to do her a service and instead he'd walked straight into a trap of his own making!

"Forgive me." He ground his back teeth together. "I am not used to playing nursemaid to innocents."

She smiled then and the gesture surprised him, but no more so than her actual words. "You may rest easy, my lord. I have no intention of repaying your kindness by demanding you make amends."

Had he heard her correctly? "I don't understand?" He had convened them into a room acting as man and wife. He had leered at her near-naked body like a boy with his first woman. He had touched her and thought of doing so much more. If she demanded he preserve her reputation and marry her, honor dictated he had no other recourse but to agree. What woman in her right mind would pass up such an opportunity? Especially a woman who had no other prospects.

"While I do not condone the liberty you took, I am willing to overlook it this once. Consider it payment of the debt I feel toward you."

"Debt?"

"You did not have to leave the ship and see to my well-being."

"Of course, I did." What other choice did he have? Her mother had made it clear she cared not what happened to her daughter. Lady Caelie was Nick's kin now and helpless, given her state of health. What kind of man would he be if he had left her sick and unattended on a dock in Portsmouth? He may be a cad and a reprobate, but he had not abdicated his honor yet.

"I know you do not want to return to London. Your reticence toward marriage is quite well known, my lord. While my own prospects would be much improved if I were to demand recompense for our situation, I have no desire to marry a man who would only despise me for it. It hardly seems a recipe for happiness, does it?"

"No. I suppose you are right." He had seen the damage resentment wrought. It was his worst fear.

"Then we are agreed."

"On what exactly?"

"You will, going forward, not take such liberties and I shall forgive this incident. There were no witnesses. No one will be the wiser. It will be as if it never happened and I trust you will not allow it to happen again."

I trust you.

She shouldn't. The image of her breast and the softness of her skin burned their memory into his consciousness. It would be a very long time before he forgot the way desire had erupted throughout his body. Longer still before he could honestly confess, he did not want to experience it again and see it through to its conclusion.

The sensation left him wholly unsettled.

"I should go see what is taking the broth so long."

"Thank you. I think I may be a bit hungry. That is a good sign, is it not?"

"I suspect so." Spence stood and gave his coat sleeves a sharp tug. He did not tarry longer. He didn't dare. He marched from the room and took the servant stairs two at a time. He would hire one of Brampton's daughters to attend

Lady Caelie, even if he had to pay her a King's ransom to do so.

He did not dare chance her reputation being left to him, regardless of her misplaced trust. Not when her innocence, and his freedom, hung in the balance.

Chapter Five

A soft knock sounded at the door before it creaked open. Caelie lifted her head from the pillow, expecting to see Lord Huntsleigh. He had made himself scarce the past two days as she convalesced. He had checked in on her, and of course he had slept here. She found him one morning stretched out between the two chairs by the fireplace looking less than comfortable, not that he had complained.

One of Mr. Brampton's several daughters checked on her throughout the day, ensuring she had enough to eat and that her health improved, which it had. She had reached the point of her recuperation where the four walls were closing in on her and she craved fresh air. She had walked across the room yesterday after Lord Huntsleigh had left and did not fall on her bottom, though her legs did wobble. Her stomach had recovered well and today, Elsie, the oldest daughter, had promised to bring her something heartier than broth and bread.

Caelie pushed herself up onto her elbows as the door opened fully. It was Elsie who poked her head through, not

Lord Huntsleigh. She ignored the pang of disappointment. She liked Elsie. The woman, a few years older than Caelie, had a no-nonsense, practical way about her she found very appealing, but Lord Huntsleigh was far more entertaining. On the occasions when he did stay, he had regaled her with tales of his boyhood and the shenanigans he, Nicholas and Mr. Bowen had gotten up to that sent his poor grandmother into fits.

The stories were amusing and demonstrated the affection he obviously felt toward his friends. He thought of them as family, the brothers he never had, including Mr. Bowen who had been raised as the ward of Lord and Lady Ellesmere. This affection only served to improve her opinion of Lord Huntsleigh and as the hours whittled away, so did the reputation he had as a scoundrel. In truth, the future Marquess of Ellesmere was a good man masquerading as a rascal, though she did not doubt a little of the rascal remained.

She flushed at the memory of two days ago when she awoke to find his gaze fixed upon her breast, a look of rapt desire burning bright in his blue eyes. It both thrilled and frightened her. Thrilled her, because she had never had a man look at her in quite that way before—as if he wanted to eat her up. And frightened, because of how her body had responded. Warmth had spread throughout her, languid and heavy. She'd reveled in it, breathed it in. Wanted more.

The sensation shocked her. She'd feigned indignation; afraid if she didn't, he would think her loose. A woman who gave in to such scandalous passion would surely invite more. But her indignation had no strength to it, nor did it dispel the sweet ache that pulled between her legs.

Elsie approached the bed and behind her two of the younger girls appeared dragging a tub.

"Lord Thurston sent us, m'lady. He thought a warm bath would help make you feel better."

"How thoughtful of him," she said. She shook the

memory from her head. She must be on her guard. She could not risk Lord Huntsleigh discovering she struggled with the same weakness her father had for such wanton desires. She did not want to share her private shame.

"Come then. We'll get you out of bed and ready while they fill it up."

Once the other girls had finished filling the tub that had been set up by the fire, Elsie dismissed them.

"Do you have oils or soaps, m'lady, that you would prefer to use?"

"Oh, yes." Abigail had gifted her with a set of soaps and bath oil that held the essence of wildflowers, Caelie's favorite. "In the bottom trunk."

Elsie strode across the room and lifted the top trunk onto the floor as if it weighed next to nothing. She opened the bottom trunk and carefully set aside the underthings. "You like to read, m'lady?"

"Yes, very much." Her face flushed. She had stashed several books in her trunk when Mother wasn't looking. "I know it isn't considered very ladylike, but—"

"Pish," Elsie said with a wave of her hand. "A lady has as much right to read as any man, is my opinion."

"Do you read?"

Elsie returned and poured a small amount of the oil into the bath then reached down a hand to mix it into the water. "I do, mum. My ma taught me when I was a girl, a'fore she died. She'd been in service before she married my pa and the house-keeper 'ad taught her, thinkin' she might elevate her prospects. Didn't work too much for her, but she thought it might do me some good."

"And did it?"

"Lean your head back, m'lady," she said and poured an ewer of water over Caelie's head, wetting her hair. "I suppose it didn't do me no harm. I know my letters and numbers and I taught my sisters, though some of 'em learned better than the others." Her wry tone made Caelie smile. She had longed for siblings, but the closest she came was to share a womb with her brother. How different would Caelie's life have been if he had lived?

An idea struck Caelie as the heat from the water seeped into her bones and the scent of wildflowers washed away the smell of illness that had clung to her like a bad dream.

"Elsie, do you enjoy your job at the inn?"

"Oh, I suppose it ain't too bad, m'lady. It wasn't the life I 'ad planned for, but it's the one I 'ave."

"What did you plan for?"

"Guess I thought Rabbie and I might have a passel of children, grow old together."

"Rabbie is your husband?"

"Was, m'lady. He died in an accident shortly after we were married. I came back home then. Didn't seem much reason to stay where I was without my Rabbie." The sadness that bled through Elsie's words touched Caelie.

"You must have loved him."

Elsie laughed a little and sunk her hands through Caelie's hair and massaged her scalp with the soap Abigail had gifted her with. "At first, I thought him a stubborn mule, but he worked hard and he treated his horse with a gentle hand, so I figured he had a kindness to 'im underneath his stubborn hide. After a fashion we learned to love each other."

"I'm sorry for your loss." She didn't know what else to say. She knew the pain of losing someone suddenly, but she suspected losing a husband brought a whole different kind of pain. Her Aunt Lorena had buried her husband and Caelie could tell a part of her had died along with him. The rest of her carried his memory around like a constant companion.

"That's mighty kind of you, m'lady. I thank you for that.

Lean back now and we'll give you a good dunking and get all the soap out."

Caelie did as the woman bade, one of Elsie's strong hands holding most of her weight while the other pulled through Caelie's mass of curls. When she finished, she handed Caelie the soap and washcloth.

"Think you can manage?"

"Yes, thank you." She took them from her. As she washed herself, she mulled the idea she had been considering. It made a good kind of sense. Smart and efficient, Elsie had proven herself competent. Caelie had never hired an employee before. That had been left up to Mother. She had no idea the things she should ask.

Caelie handed the cloth and soap back to Elsie when she was done. "Can you dress hair, Elsie?"

"Oh, aye. I 'ave seven sisters, m'lady. As the oldest, it usually fell to me, especially after Ma passed on."

"Would you..." She hesitated. How would she pay her? Caelie had no income of her own. Father's fortune had dwindled to nothing by the time he had died and while she knew Benedict would find a spot for Elsie when they returned to London, that didn't solve the issue of how she would pay her now. Then again, Lord Huntsleigh had indicated they needed to find a chaperone, so perhaps he would be willing, at least until they reached London.

"Would I what, mum? Fix your hair for you? Such beautiful curls, won't be no trouble at all. Truth be, it's pretty all on its own. Don't need much in the way of decoration or fixin'. Simple works best to show it off."

Her kind words warmed Caelie. Mother had always lamented her curls. *Dreadful, awful things.* But Mother was no longer with her. She had made her choice to abandon Caelie and as such, perhaps she should abandon Mother's dictates in turn.

"Elsie, would you be interested in taking a position with me?"

Elsie worked another towel through Caelie's hair, soaking the water out of her drenched curls. "What kind o' position might that be, mum?"

"I require a lady's maid, at least until we reach London. Permanently, if you're interested in staying longer."

"Where's your lady's maid now?"

"Oh...I...she stayed on the ship. She'd taken a shine to one of the sailors." Caelie rushed past the lie before Elsie could question it. "We can pay you a decent salary and if you find the position is not to your liking, or you miss your family, we will return you home after we reach London. You've only to say the word."

Elsie's hands slowed and Caelie held her breath and prayed Lord Huntsleigh would not balk at paying Elsie. After all, having her present would benefit them both.

"Ain't never been to London," Elsie said.

"I expect you'll have to discuss it with your father and get his permission—"

"Permission?" Elsie chuckled. "I'm my own woman, m'lady. My decisions are my own to make, not Pa's."

Caelie looked away to hide the surge of envy that filled her. Hiring Elsie was the first decision she had made on her own. Even decisions that should have been hers were often wrested from her control by Mother, who thought she didn't have enough sense to make a good choice.

But Mother was gone. In a sense, she had as much freedom as Elsie now. The prospect proved daunting, yet exhilarating at the same time. She could do and say whatever she liked without being constantly censured. Good heavens, the very idea made her head spin.

"Then you will consider it?"

"I suppose it might be a nice adventure to try somethin'

new, eh? At least for a little while. 'Course, I'd have to help Pa out while I'm here, what with Lord Iber's wedding fillin' us to the rafters. But I will come with ye to London and then we'll see from there."

With the matter of a lady's maid settled, Caelie let Elsie finish her work while her sisters came and removed the water, tossing bucketful after bucketful out the window before dragging the empty tub away.

Once she had the room to herself again, she waited for Lord Huntsleigh's return. She longed to go outside for a walk —she loathed being cooped up—but she could not risk it. She tried to read one of her books, but even that did not hold her attention for long and she took to pacing until her legs tired and finally she pulled a chair up to the window and stared at the stables below.

In time, the sun set, casting an orange glow across the skies. Caelie's stomach grumbled. She had asked Elsie to have a supper prepared for her and *her husband*, to be brought up upon his return. Whenever that would be. Did he intend to stay out all night?

She hated how the thought he might not return rankled her. She had no claim on him. He was her husband in ruse only. Granted, she had enough reason to demand he marry her for real. Marriage to Lord Huntsleigh would certainly eliminate the bulk of her problems, but she had given her word she would not trap him so, and she meant to keep it.

Besides, how good a husband would he make when he treated the institution with the same reluctance he would being marched before a firing squad? She didn't ask a lot out of a potential husband, but she would at least like a man who *wished* to be married to her.

A soft tap at the door made her turn.

"Lady Caelie? May I enter?"

A rush of pleasure sent her to the door which she opened

with a flourish. "Please, come in." She swept her arm into the room but he did not move. Instead, he stood there mutely staring at her.

"Is something amiss, my lord?" She touched her hair self-consciously. Had Elsie's attempts at setting her hair come undone?

Lord Huntsleigh shook his head but his gaze did not waver. Nor did the rest of him. He remained rooted to the spot.

"Would you like to come in?" It seemed strange to ask him, given he had bought and paid for the room. She was but a guest here at his largesse.

"Uh, yes. Thank you. I would." But still, he did not move.

"You'll have to put one foot in front of the other to manage that, my lord."

He nodded and stepped over the threshold. He stopped in front of her. "You look positively stunning. Ravishing, really."

Ravishing? No one had ever called her such. Oh, she had been a celebrated beauty when she made her introduction to Society, but Mother had repeatedly counseled not to let her vanity get the better of her, for she was no more beautiful than anyone else. Quite plain, in fact. And she had that hair to contend with, after all.

"You are kind to say so. Elsie did it. I...I hired her as my lady's maid. I hope that pleases you, my lord."

His gaze started at the tip of her toes and traveled upward until it reached her face. He smiled, slow and easy. The impact of it whistled through her body like a warm breeze and made her legs weaken.

"It pleases me fine."

"Good." She flushed. His perusal had left her...what? Wanting? Yes. But what? What did she want?

She looked at his smile and took in his rapt attention

focused directly on her and knew the answer. She wanted him. The impact of it frightened her.

"I gave instruction for supper to be sent up. Forgive me for being tardy." Lord Huntsleigh closed the door behind him.

"You must be famished, my lord."

"Indeed, I am."

She had meant with respect to dinner, but had the strange sensation he spoke of a different appetite altogether. An unexpected current in the air made the hair on her arms lift and her skin tingle, not to mention other parts of her she did not want to consider. It was as if she had wandered out onto brittle ice and one misstep would send her falling through to the cold water below.

He walked to the table set up near the fireplace and pulled out a seat. "Please, sit down. I do not want you to overtax yourself."

She obeyed his dictate, happy to rest her shaky legs. They made small talk while they waited for the food to arrive, though once it did, Caelie could not recall any of the topics they'd discussed. She'd spent most of her time stealing glances at Lord Huntsleigh. At the fine cut of his jacket, the lean muscles in his legs where he had stretched them out away from the table, and the fluidity in his hands as he arranged and then rearranged his utensils.

By the end of the meal, her entire body had warmed and while she could blame it on the fire next to them, that would be a lie. This heat generated from somewhere deep inside, somewhere she rarely ventured, somewhere that scared her beyond comprehension. She feared this part of herself. It had led her down a dangerous path once before.

They ate quietly, the silence only broken by the occasional comment on the tasty fare provided for their meal. Caelie ate what she could, being careful not to overdo it.

After one of Elsie's sisters came to take the plates away,

Lord Huntsleigh paced about the room like a caged lion. In fact, with his coloring, proud bearing, and agile gait, a lion was a good comparison.

"Please do not feel you need to stay and keep me company if you would prefer to leave, my lord."

"Very kind of you, but I'm afraid the inn is crawling with dandies." Lord Huntsleigh made a face as if he'd discovered the inn had become infested with rats. A description that was not far from the truth, should their ruse as Lord and Lady Thurston be discovered by someone who knew their true identities. "We should consider leaving soon. The longer we stay, the better our chance of discovery."

"I will be ready when you are." She felt much improved and the trip from Hampshire to London would not take overly long. Delaying their departure no longer made sense.

"Good. In the meantime, it appears we are stuck in this room for the evening." It did not sound as if the prospect pleased him.

"Perhaps we could entertain ourselves then."

He stopped pacing and looked at her, one eyebrow arched upward. "Indeed. What exactly did you have in mind?"

Caelie swallowed. She'd forgotten for a moment she shared the room with an expert in seduction. Just that one small movement of his eyebrow coupled with the mischievous glint in his eye was enough to cause a nest of butterflies to erupt in her stomach.

"Do you play whist?" They were two short but surely they could improvise. Anything to take her mind away from the wings battering against her abdomen.

"I do not. Do you play Three Card Brag?"

"I'm afraid not. Mother frowned on such games of chance. She thought them the height of debauchery." But Mother was not here, was she? "Perhaps you could teach me?"

Lord Huntsleigh hesitated, as if giving the idea consideration, then he nodded. "It normally requires four to be played properly, but I think we can make due. Do you have cards?"

"On the night table." She had packed a set away in her trunk for the voyage. She'd pulled them out when reading did not hold her attention. The repeated games of solitaire she'd engaged in had not done much better.

Lord Huntsleigh picked up the cards and returned to the table. "Are you certain you want to learn? This is hardly ladylike."

His words challenged her. Did he think she would swoon at the idea of bucking expectations? Was that the impression she gave him? If so, how tepid he must think her. The need to prove him wrong rushed through her. Maybe she had been a timid mouse before, but only because she'd had no other choice. It had been a matter of survival then. She would have done whatever she needed to in order to escape Mother's wrath. But Mother had abandoned her for Italy and Caelie's survival no longer depended on timidity but on courage. Like Elsie, she was her own woman now.

"I am quite certain, my lord."

"Very well, then." Lord Huntsleigh split the deck in half and shuffled the cards like a seasoned veteran, all the while explaining the game in rapid fire. She picked up what she could then glanced at the cards he dealt her.

It took her several hands before she finally managed to get the basics down. Lord Huntsleigh displayed great patience as he taught her the rules and she could not deny the times he came out of his chair to lean over her shoulder to assist her with her cards left her entire body aflame. As it turned out, the attraction she felt for her instructor became far more risqué than playing Three Card Brag. Part of her was relieved when he reclaimed his seat and announced she knew enough to manage on her own. The other part, however...

Well, best not to think about that.

"Now that we are playing for real, we must ante," Lord Huntsleigh said as he dealt her three cards. "Then, you can either bet, or fold."

"But I have nothing to wager with?"

"Hm." He leaned back and a slow smile cut across his face. "Well, there must be something we can wager."

Chapter Six

Lord Huntsleigh stared at Caelie but his expression had shifted from amused to something else. Something... heated. Her heart picked up speed and she pulled in her bottom lip, sinking her teeth into it to keep from responding. She did not want to say the wrong thing and break the spell that wove its way between and around them.

Lord Huntsleigh cleared his throat and looked away first. Caelie blushed. What had just happened? How foolish to think he held any interest in her. She had nothing to offer. A scandalous name and a depleted fortune. Not to mention, at three and twenty, she drew perilously close to being put on a shelf and left there to collect dust.

"Why don't we wager a question," she said with a smile, as if the strange tension had not occurred. But it had. And it had affected both of them, she could see it in the set of his shoulders, the desire that had sparked in his eyes.

She needed to distract his thoughts away from anything scandalous. As much as her attraction for him tempted her, she could not risk it. Temptation was a slippery slope and waiting at the bottom, ruination and despair.

"A question?"

She nodded. "The winner of the hand may ask the loser a question and they must answer it honestly."

"That seems a far more dangerous proposition than exchanging money."

"Are you afraid to gamble, my lord?"

His gaze narrowed. "Very well then, lay down your cards."

"You first."

Lord Huntsleigh set his cards face up on the table with a flourish. He had a straight run. "You're turn."

She twisted her mouth to one side and set down her hand. "High card. It appears you are entitled to one question, my lord."

"To the victor, the spoils!" He rubbed his hands together with unmitigated glee.

The sight caught Caelie off guard and she laughed. The sensation of it filled her with a sense of...freedom. Yes, that's what it was. Here, society's constraints could not find her. She stayed in a room with a man pretending to be her husband, playing a game that would have sent Mother into a swoon. If caught, her already dismal fate would be worsened; but in that moment, she cared not. No one could touch her here. London was far away. She would have to go back soon enough, but for now she embraced her freedom. She would relish this time for as long as it lasted.

"What is your question, my lord? I am at your mercy."

"What are your plans when we return to London?"

She'd had plenty of time to think about it over the past few days. Her prospects were few and she did not want to be a burden on her cousins. "I thought I might consider employment."

Lord Huntsleigh stopped his collection of the cards and gave her a confused look. "Employment?"

She shrugged. "The chances of my making a suitable

match are rather dismal, I'm afraid, and I do not relish the thought of being a burden to my family or sitting about idle with nothing useful to spend my time on."

"But employment?" He made it sound as if she planned on contracting the plague.

"I will hardly be toiling in the mines. I only wish to use my time to better service than working on my needlepoint and making inane conversation. I have had the benefit of a good education. I could be a governess or teach if I can find a family or institution willing to hire me."

His fingers picked at the corner of the cards as if her suggestion agitated him. She didn't quite understand his response. What did it matter to him what she did?

"Is that what you truly want for your future?"

She avoided his gaze. "I grant you; it is not what I had originally planned for, but my circumstances have changed and it is the one I am faced with."

"What is the future you had planned?"

"That is two questions, my lord."

"No, it is an addendum to the original question."

She lifted one shoulder and gave a small smile. "I suppose the short answer would be marriage, of course. I had hoped for children, a home of my own. A place to belong, a person to belong to." Lord Huntsleigh made a face and she laughed. "I assure you, my lord, marriage is not all bad."

"Is it not?" Lord Huntsleigh crossed his arms over his chest. The superfine wool pulled at his shoulders and diverted her attention momentarily. "I beg to differ."

"You may beg all you like, but not everyone shares your views on marriage. Some of us desire the chance to build a life with someone else."

"Hmph." He sat on his side of the table and stared at her until the hair on the back of her neck stood up and the butterflies that had settled down fluttered wildly once again.

"Will you deal another hand? I believe it is my turn to redeem myself."

He chuckled and dealt three more cards each. "Very well. Let's see what you have."

She placed her cards in front of her and grinned. "Three threes, my lord. I believe you called that a prial and I believe it means I win."

He scowled. "So it would seem. Ask your question then."

Caelie didn't have to think long. Her curiosity had been piqued when they spoke on the deck of the *Windswept* and again now, with his comments on her previous answer. "Why are you so averse to marriage?"

"Ah." He leaned back in his chair and once again crossed his arms over his chest.

"You do not want to answer the question, do you?"

He smiled and there was a warmth to it, a vulnerability that touched something inside of her and ignited it deep within. "It isn't so much the answering part I wish to avoid, but the honestly part."

Caelie returned his smile and propped her elbow on the table, resting her chin in her hand. "Gambling is a risky venture. One should not partake in it if they are not prepared to pay the piper."

A log in the fire tumbled into the embers. For a few seconds the flames rose and illuminated the table before they tapered off and the room became dimmer than before.

"My parents, I suppose. They did not set the best example."

"In what way?"

"That is two questions."

"No, it isn't. It is an addendum to the first question."

"You are a very quick study, my lady. Has anyone ever told you that before?"

She shook her head slowly. A strange intimacy tangled

around them. "I believe there is much more to the story. My parents did not set the best example either, but I do not cower at the thought of taking a husband."

"I do not cower."

Caelie gave him a dubious look.

"I avoid. There is a difference."

"You're avoiding the question."

"You're rather nosy, aren't you?"

"I'm desperate for entertainment." She smiled. "And you lost the wager."

He sighed, then picked at a piece of lint on his coat and after that rubbed at a spot on the table. Caelie sat quietly and waited.

"Very well then. If you must know, my father fell madly in love with my mother."

"Is that not a good thing?"

"It would have been if my mother returned his affections, but she did not. Instead, she flaunted her lovers in his face and mocked his feelings. Their relationship was a series of battles and arguments and physical altercations on both sides that I had the great displeasure to witness."

As he spoke, Lord Huntsleigh's voice grew in strength as did the anger that punctuated his words. He drew an ugly picture. That he had witnessed it all as a child was nothing short of heartbreaking. Her parents did not love each other, but their relationship had never descended to such depths. At its worst, they behaved toward each other with cold indifference, not the heated rage Lord Huntsleigh described.

"You do not have to say more."

He shook his head. "No. You are right. I lost the wager and must pay the piper. It's the honorable thing to do."

"I did not mean to—"

. . .

S pence cut her off. Now that he had started, the words tumbled out of their own accord. He couldn't have stopped them if he tried.

"One day my mother decided to leave my father and take off with her latest lover."

"How old were you?"

"It was just before my tenth birthday. I tried to talk her out of it, tell her that I did not want to leave Nick and Bowen and my grandparents. But she told me to hush. To pack a few things, that I would have a new father and make new friends."

How long had he tried to bury that day? Yet without even trying, Lady Caelie had set the words free and he found himself inside the carriage with his mother once again, racing along the rutted road as if the Devil nipped at their heels.

The carriage moved at a quick pace, faster than was necessary. Spence worried the horses might collapse from the strain. The sky had turned a purplish hue by the time he heard Father's shouts from behind.

He leaned against the window and tried to see him, but by then the darkness had overtaken the day and the only thing visible was the light bobbing in the distance, steadily growing closer. Mother yelled at the driver to go faster.

Spence's teeth ached from clenching them against the constant battering of a carriage not made to travel at such high speeds on rutted roads. Soon his father caught up, his lathered horse level with the window. Mother shouted and cursed; words he'd never heard her speak before. They were silenced when Father's foot smashed against the window and shards of glass splintered around them. Mother had screamed.

Spence glanced up. At some point in his story, Lady Caelie had reached across the table and covered his hand with hers. It anchored him to the present, but not for long.

"Did she stop the carriage?"

"No."

She had screamed for the driver to go faster. Spence remembered little after that. The carriage tilting, the pain of impact. The sickening sound of wood splintering and horses screeching. He remembered bouncing and being dragged, though he had no sense how long any of this went on for.

And then all went still.

Deathly still.

"Both carriage doors were gone, as well as a section of the exterior." It had looked as if a giant had reached down and tore it off. "The carriage lay on its side and through one empty door I could see mud from the road and part of Mother's dress."

Lady Caelie's hand tightened and he lifted his thumb to caress her fingers. The small motion calmed his heartbeat and he continued.

"My head was cut." He touched his hairline where a small scar still remained. "From the glass or the accident itself, I'm not sure."

"And your parents? Where were they?"

It had taken several attempts before Spence had been able to pull himself out of the carriage. He landed where the wheels should have been, but only two remained, one broken and hanging at a precarious angle from the axle, the other still spinning. The horses were gone. The driver laid a short distancd away near a tree, unmoving.

He had called for his mother and his voice shook in the still night air. No answer came. He did not want to go around to the other side of the carriage, fearing what he might find. Darkness shrouded the wooded area. A small fire burned where one of the lanterns had broken upon impact and caught on some of the leaves and underbrush. Spence ran toward it and stamped his feet on the low flames until he snuffed them out. Overhead, the full moon shone down and provided him with a little light. He turned away from the burned ground and a scream caught in his throat.

"Mother was partially covered by the carriage. I could not see her legs. She lay on her stomach, her arms reaching over her head as if she had simply lain down for a nap. I knew something was wrong but fear had paralyzed me."

"Oh, Spencer..." Somewhere he noted she had used his proper name. It was like a balm to his heart.

"My father called for me." Spence remembered wanting to cry, but he could not. He had to be brave. He turned to face his father. Both of his legs were twisted and bent. "His legs were broken and he wore only one boot."

"But he was alive."

Spence nodded. "I went to him. Touched his hand. It was ice cold. He told me I needed to go for help. It was dark and the horses were gone. I would have to walk the road alone. I wanted to be brave, but I wasn't."

"You were only a child."

Spence remembered the taste of fear, tinny and harsh. He took one of the lanterns that had survived the crash and did as his father bade him. "I do not know how long I walked for. It seemed forever. After a bit, I started to run. I yelled for Grandfather until my throat grew hoarse, but no one came. I thought maybe I had gone the wrong way, so I turned back."

His heart pounded in his chest; his memories as real as the day it had happened.

"When I reached the site of the wreckage..." He closed his eyes tight against the memory but it came anyway, as it always did. Her hand over his had disappeared and he desperately wished it back. He needed it. Needed her.

He wrapped his arms around himself and felt her crouch in front of him. He leaned forward until he could rest his forehead against hers and breathe in the scent of wildflowers to ward off the stench of death in his mind.

"You don't have to continue." Her hand touched his cheek and he leaned into it and shook his head. He had no choice. The words kept tumbling out and he didn't know how to stop them.

"When I returned, my father had moved. He'd managed to crawl over to my mother. I can't imagine the pain that must have caused him. He'd taken her hand, as if to offer her comfort. I knelt next to him but...he wasn't breathing."

"And your mother?"

His mother, when he looked at her, stared back at him with lifeless eyes. He bit down and shook his head.

She had been dead the entire time.

They were both dead.

He had failed.

Soft lips pressed against his cheekbone and the warmth of the gesture sent a shiver through him. How could such an innocent kiss have so much power? But it did. He lifted a hand and touched her face.

"Caelie..." Her given name whispered between his lips.

"Yes?"

He didn't know what to say. How to say it. He needed her. He had no right, but he did. Her reputation could not withstand another scandal, and he could not risk what having her would mean for him, but society and its dictates seemed very far away. In that moment, the two of them existed in their own little world where society had no place.

Dangerous thinking, but heaven help him he needed to kiss her. Just one kiss.

But before he could make good on his desires, her fingers gripped his lapels and pulled him closer. Desire flooded through him the instant their lips touched and he let himself go, let himself be lost in the sensation of his mouth on hers.

Chapter Seven

T his must be what it felt like to die. This exquisite torture of Caelie's mouth on his, her body pressed between the alcove of his legs, his hand as it slipped to her back to hold her close against him. Her kiss was that of an innocent and yet Spence could feel the passion behind it begging to burst forth.

She pressed closer to him and the pressure on his groin intensified as the thin tendril of willpower he held onto weakened. She was a beautiful woman, and more than that, she had surprised him. He'd thought her a placid little thing with barely a spark of life in her, but with each passing day she had proven him wrong. She was warm and resilient. Quick witted and intelligent. And passionate. The last had surprised him most of all.

He could not remember the last time he had been surprised.

Somehow, that left him more intoxicated than her uncommon beauty.

All of these things had worked together and enticed him into opening up. He'd told her things he had revealed to no one. Even Nick and Bowen did not know the full scope of what had happened that night. How had she done that? What bewitchment had she used to muddle his brain to such a degree emotions and memories poured out of him?

She had made him feel safe. Such an odd, unnecessary thing, yet he had reached for it the way a drowning man grasped for an extended hand.

He would not reward that by—

Her fingertips traced the line of his jaw with a gentle pressure and in that slightest touch he could feel her character, her strength and her weakness, what she needed, what she could give in return.

God help him but he wanted it all.

Whatever willpower he'd clung to snapped. His arms tightened around her and he stood, bringing her with him. His senses spiraled out of control as her body moulded against his and her mouth opened to accept his kiss. He heard her gasp when he ran his tongue along the inside of her lip and knew when her body relinquished any last shred of doubt.

Spence sunk his hand into the thick, glorious mane of her hair to keep her mouth on his as he backed her toward the bed, a dance he was well practiced at, yet somehow felt new. He eased her down onto it and when she gave him no resistance, he joined her and pulled her close. The length of her fully against him made him long for the moment when he could sink himself fully into her and find himself home—

A sharp rap caught him unaware.

"M'lady? It's Elsie. I've come to help you get ready for bed."

Reality clamoured in. Spence jumped to his feet with such force he stumbled backward and landed on his backside. He sat there, staring up at Lady Caelie in horror, though in truth, it was his own behavior that horrified him.

Sweet Judas, what had he done?

Elsie rapped on the door once again. "M'lady?"

For her part, Caelie looked equally as horrified. She sat up and stared at him then down at the quilt beneath her as if she had no recollection of how she had gone from the table to the bed. He couldn't quite recollect it himself. One moment he'd been lost in his memories and the next, she had rescued him from them.

"Y-yes, Elsie. I'm...yes, one moment please." Lady Caelie's voice had an edge of hysteria to it. She took in a deep breath that pressed her breasts against the scooped neckline of her dress. He looked quickly away. "Lord Huntsleigh—"

Spence held up a hand to ward off...what? Recrimination? Anger? The fact that his life had just been altered forever and there was no turning back? "Lady Caelie—"

She cut him off with a sharp shake of her head. "No."

"No?"

"Whatever you are about to say, don't say it." Her cheeks flamed red, though whether from the passion they had shared or the shame she felt in its aftermath, Spence could not be certain. "This was my doing."

"You were not the only one involved."

"But I initiated it."

"I have compromised you—"

"It was just a kiss."

Except it wasn't. There was much more to it. She hadn't just kissed him. She had changed him. The moment her lips had touched him something inside of him shifted out of place. Spence had kissed more women than he could count and not once in any of those kisses had he experienced what he'd felt in this one. The loss of control, being swept up into something much bigger than his own desires. The sense of coming home.

The idea terrified him.

"Either way, we must m-marry—" He stumbled over the word.

"No."

"No?" He didn't understand. "Is that not what you wanted? Marriage?"

Lady Caelie stood and ran her hand down her skirt to straighten it. Her hair had pulled free of its pins on one side where he'd sunk his hands into it. Lord, it had been soft. Like silk. Just looking at the tumbled mess he'd made of her made him want her all over again.

She squared her shoulders. "I promised you I would not force you into marriage."

"I have compromised you. There is no other choice. You are upset, not thinking clearly."

She shook her head. "No, you are the one who is not thinking clearly. No one knows what happened. There is no reason for such drastic action."

"But—"

She cut him off. "You should get up. I must answer the door. Elsie is waiting for me."

The new maid. Of course. The woman meant to act as chaperone so things like this did not occur. Spence leapt to his feet and brushed off his breeches.

"Caelie." He reached out a hand as she walked past him without sparing a glance and he could not shake the sense he had been dismissed. Dismissed. Him. He could not recall that ever happening before. He did not care for it.

Caelie opened the door where Elsie stood on the other side. The maid's gaze went to him first and then Caelie and a smile played about her lips.

"Please come in, Elsie. Forgive me, I had forgotten I'd asked you to come up."

Thank God she had, Spence thought. He did not dare consider what might have happened had they not been so unceremoniously interrupted. One thing for certain, it would not have ended at *just a kiss.*

"I will give you your privacy," he said. He needed to leave, to regain his beleaguered senses and restore his equilibrium. In the span of a few moments, he'd gone from playing cards, to revealing his darkest memories, to kissing an innocent and nearly more, then insisting they marry only to be rejected.

He needed a good stiff drink followed by several more stiff drinks because none of what had happened made any sense to him at all.

Caelie's heartbeat took its time returning to normal. Elsie bustled about the room pulling down the bed and laying out her bedclothes. What had she done? What he must think of her!

Her heart had broken for the little boy who had witnessed such devastation, who had lost his parents and been left in the dark, alone and frightened. And her heart broke for the man who was still haunted by the wreckage of that day, and all the days that preceded it, creating a vision of marriage he could not shake.

She had meant to offer comfort, but—

"Beg your pardon, m'lady if I...interrupted anythin' between you and 'is lordship," Elsie said as she pulled the pins from Caelie's hair, those that were left at least.

Caelie's skin flushed anew. "That is quite alright. I mean, that is to say you didn't interrupt anything. We were just—"

"Oh now, no need to be embarrassed. It's a natural thing and his lordship is a fine specimen, if you don't mind me sayin'. Though I suppose as lady's maid it isn't my place to say, is it?"

"I would prefer if you speak your mind, Elsie. I don't wish there to be any secrets between us." But there already was, wasn't there. Caelie motioned toward a chair near the fire.

"Perhaps you should take a seat and I will tell you the whole story. Then you may decide whether you still wish to accompany me to London."

Elsie took the offered seat. "M'lady?"

Caelie folded her hands in front of her primly and took a deep breath. "My name is not Lady Thurston."

"It isn't?"

"No. And Lord Thurston is not Lord Thurston. He is Lord Huntsleigh."

"And you are Lady Huntsleigh then?"

Caelie swallowed. "No. I am Lady Caelie Laytham."

"I see." Suspicion crept into her eyes.

Caelie flushed yet again. "It is not quite as awful as it sounds. I am not Lord Huntsleigh's mistress, though I am certain that is what it must appear and the assumption we assumed false identities to avoid."

She gave Elsie a full accounting of her illness on the ship and the need to set ashore, as well as Mother's refusal to accompany her, leaving Lord Huntsleigh no other alternative but to do so to ensure she made it home safely to London.

"It sounds as if Lord Huntsleigh has done you a great service."

"He has. Unfortunately, with only one room available at the inn, we needed to create a ruse in order to preserve my reputation. I assure you nothing untoward happened between us. Lord Huntsleigh has behaved with all due honor." A small lie, but not enough of one to make Caelie feel bad about telling it. After all, she was as responsible as he for what had happened between them.

"Shame." Elsie smiled. "He's a handsome lord and I think you make a right handsome couple. Maisy says he's as charmin' as they get with those blue eyes and devilish smile. Don't know how you can resist. Why, she tried to turn his 'ead every chance she got, but he wasn't havin' anythin' of it. Figured it was on account of you."

"Oh, I doubt that," Caelie said. "He'll be happy to be soon rid of me, I think. Marriage is not something he courts with any great enthusiasm. And I do not want him to suffer any unwanted repercussions for helping me."

"And what about what you want, m'lady?"

"I beg your pardon?"

"If he was willing, would you want to marry him?"

Yes. The answer rushed into her head but she clamped her mouth shut before she spoke it. She could not deny her feelings for him even if she didn't fully understand them, but she would not allow them to rob Lord Huntsleigh of the freedom he so deeply coveted.

"I would prefer to marry a man who returns my affections. But if I have any hope of doing that, I will need to arrive in London with the appearance of having had a proper chaperone and lady's maid. Are you still willing, Elsie?"

Elsie patted her hand. "Of course, I am. The way I see it, sometimes a body needs to do what a body needs t'do."

Relief welled inside of her. "I appreciate your understanding, Elsie, and your assistance in this matter. I have spoken with Lord Huntsleigh and he believes we should leave within the next day or so. Will you be ready?"

"Of course, m'lady. You've only to say the word and I'll be ready. Now, what say we get you ready for bed before 'is lordship comes back? We wouldn't want 'im to see you in a state of undress, given the circumstances."

"No, we wouldn't." Though the circumstances she had in mind were likely far different than the ones Elsie referred to.

After Elsie had left, sleep refused to come. Caelie tossed and turned until she gave up on sleep and stared up at the ceiling barely illuminated by the stoked fire.

Likely Lord Huntsleigh would not let the matter of the intimacies they had shared drop. If he brought up the matter of marriage again, insisting they had no choice, should she agree? She wanted to marry a man who wanted to marry her, yes, but given the passion that had erupted between them so swiftly, could there be more there than Lord Huntsleigh recognized? Could he have feelings for her? He had revealed a deep secret to her after all. That had to mean something. And if not affection, something existed, did it not? Perhaps whatever had stoked their desires could in time develop into a deeper affection.

He would need to marry in the end. He could not escape it. Eventually, Lord Huntsleigh would run out of time and places to hide and would be required to provide an heir to the title. Would it be so awful if she filled the role? They could provide each other with what they needed—she a husband and a family; he an heir.

The idea pleased her greatly, but would the reality stand up to it?

Did she dare try to find out?

S pence kept his distance from the room he and Caelie shared while Elsie helped prepare her for bed. He had no idea how long such things took—most of the ladies of his acquaintance didn't usually dress for bed when with him, and he preferred to undress them at his leisure. Although with Caelie, he'd been as eager as a green boy to strip away everything that created a barrier between his skin and hers.

Sweet Judas!

He slammed another shot of brandy down his throat. How many did he have to drink before he erased the image from his mind and the sensations from his body? Already his head swam, yet she remained firmly entrenched in his thoughts.

Spence cleared his throat and waved to Brampton for a refill.

His behavior had been deplorable. Never before had he put himself in a position where honor dictated a marriage proposal. He avoided innocents at all costs. The women he consorted with were fully cognizant of the fact their assignations were nothing more than two bodies slaking their lust. There were no complications, no expectations.

Until now.

Until Caelie had managed to captivate him with such stealth he had not even been aware it was happening.

How had he not been aware she possessed such abilities? It made him question his powers of observation. Then again, Bowen often told him he didn't take enough time to look beneath the surface of things. His friend had the right of it. If what he saw pleased him, he did not look any further. If something he saw did not please him, he did not delve deeper, but instead moved on to something else.

But held captive in a room with Caelie for several days, he'd had no choice but to see beyond the surface. He had been completely unprepared for what he discovered.

Spence shot a stealthy glance over his shoulder. The common room had filled up. He knew he should not linger, but he could not go upstairs until enough time had passed that Caelie was fast asleep. He had gone outside initially and walked until his feet hurt, but rain chased him back inside. He kept his back to the growing crowd and his head bowed over his drink.

The raucous voices of men lifted to the exposed beams above, punctuated here and there with a high-pitched giggle of a serving girl or one of Mr. Brampton's daughters.

"My Elsie is done assisting Lady Thurston, m'lord. If'n ye

want to go back upstairs." Mr. Brampton set a fresh brandy in front of him.

Spence nodded and reached for the drink, but made no move to leave. He lifted the brandy but before he could take a sip a hand slapped his back and caused the drink to spill over the edge of the glass onto his hand.

"Huntsleigh! It is you, my good man!"

Chapter Eight

Spence closed his eyes. Bloody. Hell.

He eyed the bar and gauged his ability to leap over and hide behind it. But it was a bit late for that, wasn't it? He'd already been discovered. Best he let things play out. He would make whatever excuses were necessary, then quickly leave.

He turned around.

Oh, bloodiest of all bloody hells.

Fate officially had it in for him in.

"Billingsworth." He forced a smile. "Odd to find you here."

"I could say the same about you. I had no idea you were closely acquainted with Lord Iber. I do assume that is why you are here?"

"You assume wrong. It is pure happenstance. I was on my way to the West Indies in fact when I, uh, was called back to London. Urgent business." He did not bother to mention his urgent business comprised of conveying Billingsworth's former fiancée back to the city. That would not do. The lord gossiped like an old woman. One word from him and Lady

Caelie's cousin, Lord Glenmor, Spence's grandfather, and Nick, would be awaiting their arrival with a vicar in tow.

"Doesn't one travel to the islands by ship?"

The man's grasp of the obvious astounded. "Yes. That is the usual way."

"Then how did you receive your message to return?"

Spence blinked. He liked Billingsworth better when he was being obtuse. "Carrier pigeon."

"Carrier pigeon? They can do that?"

"Obviously." In truth, he had no idea what a carrier pigeon could do, having never used such an antiquated mode of communication, but one little pigeon finding a ship in the middle of the English Channel did stretch the bounds of probability. Still, no reason Billingsworth needed to know this.

"Well, how fortuitous we have met. I do declare there are not many of Lord Iber's acquaintances I am overly familiar with. Of course, he is but a viscount and he's marrying the daughter of a French aristocrat, so I suppose it stands to reason, does it not?"

The pompous tone in Billingsworth's voice drove nails into Spence's skull. The man affected more airs than he was due. What had Caelie ever seen in him? "Are you not a viscount?"

Billingsworth straightened and his eyes widened as if Spence had delivered a most grievous insult. "It is a courtesy title, much like your own. In time, I will be an earl, as you well know."

"And I a marquess," Spence said, unable to hide the smirk. "Should I only consort with those of my rank or higher then? I should be most grieved to hear this, as my closest friends are not. Blackbourne is like you, but an earl, and I'm afraid poor Mr. Bowen has no rank at all." And both were ten times the man Billingsworth could ever hope to be.

"Indeed, I am certain you may consort with whomever

you choose, though why you have chosen those two is beyond me. As you said, Mr. Bowen, though once your grandfather's ward, is but a gentleman and no more and Lord Blackbourne...well..." He shrugged. "We all know what sort he is, don't we?"

The slight against Nick's character stoked Spence's ire. In the back of his mind, he heard Bowen's voice advising caution and a clear head. But he had not shown an aptitude for either of those things this evening and he doubted he would start now.

He leaned in and affected his most innocent of expressions. "What sort might that be? The sort to breach a promise of marriage once given? Oh no, wait—" He straightened and poked a finger into Billingsworth's soft chest. "That was you. Lady Caelie Laytham if I recall. Quite a beautiful woman."

Billingsworth sputtered before he managed to spit out his answer. "And riddled with scandal."

"Was she?" He scratched his chin as if giving the ludicrous claim serious consideration. "I thought it the late Lord Glenmor who had courted scandal. I remember Lady Caelie as being quite modest in nature."

"The sins of the father are rested upon the child!"

Spence's fists clenched. "Horse shit."

"I beg your pardon?" Billingsworth puffed up with selfrighteous indignation. If Spence poked him in the chest again, likely the pompous buffoon would burst. A delightful thought.

Spence didn't bother repeating himself as he knew Billingsworth had heard him clearly enough the first time. "You may have convinced the rest of the ton that your reasons for breaching your promise of marriage to Lady Caelie had to do with the scandal that tarnished her family name, but you and I both know better, don't we?"

"I know nothing of the sort. I made my proposal to Lady

Caelie because at the time she came from a good family with a respectable name and fortune." But the first hint of fear had edged into Billingsworth's pale brown eyes and Spence knew his suspicions were on the mark.

"I suspect it was the fortune part that caught your attention more than anything else."

"Preposterous!"

"I think not. You see, I know your father is heavily in debt. He's made several bad investments over the past five years and has had to borrow heavily to pay back his creditors. Do you know how I know this? Because my grandfather is one of those people he begged funds from due to his familial connection with my grandmother's side of the family." Spence crossed his arms leaned against the oak bar and smirked. "How humiliating that must have been, begging like a pauper."

"That is—you have no right—"

Spence ignored Billingsworth's attempt to mount a defence. "You proposed to Lady Caelie because she had a significant dowry and when her father's accounts began to dwindle, you broke off the engagement in the hope of finding a more lucrative bride."

"Glenmor lied to us. It was he who breached his promise and therefore I was under no obligation to keep mine!"

"And what of honor?"

Billingsworth reddened. The color did not suit his pasty countenance. "Her father's behavior only brought dishonor upon their family."

"Is that the argument you used with Lady Caelie? Did you use guilt to keep her from crying foul?"

"She did not have a leg to stand on."

"She had two legs to stand on and you well know it."

"Two legs she happily wrapped around me in an attempt to convince me to change my mind!"

The words took a moment to sink in but when they did,

disbelief took hold and the rashness Bowen so often cautioned him against raged forth. Suddenly Billingsworth staggered backward like a drunken fool and landed with a thud on his aristocratic ass. Spence's knuckles burned and he glanced down at them to find them inflamed. Billingsworth remained on the floor and bandied between touching his bloody nose and staring up at Spence with an equal mix of loathing and fear.

"Have you gone mad?"

It was quite possible, though Spence had no plans to announce that fact in front of the patrons of the inn who had stopped whatever they were doing to stare at him and Billingsworth, who had yet to get off the floor.

Mr. Brampton leaned against the bar and fixed Spence with a stern look. "I'll be having none of that in 'ere, yer lordships. This is a respectable establishment."

Spence corralled his anger as best he could and nodded in Mr. Brampton's direction. "Of course. My apologies, sir. But this particular lordship gave great offense to a lady of our mutual acquaintance and I merely responded in kind. Forgive me."

Mr. Brampton nodded and returned to drying the glasses lined up on the back shelf. The din of the main room lifted once again when it appeared there was nothing more to see. Had anyone else recognized him?

Spence offered Billingsworth a hand and when he took it, he hauled the other man to his feet bringing them nose to bloody nose. Spence kept a smile on his face for the benefit of anyone who still watched, his words were delivered as fair warning.

"If I ever hear you speak ill of Lady Caelie, if I ever hear you have spread such filthy lies, it will be the last thing you ever do." He squeezed the hand still in his grip until Billingsworth winced in response. "I will have you shanghaied, dragged on board one of my grandfather's ships and dropped in the middle of the ocean where you will become food for the fish. Do we understand each other?"

"What do you care what I say about Lady Caelie?"

"I care because no lady deserves to be slandered in such a way and certainly not by the likes of you. Now I ask again, have I made myself clear?"

Billingsworth looked as if he wanted to protest further. Spence squeezed his hand tighter. "Very well. I shall hold my tongue, though doing such does not change the truth of it." He yanked his hand from Spence's and jerked at the cuffs of his jacket. "Good day, sir."

S pence left the tap room of the inn and made his way to the stables. His mind raced and spun. He could not deny Billingsworth was a first-class ass, but something about what he said would not leave him.

"Two legs she happily wrapped around me in an attempt to convince me to change my mind!"

He wanted to toss the words out with the rest of the garbage Billingsworth spewed, but...

Marriage to Billingsworth would have saved her from the worst of her father's scandal—put a stopper in it more quickly by making her the respectable wife of a future earl. When Billingsworth tried to back out, would desperation have compelled her to do what she must to force him to stay? Would she have bartered her body for a husband?

Spence dodged the growing mud puddles and slipped through the slightly opened door of the stables. He found a lantern near the door and fumbled around until it lit. It provided a small glow around him too weak to penetrate the dark interior. Somewhere close by a horse nickered at the intrusion, but beyond that the stables were quiet.

Spence walked further inside and found a stray bale of hay and sat down. He set the lantern at his feet. His encounter with Billingsworth swirled in his head and refused to rest.

Was there something to what the fop had said? He didn't like to think of Caelie as being that mercenary, but...

But she had kissed him. Without provocation from him. She had enticed him into revealing a piece of his past that left him vulnerable and exposed and then she had kissed him. Had that been a ploy on her part? Had she kissed him knowing he had a reputation as a rake and would likely take it further, forcing them into a compromising position where he would have no recourse but to offer marriage? And he had walked right into it, hadn't he?

Her feigned refusal could easily be another ruse to make her appear altruistic so that he would beg her to do the right thing, then she would come away as the one who had fought for his freedom to save him from his own sense of honor.

He dropped his face into his hands and groaned.

"Well played, my dear. Well played."

"Talkin' to yerself, my lord?"

Spence's head shot up and he stared at Garron who stood just outside the halo of light. He had not heard his approach. For a large man, he moved with much stealth.

"Garron. Yes, I suppose I am. What are the chances you have some type of libation on your person?"

The bigger man chuckled, a thick, rumbling noise that emanated from deep inside his barreled chest and took a seat on another bale of hay. "Don't take to the stuff, I'm afraid. 'Sides, looks as though ye've 'ad enough."

"You don't know the half of it."

"How does our lady fare? Well, I hope."

Spence scowled. "Well enough."

Had the illness been a ruse as well? But no...not even a consummate actress could have faked that. But that didn't mean she hadn't used it to her advantage. He'd known from the moment he set eyes on her, the way she gazed longingly at the docks and the hope that soared in those beautiful green eyes when he suggested they leave the ship, she did not want to make the trip to Italy. When she fell ill, did she see that as her way out? Had she played it up enough to make him believe she banged on death's door?

Did she know her mother would refuse to accompany her and he would be forced to? If so, he'd played directly into her hands.

"Ah, then we shall leave soon?"

"Sooner than expected. We've been discovered. Or rather I have." He told Garron of his run in with Billingsworth, though left out certain pertinent details and the fact he'd left the man with a bloody nose and an earful of threats. Whether either would keep him from spreading what he'd told Spence, only time would tell.

"Best we be on our way as soon as possible. We wouldn't want 'er ladyship to be seen as well."

Spence nodded. Not that it mattered now. If she intended to trap him, she had more than ample ammunition to do so.

"M'lord?"

"What?"

"You look like death, if you don't mind me sayin' so."

"Thank you, Garron." He didn't bother arguing. Even if he didn't look like death, he now stared down into its gaping maw. Marriage. He shook his head. "Have you ever been married, Garron?"

"Oh, aye. Once upon a time."

Spence straightened and looked at him. "Truly?"

"Don't look so surprised, m'lord. I 'aven't spent me whole

life on the sea. I was a smithy once upon a time," Garron said. His voice took on a faraway quality and something akin to sadness filled his dark eyes. "Married a lovely lass. Mellie was her name. Far too good for the likes of me, so she liked to remind me."

"Were you happy?"

Garron laughed, but a sadness had seeped into his voice when he spoke. "Ah, no, m'lord. As it turns out, we were not, though I suspect she was far unhappier than I."

"What happened?"

"She took off. I went into town one day and when I returned she had left."

"Did she say why?"

"Left me a note. Said she and my cousin, Fergus, were in love and leaving for Yorkshire to live as man and wife."

"Oh. Do you miss her?"

Garron gave a sly grin. "I miss him more, I think. Much easier to get along with. And I suppose I couldn't fault him for falling for her. I had done the same."

"Where is she now?"

"Dead. She caught a sickness a year after leavin' and never recovered. Fergus was heartbroken. I almost felt bad for the lad."

"Is that why you ended up working on the *Windswept*?"

"It is. But I'm ready to go back now, I think. Maybe I'll find meself a new lassie." He winked. "Mayhap I already have."

"Truly? You would do it all over again?"

Garron laughed. "Mellie might not have been the right lass for me, but that doesn't mean there isn't another one out there who is. 'Sides, a man likes to have a warm body to come home to each night, doesn't he?"

Spence had never given it much thought. He preferred the warm bodies he shared his nights with to be gone by morning.

At least he had. In recent days, he'd found a strange peace in waking to find Caelie nearby.

At least he had. Before Caelie's machinations put the shackles of marriage on him so that the best he could hope for now was an early death or a life filled with misery.

"Off ye go now," Garron said. He reached over and patted Spence on the knee as if he were a small lad who had just been told a goodnight tale. "Ye best be gettin' back to her ladyship and lettin' her know we should be leavin' on the morrow."

Spence nodded. He did indeed need to have a conversation with her ladyship, but it wouldn't be about their departure. She had refused his marriage proposal and he did not plan on coercing her to change her mind. He would not be hauled into marriage like a blind fool.

She would know he had discovered what lay beneath the timid miss she had pretended to be—a woman who had played him as expertly as any skilled courtesan. But like any such mercenary, the best she could hope for from him was a few coins tossed her way as he left her for greener pastures.

Chapter Nine

Caelie gave up on sleep and rose from the bed, wrapping the quilt around her to ward off the chill. The fire had long since burned down, but she didn't bother trying to restart it. She wandered over to the window and glanced down toward the stables. In the pitch blackness of the night a lantern bobbed along the pathway between the two buildings. As it drew closer, she recognized Lord Huntsleigh. She watched him for a moment until he disappeared beneath the awning of the inn.

A nervous thrill shot through her.

She would accept his proposal. A bold move, and not one she had intended, but she could not deny the sense in it. He needed to marry to procure an heir and she needed a husband lest she wanted to spend the rest of her life scraping out an existence as a governess or teacher, or worse, being a poor relation.

She would be a liar if she denied something had developed between them. She lacked the naivety to call it love, but she hoped, in time, it would eventually reach that destination. She would be a fool to turn away from such an opportunity.

Lord Huntsleigh did not feel the same way toward marriage as she, but surely, she could convince him of its merits. Why, they already had people in common. One of his closest friends, Nicholas, had married her cousin, Abigail. And they got on well. They were able to talk to each other without the banality of societal small talk. They laughed together. Surely it was a strong basis to start out with.

Yes. As soon as Lord Huntsleigh—Spencer—stepped through the door to their room she would give him the news. She would be more than happy—honored, in fact—to accept his proposal to be his wife.

She did not have to wait long. The door opened and closed quietly. Spencer's boots echoed softly in the quiet of the room as he set the lamp on the table next to the door and turned down the wick. She watched him from the shadows as he struggled out of his coat, his uncoordinated efforts taking longer than she had expected. He tossed it aside as if angry. His waistcoat and cravat soon followed. Then he sat down on the chair by the fire and pulled at his boots with far less success.

"Would you like some help?"

"Bloody—!" His foot hit the floor with a loud thwack, the boot having refused to budge. "How long have you been standing there?"

He sounded cross. "Since you arrived. I couldn't sleep."

He grunted something under his breath, but she couldn't make it out. He returned his attention to yanking at his boot.

"I wanted to speak with you."

Again, silence. Had she done something? Had something happened? His last boot finally released his foot and he dropped it to the floor. He looked quite a sight standing there in his stocking feet and shirt. Rather appealing, really.

Silence lingered in the room as he stood there staring at her. Her nerves increased. Was he waiting for her to say what she had to say? Caelie took a deep breath and forged ahead before she lost her courage.

"I have given what you said serious thought."

"What I said?"

"Yes." She cleared her throat. She had not anticipated how difficult this would be and his rather remote manner did not make it any easier. "Your proposal."

"My proposal?" He drew the word out as if it was new to him and trepidation crept up her spine. She had not seen him like this before. Something was...off. "My lord, are you...are you drunk?"

He smiled at her but it lacked the warmth of the smiles he had gifted her with earlier that evening. This one held no mirth to it at all. "Drunk?"

Frustration erupted within her. "You keep repeating my questions back to me, my lord. Are you having difficulty understanding them?"

His eyebrows raised slowly and he took a few steps toward her. She pulled the quilt tighter around her shoulders. She did not like the glint she saw in his eyes once he was close enough the shadows did not interfere.

"I *am* having difficulty understanding," he said. Again, the smile. Again, the sense of trepidation. Caelie wanted to dive back into bed and pull the covers up. Something had gone horribly wrong between the time he had left the room to when he now returned. But what? He took a step closer and the scent of brandy wafted off him. "You see, I had it in mind that you were a rather lovely lady, an innocent as pure as the driven snow and as such I was horrified at my treatment of you. So much so, that I took the unprecedented step of proposing marriage."

"Yes, I know. That is what I wanted to—" She didn't get to finish.

"Which you thankfully declined." He placed a hand over

his heart and laughed lightly as if it were all a silly misunderstanding.

"I did, my lord. But you see, I—"

"Thankfully, I say, because you see I've come across some rather disturbing information and this information has placed a new light on our situation."

She stood silent a moment. "Information?" Ice filled her veins.

"Hm." He turned away from her and walked back toward the fire. His hand waved in the air. "Oh, I ran into an old friend of yours, by the way."

"An old friend?" Now she had become the parrot.

He spun on his heel to face her. "Lord Billingsworth. You remember him, I'm sure. Former fiancé. Jilted you after the heinous scandal with your father became public knowledge."

Tiny black dots pricked at the corner of her eyes. She tried to blink them away. "Yes, I remember him." How could she not after everything that had happened? After he had tossed her aside like yesterday's old newspaper.

"He told me the most amazing story."

Bile burned in her throat. "What did he tell you?"

"He told me—while I was defending your honor, I might add, and which in hindsight I find rather comical and I'm sure you'll agree—but he told me that you had tried to convince him not to break your engagement by giving yourself to him."

Caelie's heart burst in her chest then fell silent. Or she thought it had but perhaps she simply couldn't hear it over the blood rushing in her ears.

Spencer cocked his head. Was that disappointment she saw or only shadow? "So, it is true then? You are not the innocent you claimed to be."

She had no defense. "I never claimed to be an innocent." She had let go of that title when she had allowed Billingsworth to make use of her body, trading on promises he had no intention of keeping. But Spencer had the wrong idea. She had never bartered herself. Not that it mattered. In the end, nothing changed. She was soiled goods. And now he knew it.

How long before everyone else did as well?

"No, I suppose you didn't. Not in so many words, but you certainly acted the part. Tell me, were you horribly disappointed when your ruse with him did not work?"

"You think me quite mercenary."

He crossed the room to stand in front of her. "Are you not? You tried to convince Billingsworth not to break off your engagement, and tonight you tried to compromise yourself to exact a proposal from me. Well done. Great success."

"I turned down your proposal."

He let out a short laugh. "Indeed, you did. But tell me, were you standing here in the dark tonight because you intended on accepting it when I returned? I'm sure you had any number of practical reasons to give me, clever little minx that you are. I suspect you would layer each one with a heavy dose of guilt, using my reprehensible behavior toward you, an *innocent*." He spat the last word out as if it left a bad taste in his mouth.

She didn't answer him. The truth would only confirm his opinion of her.

"Well, you can dismiss the play-acting, my lady. I am well aware of what you are about and I have decided to accept your refusal. I have furthermore decided to accept your promise to me that you will not repay my kindness in saving your lovely ass by accompanying you back to London. Tell me, did you and your mother plan that aspect of it once you had fallen ill?"

"No!"

He shrugged. "Ah, well. Either way, you executed your plan flawlessly. I'm afraid the only fly in the ointment was your previous victim, Lord Billingsworth. A stroke of luck my meeting him in the common room. For me, I mean. Not so much for you."

Words jammed in her throat. She wanted to deny it all, to explain things, but his closed expression told her he had made up his mind. Anything she said now would only sound like more lies.

"But—" He came closer and picked up a curl that had escaped her braid, twisting it around his finger. "Just because your plan will not come to fruition does not mean you and I cannot still enjoy ourselves."

Was he suggesting? Did he think she would—?

He lifted the curl away and pressed his mouth against her neck. A traitorous ache pulled between her legs. Even now, after his harsh accusations, her body wanted him with a passion she had no control over. Was this what had plagued her father? What had sent him over the edge when his mistress turned her back on him?

She squeezed her eyelids shut. Heaven help her, how had it come to this? Pain wrapped around her heart and squeezed.

"Stop," she whispered.

Spencer pulled the quilt from her grip. It pooled at her feet and he pulled her closer. Her thin, linen nightgown offered little protection against the warmth of his hand as it slid down her hip and around to cup her bottom. He leaned forward; his breath hot against her ear.

"Stop? Why ever should we? Isn't this what you wanted? For me to compromise you?"

The scent of brandy wafted around him. He dragged her earlobe through his teeth and heat raged through her without mercy.

Caelie opened her eyes and they quickly filled with tears. How had it come to this?

She pressed a hand against his chest. "Stop. You are drunk.

When you come to your senses in the morning, you will regret this."

He pulled away slightly. "I regret a great number of things, my lady. I regret that I befriended you. I regret that I let you worm your way under my skin until I opened up to you as if you were someone who could be trusted. I regret that I allowed myself to—" He stopped and his mouth twisted in anger.

"You *can* trust me," she said, but it was too late. She could see it in his eyes. He believed the twisted truths Billingsworth had told him. The more she tried to defend herself the guiltier she would look in his eyes.

He scoffed and pushed her away. She bent and picked up the quilt, wrapping it around her shoulders like a shield to protect her from his anger. His disgust.

A fat tear rolled down her cheek.

He turned away from her and walked to the fire to stare at its embers. Moonlight filtered through the window and pressed against his back. "Do not think to use your tears to soften me, my lady. Nothing you say will sound like anything but lies to me."

"Do you think he has told others what he told you?"

Spencer shrugged. "I do not know."

She swiped at the tears but they continued to fall. "If he has—" She couldn't say the words.

"You will be ruined. Quite thoroughly, I imagine."

Her life had been horrible enough when the scandal had been second hand, but this—this would spell the end of her.

"I wish you had left me on the ship," she whispered. Perhaps it wouldn't have been as direct as her father's path of putting a bullet into his brain, but the result would have been the same. The pain would have ended.

"Don't be ridiculous. You would have died."

She closed her eyes and said nothing. What was there to

say? Yes, she would have died, but would that have been any worse than what awaited her in London? Her fall from grace would be so complete there would be no coming back from it. Worse still, the stigma would not be worn by her alone. Her father's scandal had taught her that. Abigail and Benedict, Aunt Lorena. All of them would wear the taint of her ruin.

She had not heard Spencer move. Did not realize he stood in front of her until his hand touched her chin and tilted it upward. She opened her eyes and stared into his. A small hint of confusion wrestled with the anger that burned more brightly than the fire's embers.

"Why did you do it? Did you truly think it would change Billingsworth's mind if you gave yourself to him? Were you that desperate?"

She stared at him a moment and wondered if she should bother to try, but something made her anyway. Some sad little piece of hope that had yet to die within her. "It was not desperation. It was sadness."

Spencer's brow furrowed. "Sadness?"

She swallowed past the lump in her throat. "Father had just died and everyone had turned away from us. Mother had locked herself away in her room and refused to come out. I was devastated and turned to the man who promised to become my husband. I...I sought solace."

"Solace? You expect me to believe you gave up your innocence for that?"

She dug deep and found a shred of dignity buried beneath her shame and straightened her shoulders. "Whether you believe it or not, that is the truth. Now, if you'll excuse me. I am exhausted and I wish to go bed."

He moved out of her way and Caelie brushed past him.

"We will be leaving on the morrow. If Billingsworth has recognized me, it has become too dangerous for us to tarry longer."

"I will be ready." She crawled beneath the covers. "And you may rest easy, my lord. I will not try to force a proposal from you. I will uphold my promise despite what has transpired between us."

She'd had such hope earlier, thinking perhaps they had something they could build a successful marriage on, but she had only been deluding herself. Spencer did not wish to marry and he certainly did not wish to marry her, especially now that he believed the worst.

She wished she could change his mind, but that would mean changing the truth, and that she could not do.

———

"You look a might worse for wear, m'lord."

Spence glanced up to find Garron leaning against the exterior wall of the stables, his hands shoved into the pockets of his well-worn woolen pants.

"That's one way of putting it," he said. His brain pounded beneath his skull and the bright morning sunshine did not help matters. The journey that lay ahead of them did not even bear consideration.

"Little too much brandy, eh?"

"Something like that." Though it wasn't the brandy that had his conscience twisted into a knot. He'd behaved abhorrently last night. Said awful things. Made horrible accusations that, in his inebriated state had made perfect sense. Some of them still did, but it didn't justify the way he'd approached it with Caelie.

He'd slunk from the room like a thief and searched out Garron. They had to move on. He'd left Caelie a note telling her to pack her things and then informed Miss Brampton to ensure she was awoken in time to prepare for travel by ten o'clock.

He followed Garron into the stables and waited a moment for his eyes to adjust to the dim light. "Can you ready the carriage? We will leave no later than ten o'clock."

"Of course, m'lord. Hopin' to get away before any of the other lords and ladies recognize you, eh?"

"It's for the best. We cannot jeopardize Lady Caelie's reputation." He may have been seen, but Caelie had managed to remain undiscovered. Better he should keep it that way.

Garron reached for the harness and pulled it off the hook on the wall. It jingled as he slung it over his shoulder. "Aye. 'Course, s'pose ye could always marry her if ye were seen together. No folly in that."

"I cannot marry her."

"Are you promised elsewhere?" Garron asked, calling the question over his shoulder as he walked down the length of the stable to where their newly purchased horses were housed.

"No! I just...can't. It's difficult to explain."

Garron's head popped up inside the stable next to one of the horses. "Can't see what's so difficult. She's a pretty lass with a sweet nature."

"Perhaps." Spence remained on the fence with respect to her nature, unsure which aspect of it to believe. "But there is more at play than that. The politics of society cannot be discounted." The excuse sounded lame.

Garron grunted; a telling commentary on what he thought of society and its politics.

"Besides, I doubt she'd have me anyway." Desperate or no, after his behavior last night he could no longer be certain how she felt toward him.

"Guess you can't fault the lady for her taste."

Spence scowled at the man. "Either way, I shouldn't have to explain myself."

Which was a good thing because he was having difficulty this morning remembering why he couldn't marry her. Then the night before would come rushing back and the knot in his belly reminded him. Even if he could see past his belief that Caelie had somehow orchestrated the situation to her advantage, likely after his behavior toward her she wouldn't have him even if he begged on bended knee.

Which he would not do.

"Well, s'pose if you can't marry her, ye shouldn't 'ave too much of a problem findin' someone who will. Beauty like her, inside and out, be a prize for any man."

"Not if Billingsworth has his way."

"That the gentleman you put on his arse last night?" Garron led one of the horses out of the stall, forcing Spence to move out of the way lest he wanted to be trampled by the beast.

"It is. He and Lady Caelie had been affianced but he broke it off when her father met a rather scandalous end."

Garron tsked. "Not well done."

Spence couldn't agree more. The situation notwithstanding, a man's honor dictated he keep his promises. Then again, Billingsworth wasn't the most honorable of men. Any honorable man would not speak of what occurred between himself and a lady in the way he had, an act that would ruin her for sure. Despite his personal feelings on what she had done or her reasons for doing it, Spence did not want to see that happen.

In the sober light of day, and after a restless night of staring at the ceiling, Spence concluded whatever Caelie had done had been an act of desperation. Her world had fallen apart around her and she had used the only ammunition she had—her body—to try and hold it together. It didn't say much in respect to her character, but desperate people did desperate things. Such as board ships heading for the West Indies in the hope of avoiding the marriage mart.

He should have been more understanding. Perhaps he

would have been if she hadn't turned her desperation toward trying to trap him. A trap she could still snare him in if he didn't find her a better alternative.

He'd ruminated on it all night and into the morning and could come up with only one solution.

He needed to find Caelie a husband. And he needed to do it before Billingsworth started spreading his tale and ruined her for good.

Chapter Ten

C aelie was more than happy to leave The White Stag behind, though she dreaded the upcoming trip, trapped inside a carriage for the duration with Spencer and his newfound beliefs. But the option to linger and potentially run into the man who had promised her the world, then robbed her of her innocence and left her ruined held even less appeal.

Caelie's face heated at the merest remembrance of the event. Not that there had been much to remember. Billingsworth had tossed her skirts up until she had to brush them away from her face just to see him. He'd pushed inside of her, heedless of her gasp of pain or request that he stop. She had not known it would hurt so and the surprise of it destroyed any ardor she may have felt. Surely, she had felt some, though in hindsight, she could not recall.

Billingsworth had assured her the pain was a common thing and she would feel fine momentarily. She'd imprudently trusted him, a mistake she'd made too often, and after a few more awkward, painful thrusts, his body stiffened and he collapsed on her, murmuring something ridiculous about her sweet, soft thighs before rolling away to do up his trousers.

The entire episode had left her feeling bewildered. Foolish even. She had come to him broken hearted; her emotions raw on the heels of Father's death. She'd sought solace in the arms of the man who claimed to love her. The man who was to be her husband in a few short months. She had imagined it would be lovely. Magical. A sharing of hearts and souls and—

Well, obviously grief had skewered her thinking for it had been none of those things.

"You look quite a sight, m'lady." Elsie pushed the last hairpin into place to secure Caelie's bonnet then stood back to survey her work. She'd proven a quick study in the role of lady's maid and Caelie was pleased she had agreed to accompany her to London. She hoped to offer her permanent employment, but she would need to speak with Benedict first. She did not want to make promises she could not keep.

"Thank you, Elsie. It is kind of you to say." She gave her reflection one last glance. Elsie had done her best, but the lack of sleep from the night before had left its telltale signs. Dark smudges rested beneath her eyes and her pale skin lacked its usual lustre. Even the red of her hair appeared dull in the morning light.

Elsie reached for the cape draped on the end of the bed and settled it on Caelie's shoulders. "The trunks have all been taken down. I thought I might say one last good-bye to my sisters and Da, if you don't mind, m'lady?"

"Of course, Elsie. I will meet you out by the stables. I expect Garron has the carriage ready for us by now."

Elsie led her down the narrow servant's staircase that brought them into the kitchens and pointed Caelie in the right direction. The carriage waited in the distance, but she did not see Spencer or Garron.

She took a moment to breathe in the fresh morning air. It

seemed like forever since she'd been able to enjoy the scents and the feel of sunshine upon her skin. How she had missed it. Confinement did not set well with her. She closed her eyes and stood still a moment, letting the wonderful sense of freedom soak in. She should enjoy it while she could. There was no telling how long it would last.

"Lady Caelie?"

She froze. Her stomach lurched and she contemplated closing her eyes tighter, as if that would make him go away. A foolish notion.

Resigned, she turned around to face Billingsworth.

"It is you. But what are you doing here?" He gave her a pompous sneer. "I cannot imagine you attended Lord Iber's wedding."

Caelie forced a cordial smile despite the stench of brandy that assaulted her. He smelled as if he had spent the morning swimming in the swill. "Good morning, Lord Billingsworth."

Whatever had she seen in him? His cravat had been hastily tied, his jacket pulled askew across his growing belly, and his hair, often more coifed than her own, had been hastily finger-brushed into place. If he had been abed, it had not been in his own.

"Are you leaving?" He stared down his nose at her, a nose which appeared rather swollen if she wasn't mistaken.

"I am returning to London."

"From where?"

"From here." She had kept her plans to leave London within the family and with Mother having no close friends and Abigail away to the country; word of her departure had not gotten out. She did not feel the need to explain it now to Billingsworth. She owed him nothing.

Her answer did not suffice. "And where were you before here? It seems an odd place to find you if you were not here to attend the wedding. All of the others at the inn are here for that purpose save for Hunts—" He stopped abruptly and stared at her, his red-rimmed eyes growing larger until she could see the blood shot through the whites of them.

She held still, afraid if she moved it would rustle the truth that lingered silent in the air. It did not matter.

"You are here with Huntsleigh!" Billingsworth's laughter cut into her and he slapped his leg. "No wonder he defended you so staunchly at our last meeting. He's made you his mistress! I suppose that is to be expected given your circumstances."

Caelie struggled to keep her composure in the face of Billingsworth's assumptions. "My circumstances?"

He gave her another pompous sneer and waved his hand in the air. "My dear lady, you and I both know you are no innocent maid. What other choice do you have? Even your cousin's marriage to Lord Blackbourne did not make you an enticing prospect on the marriage mart, did it?"

She wished to refute him, but she could not. The only invitations she had received came after Abigail and Nicholas's wedding, and even then, they were only out of courtesy. She had become a ghost. And like a ghost, people shied away when they caught sight of her.

But ghost or no, she refused to be cowed by him. She had grown sick and tired of playing the timid miss in the hope people would forget the scandal and accept her back into the fold. Tired of thinking she would find a gentleman who would take pity on her and see more than just her father's scandal.

It hadn't happened and she no longer wanted to spend her time trying to please others when they did not give her the benefit of the doubt. She certainly did not care to please Billingsworth, considering he seemed bent on ruining her.

"How gentlemanly of you to share your opinion. Though truly, I would expect nothing less from a man of your substandard character, Lord Billingsworth."

She had made a mistake seeking comfort in his deceitful arms. She had trusted where she shouldn't have, but the betrayal was his to wear, not hers. She gave herself in good faith, believing they were to be married. He had been the one to break that faith with his lies.

"My, my. I see you have developed the bold tongue of a harlot."

No one had ever spoken to her with such disrespect. Pent up anger writhed beneath her skin.

"You are a vile man, Lord Billingsworth. Let us not forget who it is who led me to this position with promises of love and forever. And let us not forget who it is who dishonored themselves by betraying those promises. You may no longer consider me a lady, but I assure you, my lord, you are certainly no gentleman."

A muscle twitched in the corner of his mouth. He had suffered his own censure from the ton for breaking their marriage contract. Nowhere near what she had suffered, but he did not get off without a hint of taint about him. Between that, and the current state of his family's finances, there were not many marriage-minded misses setting their cap for him. She may not have been out in society, but Abigail had kept her informed of the gossip.

Billingsworth leaned toward her, the stench of brandy forcing her to hold her breath. "The only dishonor would have been to drag my family's name through the mud by associating it with yours."

"An association you will have to continue if you speak of our past...association." The words tumbled out of her and built into a threat. "If word gets out, I will tell how you seduced me with lies and you will have no other option but to marry me or face disgrace. Regardless of my standing in society, I am still the daughter of an earl, a lady. No gentleman of honor can take my innocence without repercussion."

Billingsworth snorted, but doubt lingered in his eyes. "You wouldn't dare."

She smiled and felt the cold of it through to her bones. He was right. She wouldn't dare, but he did not need to know that. "If you ruin my reputation, what do I have to lose?"

"M'lady?" She jumped at the sound of Elsie's voice behind her. She issued a silent thank you to her new maid for choosing that moment to find her. At least Billingsworth would see she did not travel unchaperoned. Would it be enough? "We should make to the carriage. We'll be wantin' to be underway. His lordship will be along shortly."

"Yes, of course." She gave Billingsworth a withering glare. "Your accusations with respect to Lord Huntsleigh are unfounded. I fell ill during my travels and he, being a close friend of Lord Blackbourne's, felt honor bound to escort me home safely."

Whether Billingsworth believed a word out of her mouth she did not wait to see. Knowing him, he would make up his mind as it suited him best. He could easily use what he had seen to ruin her, without ever bringing what had transpired between them into the mix. The unfairness of it rankled.

But she was no stranger to unfairness.

———

Spence stared across the carriage at Caelie. Miss Brampton has asked to sit in the driver's box with Garron while the weather held, claiming she did not care for being stuffed inside a carriage for long periods if it could be avoided. Spence had a sense it had more to do with a burgeoning attraction between the two, but he said nothing. Caelie had acquiesced and now the two of them shared the interior while Garron and Miss Brampton sat aloft outside.

Now and again, Garron's rumbling laughter echoed against the carriage walls.

The interior of the carriage, however, did not share such merriment.

Upset colored Caelie's beautiful features. He had spent ample time in the company of enough women to read the nuances of their moods and while he may not necessarily know or understand the cause of them, he could certainly ascertain when one occurred.

At least in this instance, he knew the source. He had only to look in the mirror to find it.

He had tried several ways to approach the subject with her in his own mind, but it proved a difficult situation to broach casually. It did not help that her firm attention on the carriage window, and whatever lay beyond it, indicated a lack of receptivity to conversation.

Not that he blamed her.

He had made a right mess of things, accusing her the way he had. The more he thought about it, the worse he felt.

I was devastated...I sought solace.

Could it be true?

And if she told him yes, would he even believe her?

Spence cleared his throat. "I feel I should apologize for my behavior of last night."

Caelie did not respond. He wasn't sure she even blinked.

"I said some things...did other things... You were correct in your assumption that I had over-imbibed. My thinking had become muddled and my judgments somewhat...skewed, if you will."

Still nothing. He might as well be having a conversation with the empty space next to her.

It struck him suddenly how much he wished he could turn back time, go back to last evening before everything had gone so horribly wrong and hear her laughter once more.

Watch as it lit up her face and made her emerald eyes dance like jewels caught in sunlight. He wanted to go back to that kiss, to experience it all over again, revel in it, make it last forever. He'd do it differently this time. He'd never leave the room, never run into Billingsworth and let his vile words worm their way into his brandy-soaked brain.

Only he could not turn back time, any more than he could change the fact she had given herself to another man.

But did that mean she had tried to dupe him?

He freely admitted, though quietly and only to himself, that he had enjoyed the time spent in her company. He did not regret leaving the ship near as much as he'd thought he would. Not that he relished returning to London to face Bowen or Grandfather's wrath, but the time he'd spent in Caelie's company had been most pleasing and...confusing.

He'd never met anyone quite like her. She had proven to be a lovely and surprising companion.

And a dangerous one.

He shook his head and realized Caelie had turned her attention away from the window to rest her steady gaze on him. She no longer bowed her head, or looked away. When had that happened? He could not recall, but their gazes locked and it robbed him of whatever words he had left to complete his apology.

"I had a run-in with Lord Billingsworth," she said.

He started. "Billingsworth?" A chill settled through him. "When did this happen?"

"He saw me leaving the inn for the carriage and approached me."

"What did he say?"

"He deduced we were traveling together. He believes me to be your mistress."

Spence pounded his fist into the cushioned seat and

wished it was Billingsworth's smug face instead. "Did he indicate if he intends to speak of this to others?"

She shrugged and returned her attention to the window once again. "I do not know. I told him if he tries to ruin me, I will make it known he stole my innocence and thereby force his hand. He will have to marry me if he has any desire to save his honor."

"The man *has* no honor," Spence bit out. Caelie did not answer. "Besides, if he indicates we are...together, he will not need to use your association with him to ruin you." Billingsworth could spread his vile gossip and use Caelie's loose morals and family scandal as proof he was right to jilt her.

"Nor does he have the courage to speak of it in a direct manner," she said. "He could not even break off our engagement to my face. He did it through a letter delivered to Benedict. If he plans on using the information, he will make it appear as if the knowledge came second or third hand. He'll spread it like a virus while keeping his own hands clean. He wants to come out of this looking like the injured party."

She had the man pegged; he would give her that. Whatever blinders she'd worn during their original association had been pulled off and she now saw her former fiancé for the unconscionable bastard he was.

"Tell me what happened between the two of you. The truth of it."

Her face flamed and for a moment he thought she might tell him to pound sand. He couldn't blame her after the way he'd treated her last night. She had every right. But he needed the truth. Why it mattered, he could not say, but it did.

"It was as I said. Papa had just died." The words rasped out of her, quiet and laced with pain. "I felt...broken. In need of comfort. I wanted someone to tell me everything would be fine. That in the end, the hurt would stop. I turned to Billingsworth. He was to be my husband. My protector."

Spence had never hated the man more than in that moment.

"Billingsworth eagerly gave the comfort I sought, then turned it down a more physical path. He told me it would be fine; we were to be married after all. So, I let him..." She shook her head. "When he finished, he turned his back on me. He assumed because of the scandal my family suffered, I wouldn't dare bring more upon it by admitting what we had done. And he was right."

Spence's stomach churned. Not just over what she had gone through, but because he had added to it with his behavior the night before. He had turned his back on her as well, believed the despicable lies Billingsworth had told. And why? Because it would make it easier for him to justify not being marched to the altar?

He shook his head. He should marry her, if for no other reason than because she deserved it. If he thought that would be enough, that he could make her happy, he'd do it too. But whatever the basis for a good marriage was, he doubted pity and shame were a component. If they married based on that, their union would be nothing short of a misery, and he'd be damned if he'd drag her through a repeat of his parents' marriage.

She deserved better than that.

She deserved better than him.

"I have been giving your situation some thought and I've come up with a solution."

Her gaze left the window, the weight of its sadness landed heavy upon him. "And what is that?"

"I will find you a suitable husband."

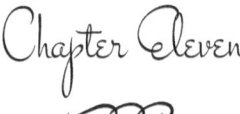

Chapter Eleven

"Forgive me, did I hear you correctly? *You* plan on finding me a husband?"

Caelie didn't know whether to laugh or cry. The idea was ludicrous. The man who considered marriage akin to misery, who had accused her of being a mercenary who had tried to trap him into proposing, *he* would find her a husband?

"I am the perfect one to do so."

She shook her head. Either the man had gone mad or he was still drunk from last night's brandy.

"In what possible way are you perfect for this task? You despise the very idea of marriage."

"True, but I am not the one marrying you."

Caelie recoiled inwardly at his remark. "I see."

Spencer's brow furrowed. "I did not mean that as a slight. Just a fact. I am ill-suited to marriage and I think you can see from my behavior of last night, not someone you would wish to be shackled to for life. But if we do not act quickly—before Billingsworth has time to spread his lies—that is what will happen."

"Perhaps my threats were enough to stay his tongue," she said.

Spencer did not look convinced. "I mean no offense, but you are but an innocent—"

"Obviously not."

"Fine, but if you think Billingsworth will pass up the opportunity to ruin you to save himself, then you are innocent in the ways of the world."

"Do you think me ignorant?" Long supressed anger burned inside of her.

"I only meant—"

But she didn't care what he had meant. Her entire life she had been treated as if she didn't have a brain in her head. And yes, she had made some bad decisions, but she had made them for the right reasons. She had trusted and she had loved and it had turned out badly. But she was not an idiot. She knew far more than he gave her credit for and she could hold her silence no longer.

"Let me tell you what I have learned about the ways of the world, my lord. I have learned that I will never be good enough to win my mother's love because in her mind, I killed my brother and therefore destroyed her life. I have learned no matter how much someone loves you; they cannot protect you from their own failings. I have learned some men tell lies to achieve their own ends and care not about who they hurt in the process. I have learned promises mean little and reputation is the difference between living and barely existing. In the past two years I have been rejected, betrayed, lied to, ruined, humiliated, and abandoned by my own mother. Do not tell me I do not know the ways of the world. I am well versed, thank you! I had no control over any of those things. The only thing I could control was how I allowed them to affect me and I was determined they would not!"

"But they did," Spencer said quietly. "If they hadn't, you would not have told me any of that."

She let out a short breath and pursed her lips. She had not meant to say any of it, but perhaps he had the right of it. Perhaps she had been blind to how the events of her life had affected her, the scars they had laid across her heart. It had hardened her. Toughened her. And somewhere in the process the young girl who had believed in love and romance and white knights had disappeared.

Life was hard. One had to be practical if they were to survive it. She would do well to remember that.

"Tell me of this plan of yours."

Spencer stared at her a moment then nodded. "I believe if my family champions you, that we will have no problem finding you a titled gentleman of good reputation to agree to a betrothal."

"If you'll recall, Mother, and my aunt, as well as Abigail and Nicholas have all tried this and had less than stellar results."

"Ah, but their attempts lacked one very important aspect." A grin spread across Spencer's handsome face. The morning sunlight bled through the window and burnished his gold hair a warm bronze and made the blue of his eyes almost transparent. He really did have the look of a fallen angel. No wonder women of the ton found him so hard to resist. Lord only knew she hadn't been able to.

"And what is this important aspect?"

His grin widened further and a glint sparked in his eyes. "The best way to make someone want something is to tell them they can't have it. If I show an interest in you, it will create a stir. Everyone knows I have no interest in marriage. Therefore, if I am seen to be taken with you, other gentlemen will take notice and wonder what kind of woman could make the marriage-averse Lord Huntsleigh reconsider his stance on the union. It will be like I've uncovered a beautiful gem that has been hidden under their noses the entire time. They'll all wonder how they missed it. And men being men, they will want to see if they can steal the gem for themselves."

"You have given this quite a bit of thought."

He shrugged. "I am well known for my schemes."

"How many of your schemes have actually come to a positive conclusion?"

"Well...I suppose it depends on your perspective. But of this scheme I have no doubt."

It hardly mattered. She had enough doubt for the both of them. "Both Nicholas and Benedict have tried to extol my virtues to others in the hope of making me a match but to no avail."

"Ah—" He held up a finger. "But they were missing the key component."

"Which was?"

"Neither of them could create the illusion that they were willing to give up their bachelorhood for you. And who better to create such an illusion than—"

"The ton's most notorious bachelor," she finished.

He grinned. "Exactly."

"And you think you can do this before Billingsworth ruins me?"

"The Season is just getting underway. If we act fast, and make a splash, I believe we can find you someone within the month."

She looked across the carriage to Spencer. Who would have believed that the man society considered an unrepentant rake through and through was in fact a man of honor and kindness, humor and gentleness? Even faced with the shameful truth of her past, he had been able to look past that and agree to help her—help them both.

A shame she had not jumped on his proposal when he first

offered it. Marriage to such a man would be a boon any woman would wish for. But she had not jumped on it, and now he knew too much about her to make her an attractive prospect even if he did want to marry—which he didn't.

"Do you agree to my plan?"

Did she have a choice? At least a husband would save her reputation from ruin and prevent Spencer from being forced to marry her.

"Yes. I agree to it."

She had nothing left to lose.

The return trip to London took two days. Two days of polite conversation and stretches of long silences. It seemed after Spencer detailed his plan to her and she agreed, there remained nothing more to say.

A vast difference from when they had shared a room at The White Stag and conversation came easy. Now, a barrier separated them, held in place by the truth that Caelie was not the person Spencer had once thought. And yet, she was the same person now as at the beginning of the trip. Only his perception had changed. Her past now infected Spencer's opinion of her. As it would the rest of society once word reached their eager ears.

Would Spencer's plan be successful before that happened? How long would her threats, or the ones Spencer had laid down, hold Billingsworth's tongue? A clock ticked in the back of her mind, but she could not say when the gong would strike.

They would have to act fast.

When they reached London, however, and arrived at the stately home where the Laythams had lived for the past three generations, her cousin, Benedict, was nowhere to be found.

Titus, the old butler who had been in service to her family for longer than her lifetime, indicated the new Lord Glenmor had gone north only two nights before to investigate a business he and Lord Blackbourne were considering investing in. It would be at least a fortnight before his return. It left the house in a rather tomb-like state with the rest of her family staying at Sheridan Park, the Earl of Blackbourne's country seat.

"You will come home with me. Grandmother will love the company," Spencer said, more of a decree than an invitation, but she took him up on it just the same. She had no interest in staying in the quiet house and she could not join her family in the country if she hoped to succeed with Spencer's plan of finding her a husband. Besides, staying alone would hardly be proper and she had already skirted too close to the edges of impropriety of late.

They returned to the carriage before Garron could unload the trunks.

"Do you think people will question my staying with you? Won't it look odd, given we have no known association?"

"Nonsense," Spencer said, waving off the footman and giving her a hand into the carriage. "Your cousin-in-law and I are close friends. It is only natural I should look out for you while your family is away. Besides, it will work well with our cover story."

She waited until he climbed in behind her and took his seat before she questioned him. "Our cover story?"

The carriage jostled as it started. The drive to Lord and Lady Ellesmere's home would take no more than a few minutes. Her nerves grew. How would they receive her? She was but a stranger to them.

"Word is bound to get out that you were leaving London for Italy and that I conveyed you back home. It is best we disseminate our own version of events first to head off any controversy. Lord Glenmor and Nick being away will aid in this."

"In what way?"

"Simple. In their absence, there was no one left to fetch you when you fell ill and needed to disembark. Nick requested my assistance as a close friend of the family to ensure your safe return. I did so—along with your chaperone, Miss Brampton, for propriety's sake—and returned you to London. My grandmother then insisted you stay with us until Lord Glenmor's return. This will also help head off Billingsworth if he tries to concoct some other story to depict the situation in a bad light."

Caelie blinked at him. He had thought all of this up from the time they walked into the house until they left, which took all of ten minutes. "You have a very nimble mind, Spenc—Lord Huntsleigh. I confess, it is a bit disconcerting."

"You may call me Spencer. I do not mind."

"It would be most improper." Though, she had already made the switch in her mind. Sometime after she had kissed him it had become more and more difficult to think of him in such formal address.

"Are we not friends?"

"Are we?" She wasn't sure. They had been at some point in their journey, but it had changed, the truth casting their relationship in shadow. "Perhaps it is best that we do not attach more familiarity to our union than need be. It is only a temporary façade, after all."

"Very well, then."

She nodded at his agreement but sensed he did not agree with her. Something in the way he straightened his shoulders and the sudden attention he paid to the street beyond the window, as if it had been a rejection. She would have thought he'd be pleased by her willingness to put a distance between them. To make it clear she understood any feelings he acted out in the name of their plan were not true and that she knew better than to get her hopes up.

"Do you think your grandparents will be put out by having me foisted upon them without warning?"

Spencer turned away from the window. "Grandmama has lived in a house filled with men for far too long. I suspect she will relish the idea of having another lady in the house again."

"Again? You mean your mother?" He had not spoken of his parents again since he'd told her of that fateful night when they died.

He shook his head. "My aunt, actually."

"I hadn't realized you had one."

"She passed away around the time I was born. She and Grandmama had been traveling and she fell ill, as I understand. She had been quite young. Only sixteen, I believe. They don't talk about it much, but I've always had the sense Grandmama carries the grief with her always."

"I can imagine she would." Her own mother still carried the loss of her son and she'd not even had the chance to get to know him before he passed. To have a child for sixteen years, to watch them grow and form into the person they would be, then to have them taken away, their future never to come to fruition—she couldn't imagine the pain such a loss would cause.

"Besides," Spencer continued. "If I am to pull off the ruse of being besotted with you, it will be more convincing if we are under the same roof, giving me regular access to you, yet having it be properly supervised to avoid any hint of impropriety."

She read the meaning that dwelled beneath his words. Any fondness he displayed toward her would be nothing more than a carefully crafted ruse. Understanding this however, did not save her tender heart from being bruised. She refused to let it show. He did her a service, despite any misgivings he had with respect to her character or past motives. She would not burden him further with any attraction she felt for him. Perhaps, in time, it would wear off. Perhaps he would find her a potential husband who would fill the spot he currently occupied in her heart.

S pence tried to push his misgivings about the plan he had concocted to the back of his mind as the carriage made its way from Lord Glenmor's house to his grand-parents'.

Spence didn't believe his grandparents would cast Caelie out. He had meant what he said when he indicated Grand-mama would enjoy the company of another lady in the house. He did, however, fear Grandfather's reaction. Lord Ellesmere had a deep and abiding abhorrence to scandal and a determi-nation to avoid it at all costs. Spence couldn't fault the man. Had Grandfather's brothers shared his feelings, perhaps Spence would not now bear the burden of being the only male heir to the title.

But alas, all three of his great uncles had shown a marked determination to ruin themselves. All had made disastrous unions filled with strife—an unsettling trend amongst the Kingsley men, save for Grandfather, though he had passed this trait to his son. All of his great uncles had met untimely ends —Gordon in a dual over a woman, not his wife; William from a disease Grandfather refused to name though rumor had it he caught it from the bawdy houses he preferred to frequent; and poor Bernard had an accident following a quarrel over a gambling debt.

None of the unions, save for Great Uncle Gordon, had borne any children – and Gordon's only child, a daughter, had run off with a Frenchman, creating a scandal of her own.

Whatever became of her, Spence had no idea. Grandfather never spoke of her, or his brothers and the numerous scandals attached to them, and he especially never spoke of Spence's parents.

It was this tendency that gave him pause at arriving with Lady Caelie Laytham in tow. Her family's scandal had barely dimmed in the past two years and now she stood poised on the precipice of another one if he didn't do something about it and fast.

If nothing else, perhaps the appearance he may entertain the idea of marriage would put Grandfather's mind at ease. It bothered his conscience to know he caused his grandfather grief, though not quite enough to be forced into a union he did not want. It wasn't so much that he loved the scandalous life, but he had hoped partaking in such activities would show Grandfather he made a better bachelor than husband. To date, however, the Marquess of Ellesmere had refused to concede this point.

"You are a million miles away," Caelie said.

Spence smiled. Her voice held a sweetness, like tasting a succulent peach and longing for another bite. Even after their long day of traveling, she appeared fresh and lovely. Her hair, always kept in a simple style, was gathered in back with soft curls cascading down from beneath her small bonnet. The soft, apple green of her travel dress and dark sage of her pelisse only enhanced the color of her eyes. She was a jewel. He would have no problem finding her a husband. In truth, he may have to fend off multiple suitors.

The thought curdled his stomach.

"Was I?"

"Do you expect your grandfather will be angry you left?"

"Without a doubt. But not to worry, he will be on his best behavior with a guest present."

She smiled but he could see the nervousness tug at the

corner of her delectable mouth. "Ah, we discover the real reason you were so quick to invite me to stay."

"I've been found out. I warned you, I am a dastardly rogue. All my motives are ulterior."

"I think you're far more honorable than you give yourself credit for."

Her words startled him; especially given how he had treated her. "You're wrong. You have nothing to base this crazy supposition on."

She shook her head and the red curls bobbed and swayed. He could easily stare at her all day and always find something new and fascinating to see. "On the contrary. I have ample evidence. You gave up your own wants to see me safely home."

"I behaved abominably. I took liberties I should not have."

Color rose high in her cheeks and she glanced down at her hands where they rested folded in her lap. "I kissed you, not the other way around."

Spence smiled. He should head this conversation to safer ground, but it was the first time since he'd behaved the drunken fool that their easy banter had returned and he was reluctant to let it go. Bantering with her held a strange exhilaration. He'd never experienced anything quite like it.

"I believe I recall kissing you back."

Her eyebrows lifted but she kept her gaze fixed on her hands. "But you offered marriage to compensate."

"Yes, I suppose I did. And you turned me down."

"I did." She looked up and the light in her eyes had dimmed. "And I mean to hold to that as I promised I would."

You don't have to.

The words came unbidden to his mind and he clamped down on them before they shot out of his mouth. He had no business saying them. He did not want to relive their last night at The White Stag. It had been ugly and not well done on his part. He'd rescinded his proposal and then proceeded to behave like a royal ass.

His behavior of that night only served to highlight the truth—he was not suited to marriage and had they gone through with it, he would have made her miserable, much as he had that night. It had been ingrained into him, generations deep. The Kingsley men did not do marriage well, Grandfather the odd exception to that rule. Spence often wondered if the man wasn't a foundling passed off as the heir. No other explanation made sense of the strange anomaly.

Spence changed the subject rather than dredge up the other night any further. "Are you prepared for the Season? It may be quite exhausting. Grandmother usually has a full social calendar and I mean to escort you to as many fetes, assemblies, teas and whatever else they throw at us. I want to create a buzz of ghastly proportions."

"I will be ready," she said, though her expression implied he might as well have asked her if she was prepared to walk the plank.

"It won't be as bad as all of that, I promise you. You may even enjoy yourself."

"Once upon a time, I might have believed you."

"I'm a wonderful escort. And who better to weed through the selection of gentlemen than me? I can easily point out which men have honor and which only wear it when it suits them."

"Men like Billingsworth, you mean?"

"Indeed. I will not allow you to marry that man."

"Is that so? And what if he is my only alternative?"

"Then I would strongly encourage spinsterhood."

"I can assure you, my lord, spinsterhood does not hold the same enjoyable benefits as bachelorhood. I do not wish to join its ranks. I would like children someday and a home filled with love and laughter."

"And you think this will be achieved if you marry Billingsworth?"

"No. I do not. But I do think it possible with the right marriage."

Her optimistic view of the institution amazed him after all she had witnessed of it. Her parents were no more stellar examples of marital happiness than his were. Yet she steadfastly clung to the belief she could achieve it. She was either a blind fool or...simply wrong.

He scowled. "And what makes a marriage right?"

She titled her head as if giving the matter grave thought. "Friendship."

"Friendship?" Hardly the answer he expected.

"Friendship creates a solid foundation to build everything else on. Wouldn't you agree?"

Spence's scowl deepened and he glanced out the window. "I'm not sure there is a foundation solid enough to sustain the ravages two people can do to each other."

"But if they are friends, why would they want to hurt each other?"

He did not have an answer to that. "We could argue this forever, but you will not change my mind. Marriage is a misery, and I have no plans to drag someone into such misery with me."

She smiled. "But you'll help me find someone to make miserable?"

"Yes, it will be my pleasure." Although how much of an actual pleasure it would be remained to be seen. The notion of her with another man left him unsettled.

The carriage turned and came to stop outside his grandparents' townhouse. He looked out the window and let out a deep breath. "We have arrived."

Time to face the music.

A liveried footman wearing the Ellesmere colors of green

and gold opened the door to the carriage and placed a step on the ground. Spence stepped out first then assisted Caelie down. He could feel her hand shake and he squeezed it in support.

"Relax."

"I am being foisted onto two people who barely know me and are not expecting me and then enlisting their help to find me a husband. Relaxing is not in my repertoire at the moment."

"It will be fine." Spence nodded at the footman. "Good afternoon, George. Will you see Miss Brampton into the house and have Mrs. Faraday settle her upstairs in the servants' rooms once the trunks are unloaded?"

"Yes, m'lord. Lord and Lady Ellesmere await you in the sitting room."

"They do?" He had not sent word ahead. He'd thought the element of surprise would work in his favor.

"Yes, m'lord. Lady Ellesmere saw your carriage from the window and called Lord Ellesmere up from his study. They have convened to the sitting room to await your arrival."

"How did they know it was me?"

"The trunks I would suppose. They weren't expecting guests."

"Ah. Yes, of course." Spence spared Caelie a glance. Her lips were pulled tight. "And their mood, George? Is it good?"

Before the footman could answer, the front door swung open and Felton, the Marquess of Ellesmere's ancient butler, stood on the other side looking his usual dour self, though one eyebrow did lift at the sight of Lady Caelie.

"Good afternoon, my lord," he said and swept a hand to usher them inside. "May I take your hat and shawl, my lady?"

Caelie fumbled with the ties. Spence could see her hands shook and suddenly regretted not sending word ahead. His grandparents may have noted his arrival, but they were not expecting her. Was it fair to thrust her into the middle of this in such a way? Likely not. But they had arrived and he could hardly toss her out and tell her to make a run for it.

He handed Felton his gloves and gave Caelie his arm. "Shall we?"

She nodded but said nothing. Likely no words could escape her tightly pursed lips.

The walk up the stairwell and down the hallway to the sitting room took forever and yet took no time at all. Felton led the way and announced their arrival before judiciously disappearing, closing the door the behind him.

The sound had a strange echo of doom to it.

Such nonsense. Caelie's nervousness must be catching.

He looked at Grandfather. His grandfather glowered back. Spence swallowed and quickly switched his glance to his grandmother, but his hopes for a warmer reception there were dashed. She sat on the sofa; her face cut from stone. In her lap, she worried a handkerchief clasped in her hands.

A sick foreboding made Spence's heart stutter in his chest. Something was not right.

"What is it?" The words came on a whisper, as if the quiet might soften whatever news his grandparents were about to impart.

"It is Marcus," Grandfather said.

Blood rushed in Spence's ears at a deafening rate.

"Bowen?" He hardly ever called his friend by his given name. It had been that way since they were boys and he'd determined Bowen had a far more dashing ring to it. The silly things boys do. He didn't know why he thought of that now. "What about him?"

"He has been stabbed."

Chapter Twelve

~

G randfather's voice cut across the room, each word landing with a hardened blow. Spence could no longer feel his hands and a strange roaring had taken up residence in his head and refused to abate.

"No." Because of course Grandfather was wrong. Bowen did not get stabbed. Such a suggestion was preposterous. Bowen had no enemies. Now if his grandfather had said it had been Nick who had been stabbed, that would be more believable. But not Bowen. Everybody loved Bowen.

Grandfather ignored his denial and stepped forward, closing the gap between them. He looked older than when Spence had left; ridiculous as less than a fortnight had passed since then.

"Marcus was returning from the dock, likely to tell me you had set sail before he could board, as I suspect you planned when you sent him on some unnecessary task." The accusatory tone of his grandfather's stern voice abraded Spence. He swallowed but said nothing. He had no defence to give. "As he left the dock, he came across Lady Franklyn who had been set upon by brigands. Naturally, he intervened. In the ensuing scuffle, one of the thieves pulled a knife and stabbed him twice."

Grandmother choked back a sob. When Spence looked at her, she had pressed a fist to her mouth as if to hold the rest of them inside. The roar in his head grew louder until it threatened to deafen him, yet he heard every word Grandfather said.

"He continued to fight despite his injuries and dispatched the brigands. It wasn't until the authorities arrived and Lady Franklyn was safe that he collapsed."

"W-what was Lady Franklyn doing at the docks?"

"She did not say. Though it appears she had packed for a trip." Grandfather's gaze pierced Spence. A trip. His stomach dropped away. She had not taken it well when he had broken off their affair and informed her of his plan to leave London. She had begged him to take her with him. She wished to escape London as much as he had, for reasons she did not give and he did not inquire upon. He had refused. He thought it nothing more than the histrionics of a jilted lover. She was married to a wealthy duke after all and her daughter had just entered society. Had she truly followed him to the dock with the intent of running away with him?

Spence needed to sit down but he couldn't move. Next to him, Caelie drew closer and tightened her hold on his arm. He leaned against her as much as he dared. He didn't want to, but his legs were doing funny things and he couldn't think straight. Save for one thought that screamed above the roar.

This was his fault.

"Where is he? He's not...tell me he isn't—" He could not say the word. He could not even think it, afraid if he did it would make it true. And it couldn't be true, because he could not live without his friend. Bowen was like a brother to him.

Grandmother sprang off the sofa and hurried toward him. "No! No." She took Spence's free hand in her own. They were cold as ice. Or was that him? "He is upstairs."

Relief swept through Spence and he stumbled back a step. Caelie's hold kept him in place though and he quickly regained his footing. Bowen lived. He was fine. Everything was fine.

Grandfather's next words brought his relief crumbling down.

"He has not regained consciousness."

The statement refused to register. Spence shook his head. "I don't understand. Grandmother said he was fine."

"No. She said he was upstairs. Where he has been since they brought him home. He had improved initially then fever struck and infection. He slipped into unconsciousness several days ago and has yet to awaken."

Spence could not remember how to breathe. "But he will."

His grandparents did not respond. Ice flooded his veins. He spun on his heel and reached the door without even being aware he had moved.

"Spencer!" Grandfather's voice stopped him. "Perhaps you would like to introduce your guest?"

Spence looked to Caelie and saw a mix of sympathy and apprehension in her emerald eyes. How he wished he could crawl inside of them and hide from what he had done, but he could not. Bowen needed him. And he needed to see him.

"Forgive me." He took a step back into the sitting room. "Grandfather, Grandmother, this is Lady Caelie Laytham. She is responsible for my return and I have offered to give her shelter until her cousin, the Earl of Glenmor, returns from up north."

His grandparents stared at him. He did not have time to explain everything. He needed to see Bowen.

"Go," Caelie whispered. He nodded and quickly raced up the staircase to Bowen's rooms.

· · ·

Once the door closed behind Spencer, Caelie turned to face her hosts. She had not expected to be welcomed with open arms, but given the current circumstances, she doubted her presence would be anything more than an intrusion. She couldn't in good conscience stay and put more of a burden on this family.

"I am so sorry to hear of the recent tragedy. I do hope Mr. Bowen recovers soon. It must be a terrible strain on both of you, as well as Lord Huntsleigh. He is ever so fond of Mr. Bowen."

While she recovered her strength at the inn, Spencer had regaled her with tales of their escapades growing up. Mr. Bowen's arrival on a rather stormy night had been unexpected. He was the only child of an older couple who had managed one of Lord Ellesmere's estates for years. Upon their deaths, Lord and Lady Ellesmere agreed to take him in as their ward and Spencer, in essence, inherited a brother, of sorts. Though he had not said so in so many words, the affection and admiration he held toward Mr. Bowen had been obvious in every story he told.

It was this affection and sense of brotherhood that had led Spencer to order Captain Moresley to leave port ahead of schedule so Mr. Bowen would not be forced to travel to the islands, a trip he did not want to make and only did so out of duty. Yes, there had been a benefit to Spencer in doing so, but Caelie suspected he would have done so either way to save Mr. Bowen from making the trip.

As much as Spencer tried to hide it beneath the image of the unrepentant rake, there was no denying he possessed a selfless side. Her being here gave evidence to that. He could have left her at the dock and sailed away. He could have left her back at the Laytham townhouse, alone. He could have left her to be ruined by Billingsworth's gossip instead of insisting on helping her avoid such ruin.

At every turn, when he could have left her to her own devices, he had instead offered a helping hand, defended her and kept her safe. She owed him her life, and, if his plan to find her a husband came to fruition, her future as well.

Lord and Lady Ellesmere stared silently at her for a moment before the marchioness collected herself and held out her hands.

"My dear, you must be tired from your travels. Let me have Mrs. Faraday see you settled."

Caelie shook her head as the older woman's soft hands encompassed her own. As much as a comfortable bed and the thought of rest enticed her, she could not accept. "No, I cannot stay, my lady. It would be too much of an imposition. You have enough to worry about without having an extra guest added to your concerns. I can stay at my cousin's townhouse. Benedict will return in a few weeks. I will be fine."

"Nonsense. It would not be proper." Lady Ellesmere squeezed her hands and smiled, though it did not reach her pale blue eyes. "And it would be no imposition at all."

"Pray tell," Lord Ellesmere said, drawing Caelie's attention away from his wife. "How is it my grandson came to bring you here? My understanding was you and Lady Glenmor were on your way to Italy."

"Yes, we were." Caelie forced her tired mind to recall the story Spencer had concocted. They'd decided to stick closely to the truth with several pertinent details removed. "Unfortunately, I fell quite ill. As it turns out, sea travel does not agree with me. Captain Moresley and the ship's doctor feared for my health should I continue the remainder of the journey onboard. The captain ordered the ship be docked at the nearest port."

"And where might the nearest port have been?"

"Portsmouth, my lord."

"I see." There was a pause. "And your mother, Lady Glenmor? Where is she?"

Caelie took in a breath and stiffened her spine. Tension tightened her jaw. "She is still on the ship, my lord."

A small gasp escaped Lady Ellesmere. "On the ship? Still? She did not disembark with you in Portsmouth, my dear?"

The tone of her voice told Caelie that Lady Ellesmere could not believe it. But the fact remained that she was here and her mother somewhere in the middle of the ocean. The truth could not be refuted.

"Yes, my lady. I'm afraid the past two years have been extremely difficult on her and she could not bring herself to return to London."

"But..." Lady Ellesmere shook her head in an effort to process the information. "But you're her daughter!" The grip on Caelie's hands tightened.

"Yes, my lady." She didn't know what else to say. She could not defend her mother's actions. She didn't know how.

"Had it been my daughter, I would have moved heaven and earth to see her safe and healthy!" Unshed tears made Lady Ellesmere's eyes glisten and Spencer's mention of his aunt that had passed away while traveling with her mother filled Caelie with guilt. The marchioness did not need that memory compounding the worry she already felt over Mr. Bowen.

"My dear," Lord Ellesmere said. He'd crossed the room and placed a hand on his wife's shoulder. "It goes without saying then that my grandson left the ship with you?"

"Yes, my lord." Caelie chose her words carefully. She needed to tread lightly to ensure Spencer's actions remained honorable and above board in the eyes of his grandfather. "He and Mr. Garron made arrangements to transport me to a nearby inn where I could convalesce and regain my strength.

They procured rooms and Lord Huntsleigh then hired the innkeeper's daughter as chaperone to safeguard my reputation and maintain propriety."

"How thoughtful of him." Suspicion colored Lord Ellesmere's tone. "And did you encounter anyone you knew while at this inn? I understand Lord Iber has his country seat in the area. Was he not married this past week?"

Caelie swallowed. She had not been prepared for that question. Did she lie and hope Lord Ellesmere did not find out? Or did she tell the truth and hope for the best? She chose the truth. She had never been a particularly adept liar. "Lord Huntsleigh encountered Lord Billingsworth in the common room of the inn."

"Oh dear." Lady Ellesmere pursed her lips and she drew in a long breath. "Did you encounter him as well?"

"He approached me as we were leaving, my lady."

Lady Ellesmere's hands released Caelie's. "Did he suspect you and my grandson traveled together?"

"I am uncertain." She left it at that. It would do neither she nor Spencer any good if she spoke the truth on that account.

"But you believe he may have," Lord Ellesmere said. A statement, not a question. Spencer had warned her of the man's astute nature. He had not misled her in that regard.

"It is possible."

"And what, pray tell, is Huntsleigh's plan for bringing you here? I assume, knowing my grandson, he has some scheme at the ready."

Caelie cleared her voice. Her face flamed with heat. "He thought the best course of action, in the event Lord Billingsworth thought to spread any untruths, would be to assist me in finding a match. Lord Huntsleigh is concerned with my...plight—" She could think of no other word to describe it.

"He is concerned Billingsworth will have garnered the wrong idea about you traveling together and wishes to ward off any threat to his bachelorhood by seeing you married off to someone else so he does not have to." Lord Ellesmere knew is grandson well, but not, in Caelie's estimation, well enough.

"His intentions are honorable, my lord, as was his behavior during the entirety of our journey. He could have left me at the dock and been on his way, but he didn't," she reminded Lord Ellesmere. "Instead, he did the honorable thing and had me safely returned to London. He has been selfless and sweet and I know he has a reputation and that he wishes to avoid marriage at all costs, but I will not have you disparage his motives after all he has done for me."

Silence laid heavy in the room as Lord and Lady Ellesmere stared at her, their features frozen in subdued shock. Perhaps she had stepped too far over the line with her outburst. She hadn't meant to come at them with such vehemence, but she meant what she had said.

Lady Ellesmere broke the silence and took Caelie's hands once again, a hint of a small smile pulled at the corners of her mouth. "You will indeed stay. I'll hear nothing more of it. You are weary and my grandson will enjoy seeing a friendly face in the morning after you're both rested, I should think."

"I really can't impose."

"You will stay," Lord Ellesmere said, his tone brooking no argument. His decree surprised her. She could not shake the sense he would have preferred if Spencer had not involved himself in her life at all and having her here, in their home, did not sit well with him. But he had acquiesced to his wife's wishes and for that Caelie was glad.

She had no desire to return to the townhouse, to wander the rooms like a ghost in a place that no longer felt like her home. Besides, perhaps she could be of some use and help

Spencer's family through this trying time. It was the least she could do to return their hospitality.

"Very well then. For a few days only."

Lady Ellesmere patted her hand. "Wonderful. You wait here, my dear. I will have some tea and biscuits sent and then I shall speak with Mrs. Faraday and we'll see about getting you settled. Then in the morning we will discuss this husband hunt."

"It is likely a fool's errand, my lady." Caelie had no illusions her chances were slim despite Spencer's belief he could make it happen.

"Most things that involve the heart are, my dear." Lady Ellesmere walked to the door, then stopped to glance over her shoulder at her husband who remained standing in the middle of the room. "My dear, go to your grandson and wish him welcome home, and try not to bark at the poor lad. He is upset enough over Marcus."

"As well he should be."

Lady Ellesmere lifted one eyebrow in a manner so much like her grandson it was uncanny.

Lord Ellesmere sighed heavily and when he spoke again his stern tone had softened. "Very well. I shall speak with him."

Despite his stoic and rather intimidating presence, warmth filled the older man's eyes when he answered his wife. Perhaps he was not as hard on the inside as he appeared on the outside.

"Have a seat, Lady Caelie." Lord Ellesmere waved to the sofa once his wife had left.

Caelie did as he bade. "I do apologize for the inconven—"

He waved her apology off then clasped his hands behind his back. His proud bearing reminded her of a general surveying his troops.

"Before we begin this...plan to find you a proper husband, I believe I should make something clear."

Caelie swallowed. "Yes?"

"I will go along with this endeavor on one condition. That my grandson is not one of the gentlemen you set your cap for."

"Oh, no. Of course. I had no intention—"

"Huntsleigh, whether he likes it or not, has a duty to perform. He must marry a lady of a certain...standing within society. A lady who—"

"Doesn't bear the stain of scandal."

"Then you agree?"

Caelie stood and faced Lord Ellesmere, keeping her shoulders straight despite the weariness in her bones. She had grown tired of bearing the mark of scandal; tired of always being judged by what her father had done, as if his last act on earth had washed away all the good he had done before his death. Why did no one ever remember that? Why did no one recall the kind and gentle man he had been before obsession turned him into someone they did not recognize?

"I agree that after everything Lord Huntsleigh has done for me, I have no wish to make his life any more difficult. Nor do I wish to attach myself where I am not wanted. I do not know if Lord Huntsleigh will be successful in his endeavor to find me a suitable husband, but I promise you I will not force him to the altar to compensate. Does that put your mind at ease, my lord?"

Lord Ellesmere did not move and his expression did not change, but Caelie had the sense of being judged. Whether the marquess's assessment of her was improved or lessened by her decree, she could not say.

"I thank you for your understanding, Lady Caelie. Now, please, make yourself at home. Tea should be along shortly." He inclined his head toward her then turned and strode from the room, leaving her alone with her thoughts and her worry and an unknown future.

Chapter Thirteen

"I never meant for this to happen," Spence said. The words whispered across the expanse of the bed and tumbled over Bowen's motionless body.

He lay still as death.

Spence came closer and leaned over his friend. His chest rose and fell in a regular rhythm as if he only slept and would awake at any minute. But the longer Spence stood there, the less likely it seemed that would happen.

Finally, he gave up and sat on the edge of the bed. "I only meant to prevent you from having to make another journey to the islands. I know how much you hated sailing. I had no idea Lady Franklyn would follow me or that thieves..." He shook his head. What did it matter what his intentions had been when he stared at the result of his actions?

This entire trip had turned into a debacle of epic proportions.

What had he done? Or rather, how did he make things better? He had no answers. Bowen was always the voice of reason amongst the three of them. Without his sensible counsel, Spence was at a loss, his confidence in his own schemes shaken, given the outcome of the last one.

"I have brought home Nick's new cousin, Lady Caelie. She's quite beautiful, had you noticed that?" He searched Bowen's features for any hint he'd heard. Nothing. "We were forced to disembark the *Windswept* when she took ill. Without a chaperone."

He leaned closer. Normally that type of impropriety would have at the very least warranted a look of censure. Perhaps more, given the fact the lady in question was Nick's cousin by marriage.

The steady rhythm of Bowen's breathing continued uninterrupted.

"As well, the inn only had one room available." Spence leaned closer. "Just one. Naturally, we were forced to share the room under the guise of being married."

Bowen didn't move. Not a flinch, twitch or furrowed brow to be seen.

"Did I mention the lack of chaperone?"

Nothing.

"I kissed her." Still nothing. "And I may possibly—" He swallowed. "I may have developed feelings—"

The door opened and Spence jumped to his feet and spun around. Grandfather stood inside of the room; his expression unreadable.

"Grandfather." How long had he been standing there?

His grandfather did not respond immediately. He walked into the room and took the empty seat on the opposite side of Bowen's bed, resting his walking stick against the mahogany night table.

Spence waited. Tension hung in the air between them, thick with unspoken words. Accusations. Grandfather blamed him for Bowen's injuries. If he succumbed to them—

But no. Spence would not entertain that possibility.

Bowen must survive. He could not fathom any other outcome.

For the longest time, Grandfather made no attempt to speak. When finally he did, his voice sounded tired. Weary. "Your grandmother sent me up here to wish you welcome home."

"Ah. And am I?"

Grandfather's stern features relented a little, but anger and disappointment remained etched in the lines of his face. "Of course, you are. This is where you belong, whether you accept that fact or not."

Spence stared down at the coverlet and traced his finger along the design sewn into it. "I know this is my home." He had never questioned that. He just did not care for the dictates that came with it, a fact he had indicated on numerous occasions whenever Grandfather brought the subject of marriage up. He did not bother repeating them now.

"What was the purpose of you leaving Marcus behind as you did?"

"He did not want to go. He never wanted to go."

Grandfather shook his head. "Whatever are you talking about?"

Of course, Grandfather would have no idea. Bowen would never have breathed a word of his displeasure to the man who had raised him and given him a livelihood far better than the son of servants could ever hope for. It had been for his own good, and as such, Spence had no compunction about holding his tongue.

"Bowen hated traveling to the islands. He's loathes the water." Spence stood and paced. He had meant to do something good, to help Bowen. Now look at him, caught in some silent world between the living and the dead.

"Don't be ridiculous. Why Marcus did not hesitate to

jump into the lake and save Blackbourne's sister when she was but a little thing. Or have you forgotten that?"

"I haven't forgotten." Nick's younger sister had been trying to catch their attention where they played nearby and had jumped into the lake. The weight of her soaked dress quickly made it impossible for her to remain afloat. "But that is what Bowen does, Grandfather. It's what he's always done. He sets aside his own wants or needs to help those he cares about. He didn't jump into the lake because he did not fear the water. He jumped into the lake because he could not stand by and allow Lady Rebecca to drown. And so, he sails to the islands even though he fears the water and it makes him ill every time because you ask it of him. That is why he's lying here now. He has an overblown sense of duty!"

"At least someone in this family knows the meaning of the word." Grandfather's claim stopped Spence cold. "Do not try and tell me your only purpose for commandeering the *Windswept* was to relieve Marcus of sailing to the islands."

Spence's sense of self-righteous indignation fizzled. Grandfather knew him too well. "I grant you, I hoped to benefit it from it as well. I have told you repeatedly I have no plans to marry."

"I know what you have told me. But like Marcus, you have a duty to this family. Had you done yours, and allowed Marcus to do his, he would not be lying here in this bed now."

Spence had no argument to that. "I will not marry. I will not drag some poor woman into the misery my parents shared."

"What makes you so certain your marriage would be like theirs?"

Spence cut the air with his arm. "Look at our family history, Grandfather! Aside from you and Grandmama, name me one other happy marriage our family has managed in recent history?" Grandfather said nothing as no such example existed. "We are not built for marriage and I will not consign myself or someone else to a lifetime of misery."

Grandfather rose and walked to the window, staring out at the limited view. "Then you leave me no alternative."

Spence did not like the sound of that. "What do you mean?"

"I have given this much thought."

He liked the sound of that even less.

"You have had more than enough time to change your ways and do what is required of you. Yet you still have shown no leanings toward doing your duty."

Spence's lungs squeezed and his chest tightened. "Grandfather, as I have said—"

His grandfather turned away from the window, the sudden movement cutting Spence off. "And I have told you, Spencer—you must marry. The succession of the title must be secured and the family line must continue. This point is not negotiable. You are the only son of my only son and so that duty falls to you."

"Well, I don't want it." He hated how he sounded like a petulant child being force fed some horrid dish of mashed peas.

"That is immaterial." Grandfather walked toward him with resolve. "You have promised Lady Caelie to see her married before the end of the Season."

"Did she tell you why?"

"She told us enough, though I suspect there is more that has gone unsaid."

Spence glanced away, unable to meet his grandfather's gaze. If he did, the older man would see the truth of his assumption and Spence did not want him to think badly of Caelie. None of this was her fault.

Grandfather let it go. "Well, enough. I will see you married by the end of this Season as well."

Spence's head snapped back. "Are you suggesting I marry Lady Caelie?"

As much a relief marrying her over anyone else would be, he would not do it. She, above all, deserved a happy life after everything she had been through. He would not rob her of that chance.

"Heavens, no." Grandfather brushed the idea away with a wave of his hand. "Her family is far too riddled with scandal to make her suitable."

"She had nothing to do with the scandal in her family." He did not know why he jumped to her defense so readily. Or why a strange sense of disappointment filled him at his grandfather's definitive rejection of the idea.

"Be that as it may, you know how I feel about attaching any further scandal to this family. We have seen our fair share and I will not willingly court more of it."

Spence straightened and held firm. "And I will not marry."

"You will. Or I will disinherit you."

"You can't disinherit me. I am the heir."

"Only to the title and the entailed property and you will not receive that until I die," Grandfather said with an incline of his head. "As to everything else, I can leave my fortune to whomever I please."

Spence blinked. Everything else included the bulk of Grandfather's wealth. He had accumulated it over his lifetime through savvy investments and lucrative businesses. Many in society had looked down their nose at such dabbling, thinking it beneath them. Yet, those same individuals thought nothing of coming to Grandfather with their hands out when their own estates could not survive on the income they generated.

The entailed property was substantial as well, but he would see none of that until his grandfather passed on, and given Grandfather's stalwart health despite his advanced age, that event would likely not occur for some time. Which meant his grandfather could cut him off completely at any moment and he would be left with nothing. Not a single shilling.

"You would leave me destitute?" The idea held as little appeal to him as marriage.

A small smile curved one side of his grandfather's mouth into a smile. "Indeed."

What did his grandfather expect him to do if he wasn't assisting in running the estates? He wasn't like Bowen. He hadn't been trained for anything else. The suggestion bordered on preposterous. "You wouldn't."

"I will." Grandfather's stoic expression told Spence the man had no intention of backing down. He'd made up his mind, and when the Marquess of Ellesmere decided upon a course of action, Hercules himself could not budge him from it.

"Why are you doing this?"

His grandfather stepped toward him and placed a strong hand on his shoulder. For a brief moment, warmth radiated from his features. "Because it needs to be done, Spencer. You cannot use your parents' marriage as an excuse forever."

But it wasn't an excuse. It was a warning. One Spence had taken to heart as he sat on the cold ground in the dark of night, his dead parents next to him.

Grandfather squeezed his shoulder. "Get some sleep, son. It has been a trying day. Tomorrow, we will discuss what is to be done."

Spence nodded but could not find the words to answer. Grandfather's decree rang in his ears with the ferocity of iron bars being slammed shut in front of him, cutting off any hope for a happy future.

Spence waited for his grandfather to leave and Mrs. Faraday to arrive. His grandparents did not want to leave Bowen unattended and Spence himself was reluctant to quit the room, afraid if he did something would befall his friend and he'd be unable to prevent it.

"I promise I will keep a close eye on 'im, m'lord."

Spence nodded as he hovered near the edge of the bed. "Do you think he'll get better?"

Mrs. Faraday's answer did not come swift enough for his liking and when it did, he heard the doubt laced around her words. "He's a strong lad, m'lord. If anyone can pull through this, it's he."

If.

Spence despised that word.

"Is Lady Caelie settled?" He had left her with his grandparents, left her to piece together the story of how they had ended up here.

"Oh yes, we put her up in the lavender room."

"The lavender room?" It had been his aunt's bedroom when she lived and while Grandmama always kept it ready to receive a guest, Spence could not recall anyone ever actually staying in it.

"I think it will be to 'er liking. She seems an easy one to please."

He could not argue Mrs. Faraday's assessment. Caelie had been easy to please. She'd taken every lump and bump thrown at her without the smallest complaint. He'd known grown men with less fortitude than her.

"Thank you, Mrs. Faraday. Well..." He cast one last look at Bowen. "I suppose I should find my own bed. You'll let me know if there's any change?"

"Of course, I will. Now off t'bed with ya." She shooed him out of the room as if he was still the small boy she used to chase out of the kitchens. The familiarity filled him with warmth. It was good to be home, he just wished it hadn't come at such a high price for everyone involved.

He made his way down the hallway to his own bedroom

but stopped as he passed the lavender room and hovered outside its door. For a little over a week, he had passed his evenings with Caelie, talking to her, teasing her, entertaining her with stories. How odd it seemed now to turn in without the benefit of her company. Without wishing her a good night. Without her smile being the last thing he saw before she turned down the lamp next to her bed.

He could sorely use her smile now. Maybe if he saw it, it would give him hope that matters would right themselves. Perhaps she could talk past the insistent chatter in his head telling him what a mess he'd made of everything.

He tapped on the door before good sense told him to turn away. Likely she had fallen fast asleep and dreamed of better days—of the husband he would find her and a house filled with children who had fiery locks and emerald eyes.

He started to turn away when the door opened. "Lord Huntsleigh." She wore a dressing gown over her nightdress. It must be her favorite as he had seen her wear the same one numerous times at the inn. Concern furrowed her brow and she opened the door a little wider. "Is it Mr. Bowen?"

"Yes. I mean, no. He's no worse." He shook his head. "He's no better."

He stared at her and, in that moment, he understood what she had done with Billingsworth. He hadn't understood before. Not truly. Now he did. It wasn't a habit created from their travels that had brought him to her door. He didn't need to entertain her with a story, or tease her, or play a game of cards.

He just needed to be near her. Her closeness made him feel better. And he needed to feel better now. He needed solace. She had done the same under far more trying circumstances.

He could not condemn her or think less of her for it.

She opened the door and stepped aside. "Come in."

Chapter Fourteen

"I should not have disturbed you."

Now that he stood inside of her bedchamber, his good sense banged on the other side of the closed door and demanded entry. He had no business being there, certainly not with her in this state of dress and no chaperone and—

He laughed. Had they not been down this road already? Had this not been the past week of their lives?

"What is so funny?"

Spence shook his head. "I just realized how improper the past week has been and yet—"

"And yet?"

"And yet it feels anything but. It doesn't feel wrong to be here with you. I know it should, but somehow it feels completely natural. I think..." He furrowed his brow. "Have we become friends?"

She smiled and it washed over him like a warm bath. He wanted to sink into it. Into her.

"I would like to think we have."

He nodded. Such a strange idea. He did not think he had

ever been friends with a woman. Had never thought to get that close. Oh, surely, he was fond of Nick's wife, Abigail, and Nick's sister, Lady Rebecca, but this felt different. Special. Something that belonged only to them.

"Tell me how Mr. Bowen fares." Caelie took his hand and placed it against her heart. Its strong beat kept a steady rhythm beneath their entwined fingers. Or was that his pulse? Either way, her closeness proved a balm on nerves ravaged by worry. Yet, at the same time, being near her filled him with a strange anticipation he could not quite nail down.

"He is just lying there. He doesn't move, save to breathe. It looks as if he is sleeping but I fear it is such a deep sleep he may never awaken." There. He'd said it. He'd given the words wings. "What if he doesn't?"

Caelie took a step closer until he could feel the warmth of her body. He closed his eyes and pulled her even closer until only their clasped hands kept their bodies apart. He rested his forehead against hers and took in a deep breath. This was what he needed.

"Mr. Bowen is strong and healthy." Her breath whispered against his skin. "If he has held on this long, my guess is he wishes to fight and find his way back. You told me he is a very determined sort. I expect he will be equally as determined now."

What she said made sense and the fear clutching his heart eased somewhat. "Thank you for saying that."

"It is only the truth, my lord."

"Spencer." He lifted his head to gaze at her. "We are friends, are we not? You should call me by my name."

"It would be improper."

He glanced around the room, at their current situation and smiled at her. She laughed lightly when he lifted an eyebrow. "Very well, then. Spencer."

The sound of his name on her lips poured through him

like warmed brandy. He closed his eyes for a brief moment to savor the sensation. "I like the sound of that."

"The sound of what?"

"My name on your lips." He opened his eyes. He pulled their hands to his side and drew her even closer until only a hair's breadth separated them. Too close for propriety, though he'd never been much of a stickler for such things. But even he knew he stood on dangerous ground.

Yet he did nothing to step away from it.

Nor did she.

"Would you say it again?"

Her lips parted and his gaze fell upon them. Heat pooled in his groin and his body shook with longing and expectation.

"Spencer," she whispered and this time she closed her eyes. Her breasts lifted against the scooped neckline of her dressing gown as she took a deep breath. Did she feel it too, this strange current that enveloped them? It was the same one he'd felt that night at the inn when she'd listened to him relive the story of his parents' death and offered him comfort with a kiss. He wished she would do that again. He wouldn't stop her. It was just a kiss, after all.

Except that it wasn't. It hadn't been that night at the inn and it wouldn't be now. It would be nothing more than a torment because for every day following, he would remember it. He would feel it all over again when he watched her dance in the arms of another man. It would worsen when she accepted another man's proposal and become unbearable when she stood at the altar and pledged her life to someone other than him.

But it would never be him.

It couldn't be.

All the things she wanted he could never give her. He could not stand the idea of the kiss they might share now turning into something terrible, and it would. That's what marriage did. It took something lovely and made it into something dark and twisted. Passion turned to contempt, loving glancing to glares of anger and resentment.

He could not stand the thought of Caelie looking at him in such a way. He would die inside. And worse, so would she. It would destroy everything wonderful about her. Her sunny disposition, her warmth, her loving nature.

Spence cupped the side of her face. She turned her head slightly to nestle into his touch. His heart twisted painfully. He dipped his head and brushed his lips against her cheek and held himself there, soaking in the warmth of her body, her enticing scent, the taste of her skin.

He had come to her seeking comfort. He had found so much more.

"Goodnight, Caelie." The words whispered out of him and even he could hear the desperation buried inside of them.

He forced himself to step away, to turn and walk through the bedroom door and down the hallway without looking back. His body screamed for mercy, his heart insisted he return to her, but his head knew better. His head knew how things would end if he did.

No, better he leave her now, that he keep the friendship they shared and protect it from becoming broken into fragments that would never fit back together.

He reached his room at the end of the long hall and pushed inside. His back pressed the door closed and he leaned there until his legs threatened to give out. When that finally happened, he sank to the floor, afraid if he moved at all his will would evaporate and he'd seek her out and ruin them both.

C aelie felt no more rested the next morning than she had been when they arrived in London the day before. Spencer's impromptu visit to her room, the kiss that almost happened, her body's response—all of it kept her tossing and turning for the rest of the night. Her body raged with unfulfilled desire and she could not close her eyes without the image of his hands exploring every inch of her skin. Bringing an end to the ache throbbing between her legs herself had only served to torment her more.

As she sat in front of the vanity while Elsie dressed her hair, she knew it to be folly to allow her thoughts to traipse down that road. Lord Ellesmere had made it clear he would not consider her as a suitable option for Spencer's wife. She, in turn, had given her word she had no intention of pursuing him.

Not that it mattered. In the end, Spencer hadn't kissed her. He had come to her for comfort, nothing more. Motives she understood only too well. She also understood the pain acting on them created. She should be thankful Spencer had shown such restraint. His ability to do so spoke volumes, for she knew she did not possess the same level of control. Had he kissed her, she would have returned it—and more.

Shame burned across her chest and up her neck.

"You're turnin' bright as an apple, m'lady. Are you well?"

Caelie cleared her throat. "Yes. I'm fine. Just a little warm. Have you heard how Mr. Bowen fares this morning?"

She did not bother to explain to Elsie who Mr. Bowen was. Staff below stairs talked amongst themselves and likely knew more about the household than the people who paid their salaries. Even in the short time they had been there, Elsie would have heard all about Mr. Bowen.

Her new maid fixed a pin into the thick folds of Caelie's hair. "Much the same, ma'am. Though Mrs. Faraday, the housekeeper, thought 'e might 'ave a bit more color today. She thinks it's on account of Lord Huntsleigh havin' returned."

"I do hope she is right."

"She also said when you are up and about you could find Lady Ellesmere in Mr. Bowen's rooms. Mrs. Faraday said she watches over 'im like he was 'er own son. Said she's wearin' 'erself down doin' it, but she won't be told no different."

Caelie had seen the strain on the woman yesterday. Fear and worry were etched in the lines around her eyes and mouth. Caelie understood such things having watched her own father descend into despondency over his mistress's rejection and the worry of where that would end. She would ease Lady Ellesmere's burden if she could in return for the warmth and hospitality she'd already been shown.

Caelie hurried through the breakfast Elsie had brought up, took one last look at her reflection in the mirror and hurried down the hallway, wondering if she would find the marchioness alone, or if Spencer would be with her.

And if so, how should she respond? As if nothing had occurred between them last night? Her head buzzed from the stress of it, but when she tapped on Mr. Bowen's bedroom door and Lady Ellesmere bid her enter, she found the older woman alone with her patient.

"Ah, Lady Caelie." Lady Ellesmere rose from her chair and crossed the room, taking Caelie's hand and drawing her toward the bed. "I think he has more color this morning. I'm sure of it. He took some broth last night. I had to massage his throat to get it down, but perhaps it helped."

Caelie glanced down at Mr. Bowen. He appeared thinner than she remembered, but given the circumstances, that was to be expected. The grey pallor she had expected, however, was not in evidence. A fact that gave her untold relief for Spencer's sake if nothing else.

"I'm sure your attentions have been most helpful, Lady

Ellesmere, but please do not make yourself sick in the process. I am more than willing to assist and allow you time to rest. I am sure when Mr. Bowen awakens, he will be most grieved if he finds you ill on his account."

"You are right, of course. But I cannot seem to help myself."

"Has the doctor given his prognosis for Mr. Bowen?"

Lady Ellesmere gave a small shake of his head. "Oh, they try to protect me from it, Dr. Bledsoe and Lord Ellesmere, but I'm not so blind. I sit with him every day. I pour broth into his mouth and massage his neck so he might swallow it and I wait for him to show some sign that he will reawaken. It has only been a few days since the fever caused him to fall silent, but I know the longer it goes on the less chance there is. I cannot bear to think of it. Marcus has always been such a strong boy. Brave, really, though I think some people miss that for all his quiet ways. If he can fight his way back to us, he will. I have to believe that."

Caelie smiled. The love Lady Ellesmere bore for Mr. Bowen emanated from her like a warm light. He may have been brought in as a ward, but they clearly thought of him as family.

"Sometimes hope is all we have to hold onto until time gives us something more."

Lady Ellesmere smiled up at her. "My dear, are you trying to placate an old woman?"

"You are not old, m'lady," Mrs. Faraday said as she bustled into the room with an energy Caelie began to realize was her natural state. "You're vibrant as a summer's day."

Lady Ellesmere smiled and went to the table where the housekeeper set a tray of tea and biscuits. "I feel more like a dark winter's night, but you are kind to say, Mrs. Faraday. I can always count on you to feed my vanity."

"Pish. Ye've not an ounce of it, m'lady. Not an ounce."

"Off with you," the marchioness waved and Mrs. Faraday's gregarious laughter followed her out of the room. "That woman is such a blessing. I know she's not as refined as most people like to see in their upper servants, but she's worth her weight in gold. Come have some tea, my dear. We'll discuss this plan my grandson has concocted and see what we need to do about it."

Caelie did as instructed and accepted the cup of tea Lady Ellesmere offered. "Should we wait for Lord Huntsleigh?"

"Oh, I suspect he's quite tired after his visit last night."

Caelie started, nearly spilling her tea. "His visit?"

Lady Ellesmere waved a hand. "With Marcus. Are you quite alright, my dear?"

"Oh yes. Yes, of course. Just anxious to get underway, I suppose." She took another sip of her tea and avoided the marchioness's pointed gaze. Heat clawed its way over her jawline and burst onto her cheeks. Of course, she had meant his visit with Mr. Bowen. "I'm sure he is quite worried."

"As we all are. He will blame himself, of course. He always does when such things happen." Her voice dipped as she said the last part.

"Do such things happen often?"

"Oh, no. Not truly. But his parents..." Her voice drifted off for a moment and the sadness from yesterday returned to her light blue eyes.

Caelie rested the tea cup in its saucer. "He told me what happened the night they died."

Lady Ellesmere looked up in surprise. "He did?"

"Y-yes." Perhaps she should have kept that to herself. "It must have been awful for him."

"It was." Lady Ellesmere released a sad sigh and took a sip of her tea before continuing. "It was a sad state of affairs, I'm afraid. We did our best to shield him from it, of course, but I don't know that we were very successful. He blames himself.

He thought it up to him to fix things, but I'm afraid they were beyond repair."

"But he must see now that their happiness was not his responsibility?" How dreadful to carry such a burden.

"Who is to say?"

"Who is to say what?"

Caelie turned as Spencer entered the door left open by Mrs. Faraday. Her instant reaction to him had not lessened in the hours since she last saw him. He had dressed impeccably in a blue jacket and brocade waistcoat. Both enhanced the blue of his eyes and the gold tones of his thick hair. Buff breeches met Hessian boots and showed his lean muscular physique to its best advantage. The blush Caelie suffered back in her room threatened to bloom anew. If he'd suffered a sleepless night as she had, it did not show.

He crossed to where his grandmother sat and gave her a quick peck on the cheek. "Good morning, Grandmama. Lady Caelie. I hope the day finds you well."

"It does, my lord." She kept with the formal address as had he. The more familiar address would be saved for when they found themselves alone, something she knew she needed to avoid whenever possible. She did not trust herself and she didn't want to give her heart any false hope that there was something worth hoping for. There wasn't.

"Perfect timing," Lady Ellesmere said as she poured him a cup of tea. "We were just about to explore our options with respect to Lady Caelie's husband hunt."

"Oh." He looked from his grandmother to her.

"I told your grandparents of our plans after running into Lord Billingsworth at the inn."

"Ah. Right. Of course. Well, let the planning commence," he said, a smile fixed upon his handsome face as if he looked forward to the process. All the better, she supposed, to rid him of the encumbrance she presented.

But before they could start, Lord Ellesmere strode into the room, his ever-present walking stick tapping against floor. Caelie had seen less traffic at the marketplace.

"Good morning, all. How does young Marcus fare this morning?"

"I think he might have more color," Lady Ellesmere offered.

"Hm." Lord Ellesmere stopped at Mr. Bowen's bedside and reached down to squeeze the man's hand before straightening. He said nothing else, yet evident in that one small gesture was all of the worry and love this small family had for the man lying unmoving in the bed. She prayed he would recover, for their sakes as much as his own.

"Come have some tea and biscuits," Lady Ellesmere instructed. Her husband stared at Mr. Bowen for another moment before joining them at the table and accepting a cup of tea from his wife. "We are discussing the matter of potential husbands for Lady Caelie. I have narrowed it down to a list of three gentlemen I think would be strong possibilities."

Spencer swallowed a mouthful of tea and winced. "A list of three? Already?"

"Well, my dear, the Season is underway and given that Lord Billingsworth may have taken the wrong impression in seeing you and Lady Caelie travel together, we cannot waste time. Wouldn't you agree?"

"I suppose."

Lord Ellesmere sat quietly but did not contribute his opinion to the conversation. Caelie suspected he would be more than happy to have her receive a proposal from anyone, so long as it wasn't his grandson. He was simply too polite to say so in the company of others.

Lady Ellesmere held up a hand and ticked the names off on her fingers. "Lord Tunston, Lord Cranbrook, and Lord Shaftsbury."

Caelie watched Spencer's expression as his grandmother listed her choices. He did not look pleased. She, on the other hand, had met them all and could claim no particular issue to the gentlemen listed, save for one. They were not Spencer.

Still, two earls and a viscount were more than respectable. Did they make her heart jump when they entered a room? No. Nor did her toes curl at the idea of sharing a kiss with them. But it did not matter. She did not have the luxury to hope for such things. Perhaps in time she could learn to love one of them and the feelings she currently experienced for Spencer would follow.

"Grandmama, honestly! You cannot seriously consider those three men as suitable for Lady Caelie."

Lady Ellesmere turned to her grandson and looked affronted. "And why ever not? Each of them is financially solvent, each is required to produce an heir and therefore must marry, and none of them has done anything scandalous enough to be worth mentioning. They are amenable men, treat their families well, and do their duty. I cannot think of any better recommendation. What possible objection can you have toward any of them?"

Spencer pushed his tea aside. "For starters, Lord Tunston waddles like a duck—"

"I grant you, he is a bit on the portly side, but that's hardly a mark against him," Lady Ellesmere said.

"Lord Cranbrook sounds like a donkey when he laughs, which he does at the most inappropriate of times—"

Lady Ellesmere shrugged. "To find a man of good humor can only be considered a bonus, I would think."

"And Shaftsbury...Shaftsbury is...he's..."

Caelie leaned forward waiting to hear whatever ghastly trait he perceived Lord Shaftsbury possessed. She had met him when she had been presented and thought him a pleasant enough fellow of moderate appearance.

"Yes?" Lady Ellesmere waited.

"He's dull!"

Lady Ellesmere laughed and for the first time since their arrival, Caelie noted a light in the lady's eyes. If nothing else, her falling ill on the ship had at least done some good. It had brought Spencer home at a time his family needed him most.

"My dear boy," Lord Ellesmere said, speaking up on the subject for the first time. "Lord Shaftsbury is a sensible man, not given to high spirits, gambling or raucous behavior. All points in his favor. We would hardly want Lady Caelie to marry a man who did not do his duty, preferred drinking and carousing and was never around when she needed him. Would we?"

Spencer swallowed. The movement made his Adam's apple bob in his throat and his lips twitched. He looked as if he wanted to argue his grandfather's point, but what argument was there?

"I recall," Caelie said, inserting herself into the conversation which seemed only appropriate given they were discussing her future. "That Lord Shaftsbury is quite fond of books."

"Indeed." Lord Ellesmere turned away from Spencer whose frustration had apparently rendered him temporarily mute. "He is in possession of an extensive library on a vast number of topics."

"I do love books," Caelie said. That was something, at least. "It would be nice to have a houseful of books."

"Well, it is settled then." Lady Ellesmere clapped her hands. "The Viscount of Shaftsbury moves to the head of the pack. We will concentrate our efforts on him while still cultivating an interest with Lords Tunston and Cranbrook."

"Now wait just a minute." Spencer waved his hands as if to ward off any further planning on his grandmother's part. "Lady Caelie and I have decided I shall act as if I have fallen under her spell, thereby giving the appearance that I am willing to give up my bachelorhood for the shackles of matrimony."

"Hm." Lady Ellesmere appeared to give Spencer's idea serious consideration. "It could work. What do you think, my dear?"

"I think it is sheer poppycock and tomfoolery," Lord Ellesmere said.

"I am not sure I agree," his wife countered. "Heaven only knows everyone believes it would take a miracle to get Huntsleigh anywhere near an altar. If Lady Caelie is seen to be that miracle, it will create a sense of intrigue. They will want to see what the fuss is about, perhaps try to woo her away for themselves. You know how competitive gentlemen can be."

"My thinking exactly." Spencer nodded and crossed his arms across his chest.

Lord Ellesmere scowled at him. "If you think for one moment this scheme to appear enamored of Lady Caelie will in any way thwart my plans to see you married before Season's end, you are mistaken."

"My dear, now is not the time to discuss such matters. It is Lady Caelie we are focusing on at the moment."

Caelie tried to catch Spencer's eye, but he avoided her gaze, having turned his attention to the window next to him. Lord Ellesmere had made it clear to her he intended to see Spencer married, but she had the distinct impression the conversation he'd had with his grandson went far beyond what he had shared with her.

A sharp rap interrupted them once again. Mrs. Faraday stood in the doorway and worried her hands. "M'lady, you have a visitor."

"Who is it, Mrs. Faraday?"

"The Duchess of Franklyn, m'lady. She says she wants to convey her appreciation for what Mr. Bowen done for 'er. I said 'e wasn't able to receive visitors, but she seems adamant someone attend to her."

Lady Ellesmere's lips pursed and Lord Ellesmere glared at his grandson.

"Lady Caelie," the marchioness said, rising from her chair. The men stood with her and Caelie quickly joined them. "Perhaps you should retire to your room while I dispense of Lady Franklyn. We will reveal your presence in our home soon, but it will be when we are more prepared. The woman is unconscionable, coming to our door when she knows we are not currently receiving visitors."

"Yes, of course, my lady."

Just as well she retired to her room. She did not relish coming face to face with Spencer's rumored former mistress. Lady Franklyn's beauty was rivaled only her vindictiveness. What would the woman think of her when she discovered Caelie now lived under the same roof as her former lover? Likely nothing good. And even less than that when they initiated their plan and Spencer's feigned infatuation became known.

Caelie was more than happy to put that particular duel off until another day.

She could not put it off forever, though. Eventually, she must face Lady Franklyn and all of the others who thought less of her due to her father's scandal. There would be no avoiding it.

She had the sudden sense of jumping off a steep cliff with nothing to break her fall.

Chapter Fifteen

"Your snoring will be the death of me."

Spence jerked and sat upright in the chair he had pulled over to Bowen's bedside. Shadows flooded the room, chased to the edges of the bed by the dim glow from the lamp a few feet away. For a fleeting moment, Spence thought the words had come from his dream, but it wasn't Bowen who had drifted through his slumber. It had been a certain red-headed lady.

It took several pounding heartbeats before it sunk in the words had come from elsewhere. His gaze flew to the bed.

"Are you...? You're—"

"Awake? Yes." Bowen's voice rasped over his throat in a whisper. "Have been for a little while."

"Why didn't you say anything?" Spence got out of his chair and went to the bedside table where a pot of now cold tea sat next to the lamp. He turned the wick up and pushed the shadows into the corners of the room before he poured a cup. Bowen winced at the light and reached for the tea.

Spence waved away his shaking hand and held the cup to Bowen's lips. The man drank greedily.

"How long have you been awake?"

"I'm not certain. I drift in and out. It always seems to be the middle of the night." He took another drink of tea and made a face as he swallowed the cold liquid. "I didn't want to wake Lord or Lady Ellesmere."

"But you were fine waking me from my peaceful slumber?"

Bowen let his head fall back against the pillow. His paleness rivaled the linens he laid upon. "I owed you one for leaving me stranded on the dock."

Spence sat down again. "Grandfather thinks it my fault you were stabbed."

A grin spread across Bowen's face, much to Spence's irritation. "Did he say so?"

"Perhaps not directly, but the inference was undeniable. And you need not look so happy about it. I felt awful. I still feel awful."

Bowen chuckled. "Good. Then perhaps you will stop trying to run away from home like an errant child."

"I was not running away. I was doing you a favor."

Bowen did not argue the point, but added, "While running away."

"Grandfather is determined to get me married. You know how I feel about that."

"There are worse fates."

"Name one."

"Getting stabbed by a knife wielding thug while Lady Franklyn screams bloody murder in your ear."

Spence groaned and dropped his head back against the chair to stare at the ceiling. Trust Bowen to put him in his place with grace and humor. "Well, I've returned."

"I see that. And unless I have been unconscious for far longer than I think, your planned trip to the islands was a very short one indeed."

"According to Grandmother, you've been lazing about—"

"Unconscious."

"—for three days. Four now. She thought you were a goner. She's quite put out with you for making her worry so. I have reclaimed my status as her favorite."

"I shall have to remedy that."

"I believe not dying will suffice."

"You didn't answer my question."

Spence avoided Bowen's direct gaze. "What question was that?"

"Why did you return? I would suggest guilt, but that would require a conscience—"

"I have a very well-developed conscience, thank you."

"I believe Lord Franklyn would beg to differ on that account."

Spence placed a hand over his heart and feigned innocence. "You befriend a man's neglected wife and suddenly you're the ne'er-do-well."

"Indeed. And she was hardly neglected. Lord Franklyn is a good man."

"Speaking of the old duke, he has offered you a sizable reward for saving his beloved."

"A reward? What am I to do with a reward?" Bowen sounded as if they'd offered him a week's worth of stale bread.

Spence shrugged and grinned. "Perhaps it will make you more attractive to the ladies, having a fortune and all."

"I already have a fortune."

"Yes, but they don't know that. Really, Bowen, you fail miserably at making yourself a viable prospect to the lovely ladies of the ton."

Bowen gave him a steady stare, his only comment on the matter. Spence shook his head. He'd never met anyone as self-assured as Bowen. The man knew little of his parents who had died when he was too young to remember them. He'd spent his life being raised as Lord Ellesmere's ward, treated as an equal but without the benefit of title or inheritance to elevate his status in society. The fortune he had accumulated by his own savvy business pursuits could help do this, yet he made no move to do so. For all intents and purposes, the man appeared appallingly content with his lot in life. It baffled the senses.

"You have yet to answer my question," Bowen said. His voice had grown tired. "And make the explanation brief. I'm tired and want to sleep."

"Well, my terribly lazy friend, as it turned out, Lady Caelie took very ill shortly after the *Windswept* set out to sea. You recall her, do you not? You and Nick arranged her passage on the ship without telling me."

"We had no reason to tell you. You were not supposed to be on the ship."

"Touché."

"What of Lady Caelie then?" Concerned darkened Bowen's gaze.

"Captain Moresley feared for her health and decided it best that she disembarked in Portsmouth."

"And you took it upon yourself to see her and Lady Glenmor back to London?"

"You need not sound so surprised." Spence scowled at his friend. "Of course, I did. She is Nick's cousin by marriage. How could I not? But, as it turned out, her dragon of a mother refused to disembark with her."

"Lady Glenmor? You mean she—"

"Abandoned her. Yes. It was a despicable thing to do and I believe Lady Caelie is quite hurt by it, though she does not say so in so many words. She's staying here for now. Glenmor is away on business."

Bowen nodded. "I put him and Nick onto a business proposition I think will prove fruitful. Glenmor has traveled north to investigate and will report back to both of us. Does this mean...did the two of you travel alone?"

"No. Not exactly. Garron came with us."

"Garron? A good man but hardly a proper chaperone. Spence, if Nick finds out you—"

"Nick should be pleased I did not leave her stranded and alone in Portsmouth. I did my best to ensure we maintained propriety. I hired a lady's maid once we reached the inn." He did not mention they had been forced to share a room, or put on the ruse of being man and wife. Bowen could be a stickler about such things and he didn't need him poking at the guilt he already felt over what had transpired between himself and Caelie.

Though, granted, most of the guilt came from not feeling guilty enough.

"Now, I must find her a husband."

"You appear thrilled at the prospect. Why don't you marry her?"

"Don't be ridiculous! Besides, Grandfather has made it clear he does not deem her acceptable. To make matters worse, he has threatened to cut me off completely if I do not marry someone of his choosing by Season's end."

"So, you have no intention of marrying Lady Caelie?"

"No." Why was it every time he thought or said that, it felt as if a stone had settled in his stomach? "She is perfectly lovely in every way you could imagine, an absolute gem. Any man would be lucky to have her, without doubt. But she deserves someone who can give her all the things she wants from marriage. I am not that man."

"I see." Bowen fell silent a moment, then, "Perhaps I am."

Spence jerked upright in his chair. "W-what? You?"

"Certainly. Why not? You said so yourself, my fortune could make me most attractive to the ladies of the ton, of which she is one. She wishes to marry and I do as well."

"Now? Right this instant? Why, you're not even upright!"

"Details." Bowen brushed his assessment aside. "And why not now? I have just had a brush with death. It has made me realize time is not something one should waste waiting for the perfect moment. Imagine that I might have died without having an heir to leave my fortune to?"

"You could leave it to me. At least then I will not be destitute when Grandfather disowns me."

Bowen ignored his suggestion. "Yes, I think I will need to give this matter grave thought. Surely neither Nick nor Lord Glenmor would have an objection. I do not have a title but I have other things to recommend me."

Spence leaned closer to his friend. "Are you jesting with me?"

"Perhaps." Bowen grinned. "Then again, perhaps not. Although I do find it curious that the thought of my marrying Lady Caelie has you so riled. Would you like to explain that?"

"There is nothing to explain." Spence averted his gaze and rubbed at a scuff on his boot. Or was it only the light casting shadow over it? Either way, worth investigation.

"Is there not?"

"No. Obviously, all this lazing about has left you addled in the head."

"Perhaps. Now, I am tired. I've grown fond of this lazing about and think I shall do some more of it. Go back to your room. No need to watch over me."

"Grandmother wants someone here at all times."

"You can tell her I sent you away on the grounds your atrocious snoring kept me up."

"I do not snore."

"You snore like a foghorn. Now go. Wait until the morning to tell your grandparents. No point waking them in the middle of the night." Bowen closed his eyes.

Spence waited a moment until the steady rise and fall of

Bowen's chest indicated he had given in to his body's need for rest. Then he took his friend up on his suggestion and left to find his own bed. Perhaps he would finally sleep tonight, now that his friend was on the mend and he did not need to fear losing him to the Grim Reaper.

But each time he closed his eyes, he could not help but see Lady Caelie standing at the altar looking stunning in her wedding dress, summer flowers blooming all around her and Bowen standing next to her looking as proud as any man marrying her should.

"Damn you, Bowen," he muttered, punching his pillow as he rolled over in an effort to escape the image.

But it followed him no matter which way he turned.

Had Bowen been serious? And what if he had been? Bowen was a far better man than any of the three Grandmama had come up with. In truth, Spence knew of no one better, and if anyone could make Caelie happy and give her the life she wanted, it would be his dear friend.

Why then, did the idea of them together leave him so horribly rankled?

"Argh!"

Spence shoved the blankets aside and stalked from his room in search of brandy.

"I am so pleased Mr. Bowen is doing better." Lady Rebecca placed a hand over her heart and tension drained from her shoulders. It had been several days since Mr. Bowen had awakened and spoken to Spencer. The change in the household since then nothing short of significant, as if a dark cloud had dissipated and left only clear blue sky.

"Indeed." The Dowager Countess of Blackbourne echoed

her daughter's thoughts. "And it is so good to hear you have returned to us safely as well, Lady Caelie. Nicholas and Abigail will be nothing short of thrilled."

Caelie smiled. "Thank you, Lady Blackbourne. It is kind of you to say." Even in her mourning dress of dove grey, the lady exuded elegance and beauty that age seemed disinclined to touch.

"How chivalrous of Lord Huntsleigh to ensure you arrived safely and with all due propriety as well." Lady Rebecca smiled.

"I will be forever grateful to him."

Lady Blackbourne inclined her head. "I will be certain to mention such on my other calls." Gratitude flooded Caelie for their kindness and support.

"How very thoughtful of you," Lady Ellesmere said. "We have sent a letter to Lord and Lady Blackbourne to inform them of Lady Caelie's return and of Mr. Bowen's improved health."

"I expect my brother and Abigail will return with all due haste if they have not already begun their journey back to London." The lavender in Lady Rebecca's half-mourning dress caught the light and reflected the same silvery eyes she shared with her brother. The distinction between her light eyes and ivory skin against her inky black hair created a startling beauty. Caelie suspected only her required absence from society after her father's passing had kept her from making a match last season.

"I am certain my son will have attempted to convince Abigail to stay behind, given her condition, but I suspect we can expect them both very soon." Lady Blackbourne smiled at Caelie, the gesture conveying her high estimation of her new daughter-in-law. "Your cousin is not one to be dictated to."

Caelie laughed at the compliment. It did her heart good to know Abigail had found such acceptance within the Sheridan family. She deserved it after all she had done to champion their own family in the wake of Father's death. "Indeed, she is in possession of a strong will."

Though it had only been a fortnight since she last saw her family, she missed them terribly. Abigail had been her closest confidante and strongest advocate. Something she needed desperately given her conflicting emotions over Spencer and the husband hunt they were about to embark on.

Then again, knowing Abigail, if she knew of Caelie's attraction for Spencer, her counsel would likely be to throw caution and good judgment to the wind and act on her feelings. It's what her cousin would have done. It's what she did do in the end.

But she was not as brave or as bold as Abigail. Nor did she wish to have her heart broken by chasing someone who did not want to marry her. And he didn't. After their near kiss of a few nights ago, he had studiously avoided her. They met at dinner time when the family dined together and on the occasional passing in the hallway, where he always seemed to be in a hurry to get somewhere else. Obviously, her original assessment had been correct. He had not come to her that night out of a sense of desire or attraction; he had merely needed someone to talk to, to gather comfort from.

Felton, the old butler who had been in service to the Kingsleys for as long as anyone could remember, appeared in the door. "Lord and Lady Black—"

"No need to announce us, Felton," the familiar voice of Lord Blackbourne preceded him into the room, cutting off Felton who looked out of sorts at the interruption.

Caelie jumped to her feet as her cousin pushed past her new husband and rushed toward her, arms out-stretched. "Caelie!"

Never one to stand on ceremony, Abigail released a small squeal of delight and wrapped her arms around Caelie. A small bump protruded from her cousin's belly where the babe grew and a rush of love filled her. She would not miss out on the birth or seeing the little one grow after all.

Abigail pulled away and held Caelie's shoulders in a firm grip. "I am so happy to see you well! Do not ever frighten me like that again. And where is Huntsleigh? I must give him a proper thanks for bringing you home to us."

"I believe he is upstairs with Mr. Bowen."

Nicholas dropped a quick kiss on the cheeks of the other ladies before Abigail stepped aside long enough to allow him to give Caelie a proper hug. "It is good to have you home, my dear. Abigail has been miserable since you left. I feared we would have to move to Italy ourselves just to improve her mood."

"I am glad to have saved you the trip, Lord Blackbourne."

"Lord Blackbourne," he scoffed. "How many times must I tell you to call me Nicholas? We are among family and friends. No need to stand on ceremony."

"Very well. I suppose with Mother no longer here to tell me otherwise, I can do just that, can't I?"

"Indeed," Abigail said. "Although I am sorry you had to suffer through such a horrible thing. Huntsleigh's message of what happened reached us as we were leaving to come see Marcus. It was atrocious what she did, but I cannot attest to being sorry she is gone, only happy that you are home."

Caelie smiled, though sadness pulled the corners of her mouth. "I am inclined to agree. It does not feel good to know Mother did not care enough to see to my well-being, but I am determined to see the bright side."

"My lady," Felton appeared at Lady Ellesmere's elbow and held out a silver salver with an expensive ivory card set in the middle. The marchioness picked up the card and glanced at it, then lifted one eyebrow in a fashion reminiscent of her grandson, causing Caelie's heart to leap in her chest.

She nodded at Felton then addressed the rest of them. "It appears the Duchess of Franklyn and her daughter are paying a call yet again."

The Dowager Blackbourne's expression mirrored her hostess's. "Again? She is rather relentless, is she not? I have heard the duke wishes to reward Mr. Bowen for his brave acts."

Lady Rebecca clasped her hands in front of her. "Mr. Bowen should accept the reward. It will enable him to make a better match. Especially if he capitalizes on the fervor once he is well enough. Why, all the ladies are sure to swoon with such a well-compensated hero in their midst."

Felton's booming voice announced the new guests as Lady Franklyn bustled into the room with her daughter trailing behind her. Much like Nicholas's mother, the duchess had not allowed the ravages of time to touch her. At forty years of age, she barely looked older than her daughter. Lady Susan, on the other hand, did not fare so well. She favored her father. Slight, yet gangly, as if she could not decide what to do with her limbs. Where her mother's hair shone a tawny gold, Lady Susan's had grown to a dull brown and her thick brow did nothing to enhance the color of her ordinary blue eyes.

To make matters worse, she wore a constant look of dissatisfaction combined with an ever-present scowl, as if she had just caught a whiff of a rather bad smell.

Lady Franklyn stopped and surveyed the group. "My, my. We are quite crowded in here, are we not?"

Lady Blackbourne and Lady Rebecca stood. "We should be on our way. Lady Ellesmere, thank you for your hospitality and please wish Mr. Bowen our best wishes. As for you," the Dowager Countess gave her son a quick peck on the cheek. "I expect to see you for dinner tonight so Abigail and I can make plans for my new grandbaby."

"We shall be there," Abigail said.

Lady Blackbourne inclined her head toward the duchess and gave a placid smile as she passed by.

"It was lovely to see you again, Lady Rebecca," Lady Susan cooed.

Lady Rebecca fixed her silvery eyes on Lady Susan and Caelie felt the frigidity in her gaze from across the room. "Indeed."

Caelie exchanged a look with Abigail, sensing there was much behind that brief exchange. No doubt her cousin would fill her in on all she'd missed during her brief absence.

Lady Franklyn extended her hands to her hostess. "My dear Lady Ellesmere, it is such wonderful news to hear of Mr. Bowen's renewed health. May I be the first to—" The duchess stopped cold as Nick shifted his position and her gaze slipped past him to land on Caelie. For a brief second her mouth hung open and her eyes blinked. "Lady Caelie. I had not seen you hiding there."

Caelie gave a brief curtsy. "I'm not sure what I was doing would qualify as hiding, Your Grace."

Lady Franklyn glanced about the room. "And your mother?"

"My mother is traveling to Italy."

Lady Ellesmere stepped in. "And as particular friends of the family, Lord Ellesmere and I are very pleased to have Lady Caelie stay with us for the Season."

Lady Franklyn's gaze flitted from the marchioness to Caelie as if she could not decide which tidbit of information proved more difficult to absorb. "To Italy? And you did not go with her?"

"I did make the attempt; however, it appears I am not made for such travel. I became rather seasick and decided it better to leave Mother to continue on her journey while I returned to London."

"I see." Yet her suspicious tone indicated she did not see at all. "How...fortunate Lord and Lady Ellesmere agreed to take you in. I had not realized you were so well acquainted."

Lady Franklyn's hesitation trumpeted her disapproval of the association. However, given the duchess's own scandalous interactions with Spencer, she was hardly in a place to cast stones. Not that it would stop her.

Lady Franklyn shifted her attention away from Caelie. "Lord Blackbourne, Lady Blackbourne. How lovely it is to see you. I believe you know my daughter, Lady Susan."

Abigail inclined her head toward them both in a regal pose they had often practiced in the mirror as girls while pretending to be the Queen of England nodding to her subjects. Caelie had to suppress a smile seeing it now leveled at the two other women. "Of course. How are you enjoying your first season, Lady Susan?"

Lady Susan took a seat on the sofa next to her mother, her sharp chin tilted upward to better allow her to look down her broad nose at the others. "Quite well. I have many suitors, as one might expect."

Lady Susan may not have inherited her mother's delicate beauty, but she did appear to share her acidic pomposity. Not that either would prevent her from making a good match. As the daughter of a wealthy duke, one expected any number of gentlemen would be willing to overlook the less than complimentary aspects of her personality and countenance for the sake of enhancing their coffers.

Lady Franklyn turned her attention back to Caelie. "Did you say you were traveling to Italy by ship? On one of Lord Ellesmere's ships?"

Caelie hesitated. The woman was fishing. "Yes."

"Hm. And, if I'm not mistaken, Lord Huntsleigh had plans to head in that same direction?"

Lady Ellesmere smiled. "Thankfully, yes. I would hate to

think what would have happened to Lady Caelie had he not been."

"It was Lord Huntsleigh who ensured my safety and conveyed me back to London."

The duchess forced a smile. "A rather scandalous trip, was it not? I would think given your family's past troubles, Lady Caelie, you would be more judicious in your decisions."

"I do not believe one gets to decide when illness befalls them, do they?" Abigail directed a cold smile in Lady Franklyn's direction. Her cousin still bristled at mention of the scandal, ready to fight for Uncle's honor whenever someone thought to disparage it. "And how is it that you were aware Lord Huntsleigh would be traveling?"

"Oh. Well, I...he must have mentioned it. Perhaps at Lady Benchley's soiree."

"He did not attend the soiree," Lady Ellesmere said.

Caelie pursed her lips to hide her grin as Lady Franklyn floundered. To admit how she had come to the information would be to admit to a rather scandalous association of her own.

"Well, either way," Lady Franklyn stood and the others followed suit. "We simply wished to pay a call and offer Mr. Bowen our best wishes on his continued recovery."

"Did I hear—oh." Spencer came to a sudden halt inside the door of the receiving room, his gaze bouncing between Nick and Lady Franklyn, then to her. "Ah. Felton informed me Lord and Lady Blackbourne had arrived but he failed to mention our other guests."

"Good help is so hard to find these days, is it not." Lady Franklyn smiled at Spencer as if they were the only two in the room. Caelie fisted her hand at her side against the sudden urge to wipe it off the duchess's smug face.

What on earth did Spencer see in that woman? Her beauty could not be denied, but nor could her pettiness. Hardly the type one would like to sit down and have a conversation with. Then again, it was not likely conversation he'd had in mind. Her shoulders sagged at the thought.

Spencer ignored Lady Franklyn's comment as he sidled into the room, skirting around where the duchess stood to take Abigail's hands and give her cheek a quick kiss. "My dear, you look lovely and you will be happy to hear Bowen is swiftly on the mend. Lazing about seems to agree with him."

Abigail laughed. "Sad that it takes such an act to get the man to slow down."

"I think he did it all for show."

"What an awful thing to say, Lord Huntsleigh." Lady Franklyn took a step closer and Spencer took a step back until he stood next to Caelie. "Why, imagine what would have happened to me if he had not been there. I could have died."

If this scenario bothered Spencer, he gave no indication. "And what is it exactly you were doing at the docks, Lady Franklyn? It seems an odd place to find a duchess."

Lady Franklyn's fair skin burned bright red. "It was my foolish driver. He thought to take a shortcut. As I said, good help is hard to find. I have since fired the man without reference. Well, we really shouldn't tarry long. We have other calls to make and then Lady Susan and I will be attending Almack's this evening. I don't expect we will see you there, Lady Caelie, so may I wish you a good day."

"You are mistaken," Spencer said, shifting closer until she breathed in the scent of sandalwood. "Lady Caelie and my mother will be attending Almack's this evening as well, and I will be escorting them."

Nicholas turned to look at his close friend as if he did not recognize him. "You will?"

Spencer cleared his throat and avoided Nicholas's gaze. "I will."

"I see." Lady Franklyn clipped the words out as if chipping them from ice. "Then I bid you good day until we meet this evening."

Lady Franklyn swept from the room, her daughter in tow.

"What a vile woman," Abigail said, re-taking her seat. "Both of them."

"And a dangerous enemy." Nicholas delivered Spencer a hard look. "Step carefully."

Chapter Sixteen

"I do not want to think at what break-neck speed you travelled to make it here with such haste," Bowen said as Spence handed Nick a glass of brandy. They had left the women downstairs to catch up and plan for the evening ahead, while the men escaped upstairs to visit with Bowen who insisted on working, his papers spread out around him like large pieces of confetti. The man did not know how to relax.

"In truth, we made plans to leave the day news arrived of your injuries. We passed Spence's man on our way with news of his return with Caelie, and your return to the land of the living." Nick took a long draw on his brandy, his silvery eyes leveled at Spence. "Perhaps now you would like to explain to me just how it was you happened to be escorting my wife's cousin back to London and the circumstances under which this occurred? You have evaded the question long enough."

"Yes, why don't you tell him, Spence?"

Spence scowled. Nick, once his comrade in arms for all things scandalous, had now taken on the new role of husband and soon to be father. In doing so, any lady with the last name

Laytham fell under his protection. A job he took on with great seriousness. It was sometimes hard to marry the once scandalous lord to the man who sat next to him.

"When did you become such a stickler for propriety?"

"Since I married a woman who has described in detail what misery she will rain down upon me if *my* dearest friend has done anything untoward with respect to *her* beloved cousin. Now answer my question?"

Spence sank a little further in his chair and stretched his legs out. "You need not look at me as if you plan to march me to the altar at the tip of a sword. All propriety was observed and if you ask Lady Caelie she will tell you the same thing."

"Caelie will cover your ass because she will consider what you did for her a good turn that deserves a measure of loyalty on her part. Whether it is the truth or not is another matter. That is just her way."

Spence could not fault Nick's thinking. Caelie did have a strong sense of loyalty and for some reason, she had extended it to him, though he wasn't sure he deserved it.

"Huntsleigh." The warning tone in Nick's voice cut through the room.

Bowen grinned. "Oh dear, he's used your title. That cannot bode well."

"You needn't take such joy in this, Bowen." Spence straightened in his chair and looked Nick square in the eye. He did not care to lie to his friend, but nor did he want to give him the wrong impression with respect to Caelie's behavior. The loyalty she extended him was more than reciprocated. "We hired a lady's maid upon arriving at the inn, a journey which took less than half a day. During this time, Lady Caelie was far too ill to be in any danger from me. But thank you for thinking otherwise. It's good to know what you think of my character."

Nick let out a long breath and had the good decency to

look somewhat chagrined. "You know I have no worries with respect to your character. It's your lack of will power around beautiful women that is my only concern. And Caelie is more beautiful than most. Abigail is extremely protective over her cousin and this most recent turn of events involving her mother's abandonment has made her even more so." He shook his head. "I cannot believe that woman!"

Spence nodded his agreement. "Lady Glenmor will have much to atone for when her time comes. It hurt Lady Caelie grievously to be abandoned with such callous disregard. I should have marched that dragon off the plank for what she'd done, but, in all likelihood, Lady Caelie would have tried to jump in and save her. She has far too good a heart to be treated in such a manner."

Nick flicked a confused glance at Bowen who smiled and gave a small shrug. The earl's attention returned to Spence and stayed there. Too long. Spence squirmed beneath his friend's unwavering perusal. "You've a soft spot for her."

"I have no such thing!" His face burned. Bloody hell, when had he become so transparent? This was ridiculous. He could not deny Caelie was an exemplary human being and the soul of kindness. He'd also discovered she had a surprising wit and an intelligence that outshone most of the other ladies of his acquaintance. That she was beautiful went undisputed.

He could not claim to be unaffected by Caelie. In truth, he had grown fond of her. Very fond. Too fond.

"You have." Nick's eyes grew wide and he leaned forward.

"He has," Bowen confirmed.

Spence glared at his friend. "Aren't you tired? Don't you need to sleep?"

"I feel perfectly fine, thank you, and I wouldn't miss this for the world."

Nick shook his head in disbelief. "Dear Lord, have we finally seen the day that the very pillar of disreputable behavior, the bastion of all things improper, has been taken down by a lady of—"

"I have not been taken anywhere! I am the same man now as when you left. And might I add that Bowen here has suggested that *he* marry her." He pointed an accusing finger and watched the smirk on Bowen's face shrink.

"Given my brush with death, it doesn't seem right to put things like marriage off any longer. I merely suggested Lady Caelie as having all the qualities a man could wish for in a wife. And seeing as Spence is determined to find her a husband—"

"You are what?" Nick bolted from his chair and threw his arms wide. "For the love of God! I have been gone for only a fortnight. Have you both lost your minds?"

Bowen folded his hands on his lap and took on that look Spence recognized as the one he used when he was about to be his most reasonable self. "I don't think one needs to have lost one's mind in order to see Lady Caelie's virtues."

"I'm not talking about seeing her virtues, I'm talking about finding her a husband. And exactly when did you decide to take this onto yourself? Without consulting me? Or Lord Glenmor, I might add?"

Spence cleared his throat and shot Bowen another glare. He made a mental note to ensure Mrs. Faraday put an extra dose of pepper in the man's broth this evening. "Glenmor is away, and I have Lady Caelie's full support on this. Given she is the one who will benefit from it, it seems hers is the only permission I need to go forward with our plan."

"Your plan? And what, pray tell, is your *plan*?"

He took a quick hit of brandy and set about informing Nick about what he, Caelie and his grandmother had concocted—Spence playing the besotted suitor in the hope of luring the interest of their short list of potential husbands. He judiciously left out his fear with respect to Billingsworth. He did not feel it right to divulge this without Caelie's permission. Besides, there was no telling what Nick would do if he considered Billingsworth a threat to Caelie's well-being. They may end up fishing the man out of the Thames. Not that he didn't deserve it for what he'd done.

"I put forth my own name," Bowen said. "But I am hardly in a position to woo anyone at the present moment."

Nick and Bowen exchanged a glance and an expression crossed Nick's face though it traveled too swiftly for Spence to pin down what it meant.

Nick rubbed his chin. "I will not deny that finding Caelie a suitable husband has been a challenge, given past circumstances, and while your scheme—"

"Plan."

"—has merit, I think Bowen is a far better choice than any of the others. Would it not make sense then to forego this farce—"

"*Plan*," Spence stressed.

"—and promote Bowen as a match to Caelie?"

"No." The word shot out before he could stop it.

Nick folded his arms over his chest. "And why not? Bowen has a fortune. He never talks about it, but we both know it."

"Why is everyone so interested in my bank accounts of late?"

Nick ignored Bowen's question. "He could keep Caelie in fine style. Besides, he's a good man, wouldn't you agree?"

"Most days," Spence muttered, slumping back in his chair.

"Then why not put him forth as the best candidate?"

"Because—" He had no argument to give. No explanation to defend his reticence. Why not Bowen? As Nick said, he was the best of men. Who better? They could marry and Caelie's worries of being ruined would be over. She could have all the things she wanted—a good husband, a happy home, children.

Then why did the idea of her marrying Bowen leave him cold inside? Why did he feel so opposed to—?

Spence sat up like a shot.

Nick and Bowen both looked at him askance. He reached for his glass and downed the rest of his brandy. It burned his throat but he didn't care.

Nick shook his head. "What is it? You look like you've seen a ghost."

A ghost, no, but something equally as frightening. "It is nothing." It had to be.

Caelie was a friend. Yes, yes, he had an attraction to her, a very strong one, but what did they expect? He had a pronounced fondness for beautiful women. But his feelings did not go beyond that. It couldn't be. They were friends. They had agreed to this fact and drew the line there. Despite Caelie's rather naïve and romantic views on friends and lovers, Spence was not convinced the two could coincide together peaceably.

Ergo, the fact that he and Caelie did coincide together peaceably, and he did consider her a friend, meant only one thing. He could not love her.

Loving her would be sheer madness.

Folly.

The road to ruin.

He looked over at Nick and Bowen and found them staring back with curious expressions. "What?"

Nick towered over him; his hands fisted at his sides. "You do have an affection for her!"

"I—I—Fine." Spence sunk into his chair once again and rubbed a hand over his face. "Yes, to some degree I do have an affection for her. How could one not? She is as lovely inside as out. But it does not matter for a host of reasons."

"Such as?" Bowen asked the question and the smug grin on his friend's face told Spence he had been played. Bowen had never had any intention of vying for Caelie, he'd only wanted Spence to admit he had feelings. There would definitely be extra pepper in his broth tonight.

Spence held up a hand and counted the reasons off on his fingers. "One—she wishes to marry and I do not. Two—I am fond of her and have no wish to see her miserable which is what would happen if she married me. And three—Grandfather has already made it clear she is not an acceptable choice." He looked at Nick. "You know how he feels about scandal."

Nick let out a slow breath. "I do. But Ellesmere has insisted you marry by the end of the Season or you'll be cut off. Can you not convince him to consider Caelie under these circumstances?"

"Even if I could, I wouldn't. The Kingsley men have proven time and again we are not built for marriage, Nick. I have no faith in the institution to have a happy outcome and I will not drag Lady Caelie into an unhappy venture. She deserves better than that after all she has been through."

Nick sat down in his vacated chair. "I cannot argue with you on that point. Then you are determined to find her another husband? Obviously, we cannot consider Bowen. No offense."

Bowen waved him off. "I would never have considered the match, truly. Spence's feelings for her were obvious—"

"They were not!" If he hadn't realized the depth of them until today, how could Bowen have known?

Bowen gave him a dubious look. "Regardless. I could not in good conscious marry a lady knowing it would cause you such grief. It's a torturous thing to see someone you love, day in and day out, yet know you can never have them."

Nick and Spence both stared at their injured friend.

"At least I would imagine it would be," he added.

"Yes," Nick said slowly before turning back to Spence. "So can I assume this husband hunt begins tonight?"

"Yes. Grandmother has procured vouchers from—" Spence shuddered. "Almack's."

Nick set his drink down and gave Spence a hard look. "I need your word of honor that you will protect Caelie at all cost. I do not wish to see her hurt beyond what she has already endured."

"You have my word."

Spence only hoped he could keep it. He could navigate Caelie through the shark infested waters of the ton, and he could advise her one way or the other where a particular gentleman was concerned, but he could not make her mind up for her. Nor could he guarantee his plan of pretending to be in love with her to make her a more attractive prospect to others would work if Billingsworth decided to begin his smear campaign against her.

This entire enterprise was a gamble with no guarantee of where the dice would fall come the end of the game.

***

Caelie had been to Almack's only one other time, shortly after her presentation to court. At the time, she had been the toast of London. Mother had not wanted to go, but Papa had insisted. He had been adamant that Caelie's mother rouse herself from her hermit-like habits and escort Caelie to as many events as possible to ensure she had the best advantage to find a suitable husband. Mother had complied, only, as she stated on numerous occasions, because it was her duty and because she wished to make her daughter someone else's burden.

Had it only been four years ago? It seemed a lifetime since the ton had lauded her beauty and poise and considered her to be the Season's shining gem. It had been at Almack's where she had caught the eye of Lord Billingsworth, a gentleman from an old and established family as well as heir to an earldom. He was considered a great catch and many of the other ladies had hoped to become the handsome lord's future countess.

Caelie had not been immune to Billingsworth's charms, of which he possessed many. An accomplished dancer, an interesting conversationalist, he had captured her attention almost immediately. It did not hurt that with his pale blonde hair, light brown eyes and most fashionable wardrobe, he cut a fine figure as well.

By the end of the Season, he had developed a special interest in her. By the beginning of the next Season, he had asked her father for her hand in marriage. Caelie had been over the moon, though Abigail had been vexingly less so.

"He has a weak chin," she'd stated. "I find it hard to trust a man with a weak chin."

Of course, Abigail had struck up a special friendship with Viscount Roxton, heir to the esteemed Blackbourne title and of course Nicholas Sheridan possessed a strong, square chin. Her cousin's mistrust of Billingsworth gave Caelie pause, but when Viscount Roxton dropped his interest in Abigail without so much as a by your leave, she had set her cousin's opinion aside and decided to trust her own heart.

A foolish decision. As it turned out, Billingsworth's lack of character went far deeper than his weak chin.

"Do not let the wolves smell your fear," Spencer warned as they entered the Assembly room.

"I will try to hide it." Caelie had expected the crush, but actually facing the horde made her stomach clench and her hands shake. What if they all turned their backs to her? What if no one asked her to dance?

Spencer leaned in, his hand on her elbow. She basked in the warmth of his touch, knowing it was foolish. She needed to direct her heart elsewhere or risk seeing it broken. "There is nothing to worry about. I will not allow them to devour you whole."

She smiled as she turned her head to glance at him. "Piece by piece then?"

Spencer chuckled. She had come to love the sound of his laugh. It came so easily to him. "Not at all."

"Do you promise?"

He placed his other hand over his heart. "On my honor."

"You may have your work cut out for you, my lord." Already she could feel the gazes sliding in their direction and the whispers that would gather strength as they traveled through the room. From mouth to ear it would spread. *Lord Huntsleigh, consummate bachelor and reviler of all things marital, was at Almack's. Not only at Almack's, but also in attendance with none other than Lady Caelie Laytham.*

The last bit would be spoken with a mix of awe and disdain.

Caelie kept her expression neutral. Mother had insisted showing one's emotions was gauche and unladylike. Caelie had never believed such nonsense but the training came in handy as she looked around. Several glances shot her way, wide eyes above fluttering fans. It did not bode well.

"I believe we have been noticed." Mischief sparked in Spencer's eyes until they danced in the candlelight like merry stars in the night sky. He bowed over her hand and made an exaggerated display as his lips brushed against her gloved knuckles. His gaze captured hers as he did so. Pleasure rippled through her and she fought to appear unaffected. "Shall we begin our ruse?"

Ruse. Of course. He did not care for her beyond friendship. She would do well to remember that. Though, for her, the real ruse would be in pretending her feelings went no deeper than friendship.

"I suppose there is no time like the present," she said.

He led her to where the other couples had started to assemble for the quadrille and insinuated himself into a group to make eight. She noted Viscount Shaftsbury among their group. He nodded toward her, though made no other indication he noticed her.

"What if I have forgotten the steps?" It had been a long time since she had danced.

"You will be fine," Spencer said.

Once the music began, she realized he had been right. The steps were ingrained in her memory and quickly came back to her.

"Remember to breathe," Spencer said as they met briefly in the middle before parting to opposite sides. They met again and he squeezed her hand in solidarity and winked. Despite changing partners throughout the dance, Caelie found it difficult to take her eyes off Spencer.

He cut a dashing figure in his black evening coat with a royal blue waistcoat that brought out the light coloring of his eyes until they rivaled even the bluest of summer skies. Black breeches fit over his lean, muscular legs that moved with the agility of a cat. Even his starched collar and stark white cravat showed off his chiseled features to their best advantage. She could find no fault in his physical presentation. He was easily the most handsome man in the room, a claim Caelie made with all confidence, despite not having seen everyone present.

But it wasn't just his handsomeness that drew her to him. Spencer had a way of bringing light and charm and a hint of mischief with him wherever he went. Life with him would be a daily surprise. One could never be certain of what he would get up to next, or what idea would grab his fancy. Yet one could always be certain that whatever it was, he would bring those he loved along and ensure they too enjoyed themselves as much as he.

What a wonderful existence that would be—to wake up

each day and wonder what new adventures awaited. It made Caelie's hope of a comfortable future seem pale in comparison.

She and Lord Shaftsbury met in the middle for a quick turn. "Lady Caelie, it is lovely to see you this evening."

She inclined her head with as much poise as she could muster. "As well you, Lord Shaftsbury." And then she went off to the side again. The constant changing and movement of the dance did not allow for much conversation, but Caelie had learned to tell from glances and forced expressions how others perceived her. And while the gentlemen did not appear overwrought by her attendance, the ladies in their group kept their gazes averted, as if scandal was like a fever and could be easily caught.

Then again, it was not the ladies' interest she needed to curry. Just as well. The Duchess of Franklyn and Lady Susan had entered the room. The duchess made no attempt to hide her contempt as she stared at Caelie. It made it most difficult to maintain the steps properly with such dagger-like eyes boring into one's back. Relief filled her when the woman snapped open her fan and turned her back.

Whatever relationship Lady Franklyn had shared with Spencer, she apparently did not appreciate someone else waltzing onto the stage and usurping her position in his heart. She had almost forgotten how treacherous the ton could be. Somewhere during the two years she had been exiled from society, she had lost her taste for such nonsense.

When the dance ended, Spencer rejoined her but his smile from earlier had disappeared.

"You are frowning, my lord."

"Am I?"

"You are. Did you not enjoy the dance?"

"I did. Perhaps I am only disappointed it is over." He offered her his arm. "Shall we take a turn about the room?"

"Together? People will talk."

He wiggled his eyebrows and his smile returned. "Precisely."

As they made their turn about the room, Caelie could feel the gazes that followed them. Spencer made a great show of attentiveness, throwing his head back with laughter, though whatever quip she had said likely did not warrant such a response.

"Shaftsbury appeared rather attentive," he noted, though whether this pleased him or irritated him she could not be certain as his smile came through gritted teeth.

"He did speak to me during the dance. He was very polite and gentlemanly."

"I believe it will take little effort before politeness turns to passion and he is begging you to accept his offer of marriage." His frown had returned.

"I think we may still have an uphill climb on that one. Lord Shaftsbury has never been the type to go against the grain. To offer for me will mean we must first turn the opinion of the ton in my favor."

Spence scowled. "If the man is unwilling to court the ton's disapproval on your behalf, then he is not worthy of your hand in marriage."

He spoke with such vehemence, it rendered Caelie speechless and an awkward silence fell upon them. "That is kind of you to say, Lord Huntsleigh."

"I prefer it when you call me Spencer."

All this *my lording* made Spence uncomfortable, given what they had shared. For heaven's sakes, they had kissed. Quite passionately, in fact. He had tasted her and desired her and had wanted to toss her onto the bed and bury himself deep inside of her.

Sweet Judas, he still did. He could not help himself. The vision of her being betrothed to Shaftsbury made him want to retch. For all his polite, gentlemanly ways, Shaftsbury was rather bland. He never said anything that startled the senses, he always did exactly what people expected of him and never once, in the entire time Spence had been acquainted with the man, had he ever done anything even remotely adventurous. In short, the man was as dull as dirt.

Caelie would be bored to tears if she married him. How could she not be?

This plan of his was sheer madness. It would never work. Or worse, it would work and then, as Bowen had said, he would be forced to live day in and day out knowing she was with another man.

What had Bowen called it? Torturous.

"My lord, are you quite alright?"

"Spencer," he whispered but the sound barely reached his ears.

Caelie leaned in to him and the scent of wildflowers enveloped and teased his agitated senses. "I cannot call you by your first name here. Someone might hear."

She had the right of it, of course. His brain knew this, but his heart, which had become the most confused organ in his body of late, rejected the idea completely. His heart wanted to hear her say his name with a desperation that bordered on ludicrous.

He nodded. Swallowed. Searched for his voice and finally found it. "Yes. Naturally. Improper." He needed to stop this, to remember all the reasons he had rhymed off to Bowen and Nick as to why their being together would never work. How many had there been? Three? Surely that was sufficient to get his brain to override his heart and make it see sense.

The problem was, Caelie had slipped beneath the walls

around his heart and invaded every part of it until the stupid thing had turned deaf to his pleas.

What did one do in cases such as this?

"Shall we continue on?" she asked.

"Indeed." They walked on but his legs had turned to lead and his body shook as if he had contracted a deathly fever. He spied Grandmama seated with the other dowagers. They watched the festivities behind their unfolded fans and leaned from one side to the other to whisper to their neighbor when something of interest caught their attention. "Shall we stop by and visit Grandmother?"

He didn't wait for her to answer but steered her in the direction of the dowagers and deposited her there. He needed to get some fresh air and retrieve his scattered sanity. To talk some sense into himself before he lost all connection to the reasonable portion of his brain.

"Punch? I'll get you some punch."

He did not wait for an answer though he had no sooner walked away when he heard her laughter and, God help him, it flowed through him like a tall glass of ale on the hottest day. She had a way of quenching his thirst, but the startling thing was he hadn't realized he'd been thirsty. Now that he had, he didn't know how to proceed. Should he drink until he got his fill? Or turn away and return to the dry, desert plains that had become his life?

Chapter Seventeen

S pence reached the refreshment table and mindlessly filled a plate with biscuits then took a small cup of punch.

"Lord Huntsleigh." Spence turned and looked down. Lord Cranbrook stood half a head shorter, barely coming up to his nose. "I must say, you are the last person I would have expected to see here."

Spence twisted his mouth to one side. No doubt the entire room buzzed about his appearance at Almack's. "Your surprise is no more than mine is, I assure you."

"The marriage-minded mamas practically swooned the moment you walked through the door with your grandmother and Lady Caelie. What is that about, my good man?"

Spence took a sip of the punch, forgetting for the moment he had procured it for Caelie. The overly sweet beverage tasted more of sugar than whatever berry concoction it contained.

"What is what about?" He tried to buy himself some time. Lord Cranbrook was on the list Caelie and his grandmother had developed but again, up close and personal, he found the man lacking and nowhere near good enough for her. Too short for one. Possibly even shorter than Caelie herself. That wouldn't do. And the top of his head shone like a cue ball where his hair had receded backward to leave it exposed. And... did he have hair sticking out of his ears?

"It appears as if Lady Ellesmere has taken Lady Caelie under her wing. That is quite the coup, considering."

Spence ground his back teeth against each other. "Considering what?"

"Well given the—" Lord Cranbrook leaned closer and dropped his voice. "—scandal." He whispered the last word and Spence wanted to punch him in his bulbous nose and likely would have if his hands hadn't been full of over-sweetened punch and a plate of less than appetizing biscuits.

"The scandal of which you speak is nearly two years old. Must you all beat it like a dead horse? Surely you can find something else to occupy your time. I had thought you possessed a broader mind than that, Cranbrook. I shall consider myself corrected on that account."

Spence's words shot out like sharpened darts and the surprise written across Cranbrook's face told him they had hit their mark.

"I say, Huntsleigh—"

"No, I think I have heard enough of what you said, Cranbrook. I suggest you go back to your lack-witted cronies. Perhaps they will be interested in such banal conversation, but I am not. Lady Caelie is a warm-hearted, impeccably mannered young lady and I will not hear her disparaged by such ignorant inferences of past actions she had no part in."

Cranbrook's gaze slid from one side to the other and too late, Spence realized he had raised his voice enough to be heard by anyone within arm's reach, garnering curious stares.

Bloody hell.

"Please accept my sincerest apologies," Cranbrook said. His Adam's apple bobbed in his throat and his face had turned an unpleasant shade of red that was nowhere near as flattering as the blush that colored Caelie's cheeks on a regular basis. "You are right, of course. I did not realize your, uh, feelings on the subject ran so deep."

Spence straightened and strained to moderate his tone. "Well, they do. And I would appreciate you letting others know this. Lady Caelie does not deserve the censure she has received and my family is determined to see this wrong is quickly righted."

"I see." Cranbrook nodded slowly. "Yes, indeed, I will be most happy to let others know and of course, we will welcome her return, we will. Perhaps, if you are not averse to the idea, I might request a dance of her, to recompense my behavior."

Spence abhorred the idea but there was little he could do about it. He had promised to assist Caelie in finding a husband and for reasons he could not fathom, she and his grandmother considered Cranbrook a likely prospect.

"Of course. If she is amenable to it, that is."

"And you, my lord? Are you amenable to it? I wouldn't want to step on any toes."

Spence swallowed. The air in the room had turned stifling. "I believe it is Lady Caelie's toes you will need to be most concerned about."

Cranbrook laughed, a strange snorting sound that reminded Spence of a pig at a trough. The man hurried off in Caelie's direction with Spence glaring after him. He had done the right thing, pushing the ridiculous Lord Cranbrook with his five thousand pounds a year toward Caelie as she and Grandmama had wished.

But the idea turned his stomach. He set the plate back onto the refreshment table and went in search of an exit. He needed fresh, unfettered air to clear his head, but the London night air would have to suffice for now.

"I thought it a most successful evening," Grandmama said as they made their way up the staircase to the bedrooms on the next floor. "Do you not agree, my dears?"

Spence glanced at Caelie who walked on the other side of his grandmother. She looked weary, but pleased. As the night wore on, more and more gentlemen had made their way to her and requested a dance, or offered to bring her punch. Why he'd barely been able to find a moment alone with her.

It had not helped that he spent far too much time fighting off the match-making mamas who insisted on foisting their daughters on him while simultaneously avoiding the rather determined Lady Franklyn who seemed to be having difficulty understanding their brief affair had ended.

"Yes, Lady Ellesmere. I must admit, once my nerves calmed, I enjoyed myself more than I expected to," Caelie said. She caught Spence's gaze and smiled, he forced one back though he felt far less jolly than when the night had begun.

Who knew success would be so disappointing?

He'd had to practically beat his way through her new throng of admirers just to request another dance and by then there was no dances left to claim . They treated her like a returning hero from the wars. Not too far from the truth, he supposed. Though he found it the height of hypocrisy that the same men who had avoided her because of the scandal now clamored to her as if she were a shiny new toy simply because he had sung her praises.

The ladies were slower to warm up, though some did approach her. Even the very proper Miss Eugenie Caldwell, who despised anything indecorous, made her way over to say hello. Having such a pillar of propriety make an overture brought forth other ladies who had so far held back their own

greetings. Perhaps Miss Caldwell had a few redeeming qualities after all. Though, after what she had done to Nick, he
would reserve judgment for now.

Oh, there were a few hold outs. Lady Franklyn, of course,
and those too afraid to go against the duchess for fear of
reprisal. And Lord Tunston did not seem to be taken in by
Caelie's sudden return to popularity. Perhaps they would have
to strike the earl off their prospect list. Which left Lord Cranbrook and the Viscount Shaftsbury, both of whom appeared
to show an interest.

Unless one of the other gentlemen who had fawned over
her decided to step up and make his intentions known.

Spence sighed and ran a hand down his face. A night of
frivolity did not usually leave him so exhausted. If one could
call it frivolity. In truth, it had been a rather torturous experience he did not care to repeat, yet knew he must in order to
keep his promise to Caelie. All he wanted to do was find his
bed and bury his head in the pillows, then wait for oblivion to
find him.

"Well, I for one am ready to retire, but I believe I will
check in on Marcus first," Grandmama said. "Sleep well, my
dears." She patted Caelie's cheek and kissed Spence's before
disappearing through the door to Bowen's bedroom.

Spence pulled his gaze away from the closed door of the
bedroom and rested it on Caelie. Even after a night of dancing
and entertaining she remained as ravishingly beautiful as when
they had set out hours earlier. He, on the other hand, felt
bedraggled and...and...

Irritated.

He offered her his arm and escorted her down the hallway
to her own room, one door down. When they stopped, she
turned to face him.

"Did you enjoy yourself this evening?" she asked.

"I did not."

"Truly?" She sounded surprised.

He shook his head. He was out of sorts. Caelie stood in front of him, her back pressed against the door to her bedchamber as she looked up at him with those lovely green eyes a man could lose himself in if he wasn't careful.

And he hadn't been careful. He hadn't even realized he'd been at risk until it was too late.

"My apologies. I enjoyed part of it."

Her smile returned and the confusion in his heart eased. The glow from the sconce on the wall next to them bathed her ivory skin in a golden light.

"Which part did you enjoy?"

"Dancing with you."

Her smile grew wider. "I worried I might have forgotten the steps."

"You did exceedingly well. I'm sure all the other dancers were extremely jealous."

"I am certain they were not. Which part did you dislike?"

Where did he start? The part where other men fawned over her like slobbering puppies awaiting a pat on the head? He particularly disliked the part where that idiot, Cranbrook, claimed the last dance, a waltz, and held Caelie in his arms. But the most unbearable part had been standing on the outskirts, pretending to be happy for her with her bevy of admirers when all he really wanted to do was toss them aside, grab her hand and run away with her.

"Spencer?"

He blinked. How he loved the sound of his name when she spoke it. "It must have been all the marriage-minded mamas stalking me like prey," he quipped. He could not tell her the truth. There was no point. As much as he wanted her, she did not belong to him. She would never belong to him.

But sweet Judas he wanted her to.

"I should go," he said. "You need your rest and I need—"

No. He could not tell her what he needed.

He mustn't.

"What do you need?" She whispered the question and he closed his eyes, let her words wash over him.

"I'm not sure I know anymore."

Her hand touched his face, lightly. Even through the barrier of her glove he could feel her warmth. It bled into him, set fire to smoldering embers. He opened his eyes and discovered he'd moved closer, though he had no recollection of it. His heart pounded against the walls of his chest and blood rushed to his groin. He lifted a thick curl that rested against her collarbone, then let his fingertips touch the soft skin beneath it. Her breath hitched.

He was close enough now to feel the rise and fall of her breasts.

How desperately he wanted to reach behind her and open the door, back her into the room, onto the bed. He wanted to lose himself inside of her, let her consume him until nothing remained. Maybe then he could move on, continue with this farce of finding her a husband and let her go.

He bent his head and his lips brushed the delicate skin on her neck where her pulse beat. She tasted of sweet aphrodisiacs, drawing him in, enticing his senses. She leaned into him; her hands fisted into his lapels. She wanted it to. He was certain.

He reached a hand behind to find the door knob.

But the door that unlatched came from behind him, not in front. The sound rushed down the hallway and doused him like a bucket of ice water. He leapt backward as his grandfather stepped out of Bowen's room, his head turned to address Grandmama who remained inside. When he did step out, Spence held his breath as his grandfather's gaze swept across both of them.

Spence did not dare look at Caelie, afraid if he did, his

grandfather would see the guilt and desire stamped over every inch of his face. Perhaps he had seen it already as he stood silent for far longer than necessary before finally speaking.

"I understand this evening was a success?"

"Yes, my lord," Caelie said. Her voice shook slightly. Did Grandfather notice?

The older man nodded. "Very good. Spencer, when you are done saying goodnight, if you could join me in my study, I would like to discuss certain matters with you."

"It grows late, Grandfather. Could we perhaps discuss it on the morrow?" He needed time to compose himself, to find his scattered wits and cool the ardor that had thundered through his body only a moment before.

"We can discuss it now. I will await you downstairs."

Caelie closed the door behind her and collapsed on her bed, her limbs limp and her mind racing. What had just happened? They had been having a pleasant conversation one minute and the next...

The next her entire body had been on fire with a desire she had been helpless to stop. Worse yet, she hadn't wanted to stop it. She had wanted to let it rage, to burn through her until only cinder and ash remained. She wanted to know the sensation of his touch on her bare skin, the weight of his body on hers, the feel of him inside of her.

Her hands flew to her mouth to muffle the sob of shame that tried to escape. Mother had been right. She did have too much of her father in her. His heedless passions had been their family's downfall, and now her recklessness had very nearly been hers.

Oh, but how she had wanted him.

When he leaned in and kissed her neck, she had a vision of

everything they could be. Their lives rolled out in a flash of vision that had rocked her to the very core. The happiness she had always dreamed of dangled at the tips of her fingers. She had only to reach out and grab it and it would be hers. There would be no turning back.

If she allowed it, he would have to marry her. He would insist upon it.

And he would hate her for it.

Tears streamed down from the corner of her eyes, across her cheeks and into the quilt beneath her. The very notion of his resentment, growing year after year as he was consigned to a life he did not want, grew uglier with each passing moment.

She had lived that life. And she had hated it.

Every day until the day Mother abandoned her in Portsmouth, she had been under the rule of someone else, of dictates and desires not her own. She had accepted it. Unlike Abigail she did not possess the fearlessness to buck convention. The consequences of doing so, of dealing with Mother if she even dared, were too great and not worth the risk. Her only hope of escape had been marriage to a man who would treat her more as an equal and less like a piece of property.

Billingsworth had promised to be that man but she had soon learned what his promises were worth.

She had promised Spencer she would not trap him into a marriage he did not want.

She sat up and sniffed.

She would not be like Billingsworth. She had given her word and she would uphold it. If she did not, she was no better than a man who had used and betrayed her, then threatened to use that betrayal to ruin her in the eyes of others.

Caelie swiped at the trail of tears across her cheeks. She would not be that person. With Mother gone, the only guidance she had came from within. The decisions she made were hers to live with. She could not, in good conscience, do something that would make Spencer so unhappy. He was a good and honorable man, but a man nonetheless, and he had a man's desires. She could not expect him to be otherwise.

She must be the stronger one. Diligent. She must stamp down this scandalous passion before it destroyed them both.

There was no other way.

S pence walked into Grandfather's study. A low fire burned in the hearth and cast a warm glow against the back of his grandfather who stood at a nearby window, his hands clasped behind his back as he looked out into the night.

"You wished to see me?" His grandfather often summoned him to speak about estate business or listen to yet another list of reasons as to why he should marry. It seemed rather late for a discussion on the Ellesmere estates, which left only the latter.

"Your grandmother indicated tonight met with success. She believes finding Lady Caelie a suitable groom will take no time at all. Apparently, your ruse of pretending you were enamored of her proved worthwhile after all."

"Yes. So it would seem." He dragged his finger along the edge of Grandfather's desk then picked up a paperweight and bounced it in his hand. He had given it to him one Christmas over two decades ago. He'd given a similar one to Bowen as well. It was nothing more than a rock he'd found and cleaned. The man had kept it all these years as if it was worth its weight in gold.

His grandfather turned. "I am glad to hear."

"Because it will mean she is out from underfoot sooner rather than later?"

"You judge me harshly."

"You've made your feelings toward Lady Caelie perfectly clear."

"My feelings toward Lady Caelie are irrelevant. In truth, I think her a fine young lady of upstanding quality. It is the scandal that comes attached with her that I do not countenance. We have seen enough of it in our own family, do we need to court it in others as well? I will not apologize for trying to avoid further association with scandal, ours or anyone else's."

He didn't bother arguing. Grandfather felt as strongly about avoiding scandal as Spence did about avoiding marriage. Likely, in the end, neither of them would get their way, for if Spence was forced to marry nothing but scandal and misery could follow. It was the way of the men in this family, save for the one standing before him. He had avoided it. He had copiously stepped around it at every turn, lived a life of exemplary goodness.

Spence had not. He had lived recklessly, with abandon, determined to outrun his fate. A fate that would leave him miserable and broken in body and spirit.

"The time has come," Grandfather said, as if reading Spence's thoughts. "I have been in contact with several families who I feel are suitable."

"Grandfather, I won't—"

"You will." The words came down with a stony finality. "Enough is enough."

Fear roiled in his gut and a vice clamped around his neck making it difficult to breathe. He watched his future slip away, dissolve into something bleak and ugly. "Please, don't force me to do this."

Grandfather fell silent a moment and in those few seconds hope grew only to be crushed by what came next. "Baron Caldwell is amenable to discussing a match between you and his daughter, Eugenie. As well, I have been approached by Lord Renfrew with respects to his daughter, Lady Beatrice."

"Lady Beatrice?" Grandfather couldn't seriously be considering her. Why he would choose the icy and remote Miss Caldwell who had done everything in her power to trap Nick into marriage, before he chose Lady Beatrice. It did not matter how large her dowry; it could not make up for her constant snuffling nor drown out her incessant complaining over everything that crossed her path. There was a reason she had been out in society for the past five years without a single proposal.

His stomach lurched. Was this how Caelie had felt when the seasickness took hold? As if her insides were being battered against a cliff and nothing she did could stop it?

"If neither of these options are to your liking, I have also considered approaching Lord Blackbourne with respect to his sister Lady Rebecca. Given your friendship, I am sure he would be amenable to a match."

Spence's head shot up. "Lady Rebecca? But she is a child!"

"Lady Rebecca is twenty and has been out in society for the past two years."

Perhaps, but in his mind, she was still the little girl who chased them as boys and refused to be ignored or left behind.

He shook his head. "Grandfather...no. I can't do this. I can't marry any of these women."

"And who, pray tell, would you like to marry then?"

"I—" One name popped into his head unbidden but he pushed it aside. Caelie deserved to be happy. He would not rob her of that. "No one. I wish to marry no one."

Grandfather took a deep breath and slowly let it out. "I have given you three viable options of women I find to be acceptable, Spencer. Once you have found a suitable candidate for Lady Caelie to marry and the ruse of your being enamored with her comes to an end, you will have until the end of the

Season to choose one of these three as your bride. If you do not, you will have nothing. I will not provide a roof over your head. I will not put food in your belly. I will not put clothes on your back. I will not pay your debts. Do you understand me?"

Spence had the sense of being shut inside a dark room where the walls closed in inch by inch until he became trapped with nowhere to go. Part of him wanted to break out of it, tell Grandfather to go to hell; he'd make his own way, but doing what? The only skill he possessed was being lord of the manor. He'd spent his entire life training to take over his grandfather's role when the time came. It wasn't as if he could hang out a shingle: Lord for Hire.

He had no choice.

"I understand."

Though understanding and accepting were two completely different entities. The only question remained which of the two could he live with—destitution until the title reverted to him and he had some level of income once again, or marriage to a woman he did not love, did not want, and certainly could not make happy?

Chapter Eighteen

"You've been very quiet this afternoon, Lady Caelie. Are you quite alright?"

The Dowager Countess of Blackbourne's voice drew Caelie's attention and her guilt. She was not being a very good guest. Lady Rebecca and her mother had invited her for an outing to Hyde Park and yet she could not seem to pull her mind out of the fog it had been in for the past few days.

Oh, how she wished Abigail had stayed in town, but Nick had insisted they return to the country so as not to overtax her during her confinement. Caelie had not argued, wanting the best for her cousin, but her absence left her without a confidante when she sorely needed one.

"Forgive me. I was wool-gathering, I'm afraid." She straightened in her seat as the carriage conveyed them past a pair of gentlemen who strolled along the side of the pathway. Both tipped their hats to offer a good afternoon. She should be enjoying the unseasonably warm day, made even lovelier by the hint of newly budded flowers and the twitter of birds in the trees heralding spring's long-awaited arrival.

If nothing else, today's outing was a far sight better than

her last trip to the park. Was it almost a year ago that Abigail had coerced her into coming out after the fashionable hour to take a row in the lake? Unfortunately, things had not gone as planned when they encountered Nicholas, then still Lord Roxton. The combination of water, Abigail's temper and Nicholas's presence had the end result of her cousin landing in the water and Caelie being left adrift, while the lords and ladies of the ton gathered along the shore to watch the entire debacle.

Her fortunes had turned since that day, mostly due to Lady Ellesmere and Spencer squiring her about. The past few days had been a whirlwind of parties and teas and even a trip to the theatre. But through it all, something had changed. While Spencer played the part of the doting escort, making it appear that he fancied her, a remoteness had crept into his demeanor. Gone was the warm, engaging man she had come to lo—

No. Not love. She shook her head. Not that.

Lady Rebecca reached over and patted Caelie's hands where she held them clenched in her lap. "You have every right to lose yourself in your thoughts. Did Mother tell you every house hummed with the news of your latest sightings when we paid our morning calls?"

"Truly?" Funny how once she would have coveted this information and now it hardly seemed to matter.

"Indeed," Lady Blackbourne said. She inclined her regal head and the ostrich feather perched dramatically on the side of her lavender hat bobbed with the movement. "Well done. People are saying Lord Huntsleigh looks every inch the smitten suitor, as do Lords Cranbrook and Shaftsbury. I would not be at all surprised to see those two gentlemen try to race the other to a proposal."

Lady Rebecca smiled, her delicate features protected from the late afternoon sun by a fashionable bonnet. "You are a much sought-after prize. If this keeps up, by the end of the Season, you may have your pick of gentlemen!"

Caelie forced a smile. Indeed, she should be happy. She wanted this. Or she'd thought she had. To be accepted back into the folds of society. To leave the taint of scandal behind her. To have a husband and a family of her own.

Why then, did she feel so unhappy, as if she were trying to squeeze into an old pair of shoes that no longer fit? They pinched her toes so tightly she wanted nothing more than to shuck them off and run barefoot through the grass.

Ah, the freedom of that notion.

Perhaps that was why she missed her time at The White Stag so much. It wasn't as if the inn provided all the comforts of home, but at least while during her stay, she did not need to worry about saying or doing the right thing, of ensuring she wore the latest fashions or upheld all the proper strictures society demanded. At the inn she had been free of such things. Free to speak her mind, to laugh as loudly as she wished, to spend time unencumbered by chaperones and propriety with a man who kept her entertained and made her feel alive despite how ill she had been in the beginning.

It was as if she had been released from shackles she hadn't realized she'd been wearing. Yet now, with each passing day, she could feel the shackles slipping back into place. The rules and etiquette and judgment brought back Mother's harsh admonishments as if she still stood next to her, whispering them in her ear.

Would it always be like this? Even after she married, would she still have to play the part of the proper lady, always worrying about the censure and criticism from others? From her husband? It did not seem a very happy way to spend one's future.

Suddenly, and with startling clarity, she understood Spencer's bid for freedom in sailing away from London. Guilt clouded her heart. She had kept him from succeeding and thrown him back into the fray.

Her heart sank. Was it any wonder he'd withdrawn from her? Despite what had occurred between them the night they returned home from Almack's—and something *had* occurred, though she could not put a name to it—Spencer now avoided her.

She hated how dismayed this left her. The desperation she felt for him bordered on shameful. Every inch of her skin had begged for his touch that night. What would have happened had Lord Ellesmere not chosen that moment to step out from Mr. Bowen's bedchamber? But he had, and any hope she'd had of anything happening crashed and broke into a million tiny pieces.

She was such a fool.

Had she left every last moral, every last ounce of propriety adrift in the English Channel? Had she learned nothing from her past mistakes?

"Oh bother," Lady Rebecca muttered under her breath.

Caelie glanced at her companion. "What is it?"

"Lady Susan and her mother."

"You do not like her much, do you?" Hardly surprising. A spiteful sort, Lady Susan rarely said anything pleasant if she could say something nasty in its place.

"No. And it does not help that she has set her sights on Lord Selward. How am I to compete with the daughter of a duke?"

Caelie squeezed Lady Rebecca's hand. "I am certain your beauty inside and out far outweighs the merits of marrying Lady Susan, despite what title her father possesses."

"I hope you are right. If I do not procure a proposal from him this Season, I do not expect one will ever come. And then what am I to do? My heart is quite set on him and I cannot imagine marrying anyone else."

"My dear," Lady Blackbourne said as they neared the carriage conveying Lady Franklyn and her daughter, as well as another gentleman. Both Lady Franklyn and the gentleman sat across from Lady Susan, their backs facing Caelie. "If Lord Selward does not offer you a proposal, he does not deserve you. Now smile ladies, we are about to enter the lion's den."

"Lady Blackbourne, how lovely to see you again!"

Their carriage came to a stop next to Lady Franklyn's more stylish barouche. Both ladies were decked out in the latest fashions until they rivaled the most colorful of peacocks. Caelie thought it a bit hard on the eyes, so many colors and feathers and beading and such. She paled in comparison in her much more sedate attire.

"Lady Caelie," Lady Franklyn said, her grin brittle and lacking warmth. "I understand you have become quite the spectacle of late."

"I believe the word you are looking for is sensation," Lady Blackbourne said, coming to Caelie's defense for which she was imminently thankful. Such criticism was rarely delivered in such an open and snide manner. Most of the attacks on her had taken place behind a fan and well behind her back. Apparently, Lady Franklyn preferred a more direct approach, though she couched it in pleasantries and an insincere smile, as if she were paying a compliment.

Lady Franklyn ignored Lady Blackbourne's admonishment though and lifted a hand toward her gentleman companion, his face obscured by the ornate feathers dripping from the duchess's hat. "I believe you are well acquainted with my dear friend, Lady Caelie."

Caelie's heart froze as Lord Billingsworth leaned forward past the feathers and tipped his hat toward her. "My lady. Lovely to see you again."

"Again, yes," Lady Susan smiled though there was nothing pleasant within the gesture. "Lord Billingsworth has indicated he ran into you in Hampshire. How lovely it is to run into old friends when one travels, is it not?"

Caelie struggled to breath. "Indeed." Though from the spiteful gleam in Billingsworth's gaze, friendship had no part in this.

His plans were for ruination.

Hers to be exact.

"I have only just returned from Hampshire myself. Imagine my surprise at hearing of your successful re-entrance back into society," he said. "Quite a boon for you."

"You are kind to say." She choked on the words. Kindness had no place in Lord Billingsworth's repertoire.

Lady Franklyn inserted herself into the conversation. "Was your journey home from Hampshire a pleasant one, Lady Caelie? We had so little time to discuss it when I visited you at Lady Ellesmere's."

What had Billingsworth told her? What had he intimated? Lies or truth, either one could destroy her.

Fear crawled up her spine like a spider. "Pleasant enough as far as journeys go."

"So good to hear, though I am certain there must be more to tell. Is there not?"

"Mother," Lady Rebecca, interrupted. "As we are planning on attending Lord and Lady Remington's fete this evening, we really should be on our way."

Lady Blackbourne nodded at her daughter and Caelie wanted nothing more than to hug her on the spot. "We truly should and I'm certain Lady Franklyn and Lady Susan will wish to be on their way as well, as they will likely need much time to prepare, will you not?"

The veiled barb caused Lady Franklyn's false smile to tighten. "Indeed. I suspect we will see you there then."

"Good day, ladies." Billingsworth tipped his hat at them again, though his gaze remained on Caelie. "I wish you all a good day and am certain I will see you again soon."

The barouche traveled down the path and around a bend before Caelie breathed again.

"Oh, Caelie." Lady Rebecca took her hand and held it. "How awful it must be for you to come face to face with him after what he did."

Lady Blackbourne looked at her and concern creased her brow. "I had not realized you had run into Lord Billingsworth before your return to London?"

Caelie nodded. She had hoped not to reveal that fact but it appeared Billingsworth did not share the sentiment. She had suspected he wouldn't, but the reality of what she now faced frightened her far more than the possibility of it had. "Yes, as we were leaving the inn where I convalesced, we encountered Lord Billingsworth."

"And he saw you with Lord Huntsleigh?"

"Yes."

Lady Blackbourne pursed her lips. "Do you fear he will suggest something inappropriate took place?"

Lady Rebecca spoke up in her defense. "Why would he? She was properly chaperoned."

But the sharp look in Lady Blackbourne's gaze told Caelie the Dowager Countess had put several pieces of the puzzle together. "Several doors have been closed to Lord Billingsworth since he broke off his engagement with Lady Caelie. Many families are unwilling to consider him as a viable prospect for their daughters. They view his actions as dishonorable despite the circumstances and do not want to take the risk he may prove fickle with their own daughters."

"But what will his spreading rumors about Lady Caelie do to change this?"

Caelie closed her eyes. "If he suggests I am...dishonorable, that my morals are wanting, then it will provide justification as to why he broke our engagement. If he can do this, the doors now closed to him will open once again."

Shock widened Lady Rebecca's eyes and she pulled away slightly. "He wouldn't dare!"

"He may," Caelie said. In all likelihood, he would. Had he not already proven how little honor he possessed?

"Is this the sudden haste in finding you a husband?"

Caelie stared down at her hands. "Yes."

"But that is ridiculous. The worst that would come of that is Lord Huntsleigh must marry you to save your reputation. Hardly an undesirable fate for any lady, I would think."

Caelie gave her head a vehement shake. "I would never put him in such a position. He has done me a great service, safely conveying me home and then assisting me in finding a husband. I will not reward him by forcing him into a marriage neither he nor his family wants."

"Even at the risk of your own reputation?" Lady Blackbourne asked.

"Even then."

Lady Rebecca's voice turned panicky. "But you will be exiled. A lady without her reputation is...is—"

"Nothing." Caelie bowed her head. "As I have discovered. But that I could live with. What I could not live with is the thought of forcing Lord Huntsleigh or his family into circumstances they do not wish for."

"While I do not support your decision with respect to this," Lady Blackbourne said. "I will do whatever is in my power to aid your cause of finding a husband. We will not leave you to be damaged by the likes of Lord Billingsworth, will we, Rebecca?"

"Absolutely not!"

The solidarity shown by these two women warmed Caelie's heart and chased out some of the chill put there by their encounter with Lord Billingsworth and his new association with Lady Franklyn, who had her own stake in the game. "Thank you."

"Think nothing of it," Lady Blackbourne said. "I only hope your sense of honor toward the Kingsleys does not prove to be your downfall."

Caelie wished the same thing.

S pence was surprised to find Lady Blackbourne and Lady Rebecca in the drawing room with this grandmother. He had seen them leave only a short while ago to take Caelie to the park and promenade her amongst the most fashionable lords and ladies.

Except that Caelie was nowhere to be seen. A fact he asked after once the pleasantries were out of the way.

"I'm afraid we had a bit of a run in with Lord Billingsworth and Lady Franklyn," Lady Blackbourne informed him, her voice grave.

Spence's hands clenched into fists. "What did Billingsworth say?"

"He made reference to having seen you both in Hampshire. It seemed to upset her greatly."

Spence's blood heated to a boil and his fisted hands wished to wrap around Billingsworth's neck and choke the words out of him. He struggled to keep his composure but he danced a fine edge.

Lady Rebecca stepped forward. "She explained to us her fears that he might try to clear his own reputation by sullying hers, insinuating something untoward occurred between the two of you."

He nodded, too angry to speak. He had hoped they would have more time, that his threats would have given Billingsworth pause before he acted. Apparently not. And if

Lady Franklyn had inserted herself into the mix and knew of what had occurred between Caelie and Billingsworth, he feared what she might do with the information.

The whole thing sickened him. As if ruining Caelie could justify Billingsworth's own lack of honor or make Lady Franklyn more attractive to him. It would do neither, but in their attempt at both, it would give the ton exactly what they wanted. Another salacious scandal to sink their teeth into and take their minds off their own petty existence.

After Lady Blackbourne and her daughter said their good-byes and promised to do whatever they could to ensure Caelie's reputation remained intact, Spence turned to his grandmother. "Where is she now?"

He needed to see her, to put her mind at ease and promise her he would not let anything happen to her. As if he could stop it. He shook his head. He could offer her little protection as today well proved. Rage coursed through him.

"She was quite shaken," his grandmother said. "She went to her room to rest."

"I will speak with Billingsworth."

"I think it best not to poke the bear where Billingsworth is concerned, my dear. Or Lady Franklyn for that matter." His grandmother stepped forward and rested a hand on his arm. He had yet to unclench his fists and the strain ran up his arms and into his neck.

"I cannot stand here and do nothing!"

"Of course not. But the best course of action now is to continue on with our plan of finding Lady Caelie a husband. If we can hurry things along, all the better. Given the number of callers we received today, I do not anticipate it will be a problem, but we must have the proposal before any scandal breaks."

Marry her off. The ton's solution to everything. As if binding her to some gentleman—Shaftsbury or Cranbrook or some other fop—would improve her situation. Yes, she would have respectability, but would she be happy? Would they make her laugh with abandon the way he had? Would they make her eyes burn with desire the way they had when he stood with her outside her bedroom door only a few nights before?

Would they protect her? Cherish her? Allow her to flourish?

Could he stand it if they didn't? Or perhaps the better question was—could he stand it if they did?

Deep inside he knew it didn't matter. He had made her a promise to find her a husband and honor dictated he keep his word, regardless of his conflicting feelings on the issue.

"We are attending Lady Remington's fete at Vauxhall Gardens this evening. Both Lords Cranbrook and Shaftsbury are expected to be there. I believe they are our best opportunity to cultivate an offer as both have shown particular interest in her. Lord Shaftsbury called on her earlier today and Lord Cranbrook sent flowers." His grandmother waved at the colorful bouquet blooming from a vase on the table behind the sofa.

The flowers were positively ghastly in his estimation.

"Fine. I will be there," he said with as much enthusiasm as he could muster.

"Good. Perhaps you should go see her." His grandmother patted his cheek. "She may need some encouragement to attend this evening's festivities."

Chapter Nineteen

S pence heeded his grandmother's advice but when he knocked on Caelie's door, he received no response. He continued on down the hallway and eventually found her in the solar Grandmama kept. It was a small room, but the sunlight that poured in from the large windows made it perfect for reading and needlepoint.

He hovered near the open door of the small room that captured the last remnants of afternoon sun before it made its descent from the sky. Caelie sat on the chaise, turned slightly away from him to peer out the window on the far side of the room from where he stood. An open book lay on her lap and her shoes rested on the floor. She had tucked her feet up beneath her skirts.

The vision knocked the breath from him. Sunlight bathed her pale complexion and made her red hair glisten like liquid fire. He had almost kissed her twice now since their return to London. It took every last ounce of his will since then not to try again, but he had conquered his desires for her sake and for his own sanity.

Yet, when he tried to conjure up that same will now, it

deserted him and before he could stop himself, he had quietly shut the door behind him and turned the key in the lock.

She glanced up as the door latched but made no motion to reprimand him for the impropriety of it. He crossed the room and sat down next to her on the chaise to face her. One fat red curl had escaped the elaborate hairstyle Miss Brampton had concocted, refusing to be confined. It rested against her cheek where a hint of pink bloomed. Spence longed to touch it, but kept himself in check.

"I understand you had an unpleasant encounter with a certain individual at the park this afternoon."

A small smile softened her features. "Yes, with three individuals to be exact."

"Was it upsetting?"

Caelie shrugged. "Lady Franklyn was her usual mean-spirited self." Bewilderment livened her expression for a moment. "Whatever did you see in that woman?"

"I no longer remember. Likely that she was married and therefore no threat to my bachelorhood."

"Cad," she said, though her tone lacked any true admonishment. If anything, the word sounded almost affectionate.

"Indeed." He reached out and touched the curl, unable to help himself any longer. She didn't pull away. "Tell me about Billingsworth."

"There is little to tell, though I do not believe he intends to keep his silence with respect to our encounter at inn."

"Even though you could expose him for taking your innocence and ruin him as well?" He hated speaking of it, hated the image it put in his head of Caelie being with another man. Most of all, he hated that he would have to get used to the idea once she married. How he would manage such a feat he did not know.

"Perhaps he believes people will think I am lying to save myself. To trap him into marriage to avoid the shame."

She dropped her gaze but he caught her chin and lifted it back to him. "You have nothing to be ashamed of. You did nothing wrong."

"Then you are the only one who thinks so. I behaved a reckless fool."

His hand slid along her jawline to the curve of her neck. Her skin was smooth and warm. "I have made a career of being a reckless fool."

"You wear it much better than I," she said. "And you will not be ruined because of it."

"I will not allow him to ruin you."

"Why do you care?" She asked, her voice filled with wonder, as if she couldn't determine a good enough reason that made sense to her. "Before we became acquainted on the *Windswept,* I meant nothing to you. Why does it matter so much to you now that you protect me?"

Because now you are everything to me.

But he could not tell her that. It would not be fair. "We are friends, are we not?"

"Yes."

"Good friends, I think." She was as dear to him as Nick or Bowen, even Grandmama and Grandfather, though the affection he felt for her was vastly differently. He did not fear what he felt for Nick or Bowen. They were like brothers to him. But Caelie...

"Very good friends," he added and leaned closer until he could feel her breath on his skin and smell the sweet scent of wildflowers.

He feared what he felt for her. It had come upon him without warning and had turned him upside down until every nerve he possessed stood on edge. His feelings for her made him want things he didn't want to want. Made him think of a future he had never envisioned for himself. It made him want to risk a lifetime of misery if only he could reach the peak of ecstasy with her for one day.

Had his father felt this way about his mother? Had it been worth it?

He remembered his father's hand covering his mother's as they lay in the scattered wreckage of the carriage. Before he died, his father had pulled his broken body over to where his wife laid and rested his hand on hers.

Had she known? Had she even cared? Or had the acrimony between them grown to such a fevered pitch she would have crawled away from his touch had she been able?

Spence shook the image from his head. He didn't often think about that fateful night, and he didn't want to now.

"I will protect you from Billingsworth."

How, he had not determined yet. His thoughts had scattered. Being this close to her muddled his thinking and try as he might to regain control, he lost the battle before it even started. The moment he saw her sitting on the chaise with the sunlight haloed around her, he knew what would happen.

He knew he would end up here, sitting next to her, telling himself he would not kiss her, knowing full well he would anyway.

"I almost kissed you the other night," he said.

"I know."

"I didn't, though."

"Your grandfather interrupted us."

"I thought I might remedy that."

She said nothing.

He needed no further encouragement. His hand slid up the back of her neck and his lips brushed hers, softly, teasingly. Her breath caught, or had that been his? He couldn't say. Didn't care. When he kissed her again, her tentativeness disappeared. Her mouth moved against his and her hand slid beneath his coat and waistcoat until its warmth permeated his linen shirt and burned into his skin.

She tasted as sweet as she smelled, though far more intoxicating, and in that moment, he understood his father's torment, about loving a woman who would never truly be his, about knowing her happiness resided elsewhere and not with him.

Caelie did not belong to him. It didn't matter how much he wanted her to. In the end, he would never be able to make her happy. The Kingsley men weren't built that way. But those facts turned to smoke caught in a breeze once he touched her, there one moment and gone the next. Forgotten.

He deepened his kiss and she responded. He pulled her closer until she reclined beneath him. She did not resist. The small part of him that knew of honor and character scrambled to find something to hang onto, but when her hand touched his face, so gentle and sweet, everything inside of him broke. He needed to lose himself, to forget his past and the damnable future hanging over both of them.

Spence settled himself over her and explored the length of her neck as his body reveled in the sensation of her curves and softness as they welcomed his weight. The feel of her against him turned him rock hard in an instant and the need to have her burned through his veins and incinerated any last scrap of restraint he possessed.

His hand ran down the length of her leg until it found the edge of her skirts and slipped beneath. With slow deliberation, he drew his palm over her stocking until it reached the bareness of her thigh. She gasped and for a brief second, she froze. Just as Spence thought to pull away, to end this madness, she relaxed and her legs parted further in invitation.

He was lost.

Need and desire and desperation pummeled anything good that might once have existed within him.

His hand moved to the juncture of her thighs. He slipped his fingers through the slit in her drawers. She was slick and warm. Welcoming and waiting. He slid a finger inside of her and she arched into his palm. He did it again, and again still until her rapid breath told him she was close. He reached between then and quickly undid his trousers, setting his erection free. He pushed her skirts out of the way and settled between her thighs.

"Look at me," he whispered. He needed to see her, to gaze into her emerald eyes as he filled her, as he gave her a piece of himself he knew he would never get back.

She opened her eyes and gazed at him. Into him. And in that moment, Spence understood. This was it. He had found home. And suddenly nothing else mattered.

He pushed inside of her and let her soft heat envelope him. He held himself there for a moment, staring at her. What a wonder she was. He had been so blind to not see it at first, but bit by bit she had turned him around until he became so dizzy from discovery he could no longer remember how to run away. Nor did he want to.

Her hips arched and drew him further in, stoking the madness until any resistance he had left fell away. She closed her eyes and her head fell back against the pillows, exposing the delicate column of her neck. He kissed her heated skin and brought the rhythm of their bodies to a peak before driving them both over its edge into a sea of oblivion.

Spence did not know how long he lay collapsed against her, their bodies entwined. His breath still came in rapid gasps and his mind spiraled in more directions than he could track, but one fact he could not deny.

He had done the unthinkable.

And he did not care. In fact, he wanted to do it again. Every day. For the rest of their lives. He had never experienced anything like this before. He had reached a height he had never known existed and his heart swelled from even that one brief touch. He wanted to hold onto it forever, but as his breath slowed, reality crept in.

Could he make her happy for a lifetime? Did he even know how?

And what if he couldn't?

He had seen the devastation of what failure looked like.

Not that it mattered now. He had sealed his fate the moment he walked into the room and saw the sunlight caressing her fair skin and fine features.

Caelie pushed at his shoulder and he lifted his head to look at those features once again, to know she had been as affected by what they had shared as he. But when he gazed upon her beautiful countenance, he found none of that. In truth, he found nothing at all save for a hint of color in the apple of her cheeks.

Her features were void of expression.

He shifted and sat up, adjusting his trousers at the same time she pushed down her skirts.

"Caelie."

"Yes?" She didn't look at him. Instead, she pulled herself back into a sitting position and moved so both of her feet hung over the edge of the chaise.

He did not know what to say. She acted oddly, as if the woman he knew had quietly slipped away when he wasn't looking. "Are you...all right?" It seemed a foolish thing to ask, but her behavior threw him and he could think of nothing else.

"Yes, of course." She tugged at the bodice of her dress to pull it back into place.

When had he lost her?

She slipped her small feet into her shoes. At some point, the book had slipped off her lap onto the floor and she bent to pick it up. He watched her as if he was a ghost she couldn't see. She avoided his gaze and when she did meet it, all too briefly, she looked straight through him.

"I... We will marry, naturally." He did not want her to think he took their actions lightly, or that he would have done such a thing without full understanding of how it would end. How he *wanted* it to end.

"Don't be foolish." Her voice remained calm, but distant. She smiled at him, the same polite smile he'd seen her give others over the past week at parties. It meant nothing. A façade she wore like a shield. She stood and he joined her but his legs felt strange, heavy and weightless at the same time.

"There is nothing foolish about it. I...we...." He waved a hand at the chaise. "There is but one solution."

"I am not a problem that requires a solution," she said and for a brief moment, fire burned in her eyes before the shade dropped down and shut him out once again.

"That is not what I meant. It is only that...we made love, Caelie." And that was it. Love. Such an odd feeling. It defied description no matter how hard the poets tried to capture it. It filled you and emptied you. It made you whole and yet left you broken.

And it scared the bloody hell out of him.

"It was nothing of the sort." Her words cut into him. She sounded nothing like the Caelie he knew. "Do not trouble yourself over it."

Do not trouble himself over it? Had she lost her mind? How could she dismiss what they had shared as insignificant? It had been anything but insignificant. It was a landslide, pure and simple. It had scooped him up and tumbled him around then buried him completely.

How could she say it was nothing?

She touched her hair and tucked a curl back into place. "I should go ready myself for this evening's party."

Spence shook his head. "No. There is no need. I will marry you."

She stood in front of him and stared as if he had suggested they take a walk in the pouring rain. "I will not marry you."

"But...why?" Even he knew what a good catch he was. Why, he could have his pick amongst the unmarried women of the ton and be assured any one of them would say yes and be happy to do so. Yet Caelie, who needed a husband more than most and had few prospects to claim, refused him? It made no sense.

She lifted her chin. "We are not suited. You have said numerous times that you have no wish to marry, that you would be miserable. And I have no wish to live with someone who considers each day with me a misery—"

"I would not be even remotely miserable if we were to do this every day." He waved a hand at the chaise.

"And on the days that we didn't, then what? Would you be miserable on those days? And what about when the children came and responsibilities weighed upon us? When duties demanded our attention and made our tempers short and our time together even shorter? How would you feel then? How long before you began to resent your circumstances and me along with them?"

He stared at her. He did not know what to say. She drew a picture of the future he feared most and the effect left him cold.

"Do you love me?" She asked.

"I—I—yes, of course. I think so."

"You think? Well, that's a hearty endorsement of your feelings."

Spence pursed his lips. Why was she being so difficult? He offered her the world. Or, if not that, then at least a way out of the world she had been living in, the one she may soon be consigned to if Billingsworth and Lady Franklyn had their way. If they married, she would never have to worry again about censure or exile or finances.

"Do you think Cranbrook or Shaftsbury love you? They barely know you!" Not like he did. He had learned what made her laugh, what hurt her heart. He knew her fears and her strengths and how dearly she loved her family.

"No, I do not think they do. Which is better."

"Better? I thought you wished your husband to have an affection for you." She had said that, had she not? Some nonsense about friendship and foundations to build on.

"Of course. But I expect that affection to grow over time."

"But mine has already grown. It is here now. You should accept it." He gave her his most charming smile, but it failed to penetrate the unreadable expression she wore.

"This," she moved her hand between them. "This is not affection. It is...lust. Infatuation. It will wane and you will be left with resentment that you boxed yourself into a corner because of it and, in the end, it will color any fondness you have for me. You are not the only one who has witnessed what resentment between two people can do to a marriage."

"I will never resent this."

She shook her head and the corners of her mouth turned downward. "You already do. You are just not aware of it yet." Caelie turned from him and walked to the door, then stopped. "I am touched that you are willing to do the honorable thing by me, but you do not need to. My fall came well before you and is not your concern. This was a mistake best forgotten."

Her words drove a sharp pain straight through his heart. Who would have thought a man could receive such a wound and still remain upright.

"Right, then. A mistake." He did not know what else to say, or do. He glanced out the window unable to hold her gaze, to let her know how her adamant rejection had affected him.

He cleared his throat. "Do you still intend to go to the Gardens this evening?"

"I do. Your grandmother thought it best that we concentrate on Lords Cranbrook and Shaftsbury and try to hasten an offer before Billingsworth can make his move."

He nodded but every word, every gesture he made felt faraway. Removed. As if he stood outside of his body watching the events unfold. Had nothing that transpired between them touched her in the least?

"Of course. That is likely your best course of action."

She said nothing at first, then, "I must go prepare for this evening, my lord."

My lord.

"Spencer," he whispered but she had already left. Her footfalls echoed down the hallway briefly then disappeared.

Humiliation and hurt curdled in his gut.

Caelie stood in the middle of her bedchamber and let the tears come.

She had failed. Miserably.

On such a catastrophic level there could be no going back.

She and Spencer had made love. She could have stopped him, but she hadn't. Desire had swelled inside of her when he kissed her and she let it pull her under until it crested and broke into a passion she could no longer contain.

When she had arrived home after her encounter with Billingsworth and Lady Franklyn, she had sought refuge in her books and did her best to put the matter from her mind. To quell the fears growing in her belly. Yet the entire time she wanted nothing more than to run into Spencer's arms and find comfort.

Comfort.

Why was that always her downfall? Was she so weak and pathetic she could not withstand ugly emotions without needing someone else to bolster her? And when she did seek it, why did it always end with her allowing a man to use her body—

But no. That was not fair. This had been different.

Billingsworth had taken what he wanted and nothing more. When he left her, she had felt used and foolish and... dissatisfied. But with Spencer. Oh, it had been different indeed. He had not taken, he had given. He had touched her with an intoxicating mix of boldness and gentleness. He had stoked a fire within her that burned through every last inch and left nothing as it had been—not her body, not her heart, not her soul. He'd lifted her to heights she hadn't even known existed and held her tight when everything broke away and left her unable to speak or think or move.

For the first time in her life, she'd had something she wanted within her grasp and she grabbed it. She clasped it to her and basked in the glory it gave for as long as it lasted.

And what a glory it had been. She had never imagined such completeness could be found between a man and woman. Their hearts had entwined as much as their bodies. But when the coupling ended, when the ecstasy of their bodies receded and disentangled, her heart had not returned.

She had left it with his.

She would not need it.

Oh, what a jumbled mess she had made of this! Reality intruded almost immediately. The weight of his body on hers, the slickness between her thighs, the horror of the consequences of what she had done crashed down around her.

How could she marry another man knowing she would never crave his touch the way she did Spencer's? Knowing she would never be able to give her heart fully and completely, as it no longer belonged to her?

And what man would want her now that she had given herself to another man in such a way? Surely there were ways around that, but she did not have the heart for such trickery.

Yet she must. She had no other choice.

She swiped at her cheeks but it did no good. More tears fell to replace the ones she'd wiped away.

Spencer had proposed for honor's sake, but she had honor of her own. She had made a promise—to Spencer, to Lord Ellesmere, and to herself. She would not marry him. For his sake, for his family's sake.

Lord Ellesmere feared bringing more scandal into his family and Caelie did not blame him. She knew what damage it wrought and no matter how hard you scrubbed you could never fully wash it away. Her father's scandal had been bad enough, but if Billingsworth had his way, the scandal that would captivate the ton's attention next would be her own. She would not bring that into the Kingsley family after all they had done for her.

The mistake she had made had been her own, and she would be the one to wear it.

Even before Spencer had pulled away from her, Caelie had known what she must do. She must distance herself from him, put up a wall. Pretend she felt nothing, that what they had shared had not affected her.

It took every last bit of fortitude she had, and some she didn't even know she possessed to pull it off and walk from the room as if what had happened between them meant nothing.

When in truth, it had meant everything.

She did not regret it. To her everlasting shame, she could not. For the rest of her days, she would hold onto the memory of what happened between them and try her best to revel in the fact that for one afternoon she had known how it felt to be loved. To be cherished. No matter that it was only an illusion created in the moment.

But now the ruse must continue. Tonight, she must be charming and beguiling. She must endear Shaftsbury or Cranbrook to such a degree that one of them would be prompted to propose with all due haste. She could not tarry any longer.

She must end this now.

Chapter Twenty

*"B*ut I don't understand."

Spence avoided his grandmother's questioning gaze as he stepped aside and let the footmen carry his trunk to the awaiting carriage. It had not taken long after Caelie had left him standing alone in the solar to realize he had to leave. He could no longer stay under the same roof as her.

"It is for the best, Grandmama. Propriety and all."

What a rip! The horse had run out of the barn on that one, yet here he was trying to slam the door anyway.

His grandmother stood in front of him, her hands on her hips like a general commanding her troops. "Since when have you ever given one whit about propriety?"

He didn't. Not really. What he cared about was not suffering any further humiliation by claiming his feelings for a woman who had no interest in him. He'd had her pegged all wrong. He had thought she wanted love and romance in a husband, but as it turned out, Caelie was far more pragmatic than he'd given her credit for. And he far more egotistical. He'd assumed that because he had wanted her, she would feel the same way.

Had she even wanted him to make love to her? Or had she simply laid there and accepted his attentions because...why? Out of politeness?

Anger burned deep in his gut.

"If I stay, Lady Caelie's reputation may suffer. If Billingsworth is set on trying to sully her good name and using me to do it, then it is best we do not give him more fuel to add to his fire. He cannot suggest anything improper is going on under this roof if I am not under said roof."

The words tasted bitter on his tongue.

"He wouldn't dare suggest such a thing!"

Spence smiled, the motion disingenuous and hollow, much like the rest of him. "If Billingsworth is willing to ruin a young lady's reputation to repair his own, I would suggest he is capable of doing any number of despicable things."

"He is a vile man. I have always thought so." His grandmother turned away and paced the hallway. She stopped when one of the footmen reappeared to let him know the carriage was ready. She gave him a pleading look. "Where are you going?"

"To my bachelor apartments. It is not so far away." He had purchased them from Nick who had given them up upon his marriage to Abigail. The only issue with the location was it gave him a perfect view of the Glenmor townhouse.

Thankfully, the one Laytham who caused him such distress would not be in it.

It was better this way. He had danced too close to the edge of the knife this afternoon and now carried a deep wound across his heart, one he would bear the scar of for many years to come. He'd had no right to do what he had done. She had not enticed him, nor encouraged him. He could not lay the blame for this at her door.

What had been done, he had done to himself.

That what they shared had left her unmoved, she'd made

clear. She did not want him. She did not trust him to love her over the long run and he could not blame her for that, either. How many times had he told her of his complete aversion to marriage, his disparaging thoughts on the institution? His complete ineptitude to be happy within its confines? Was it any wonder she did not take his feelings for anything but transitory?

He did not believe that any more, but nor did he trust himself. What did he know of love? How did he know the picture she drew isn't exactly how it would unfold over time? The thought of them ending up like his parents, the rages and accusations and acrimony, it chilled him to the bone. Even more so if there were children, for no child should have to witness what he had.

"Will you still attend Lady Remington's fete at Vauxhall Gardens this evening?"

"Yes, of course." He had made a promise. And as much as it pained him to partake in this farce, he would uphold his end of the bargain. He would act as if he had fallen madly and deeply with Caelie in the hope it would hasten an offer from Cranbrook or Shaftsbury.

The problem being, it had stopped being an act.

Fate, it turned out, had a twisted and ironic sense of humor.

What else could explain the fact that the one woman he could conceivably see himself married to, he could not have? Not just due to Grandfather's refusal to consider her as a viable option, but because she did not want him. Even after they had—

His grandmother tapped him on the wrist. "You are wool-gathering, my dear."

"Forgive me, Grandmama." Spence shook his head and let the thoughts recede. There was little point dwelling on them. It would change nothing. Even if he went against Grandfather's wishes and convinced Caelie to marry him, without his inheritance he had no means to support her.

Spence rubbed a hand over his brow. How simple his life had been just a month ago.

He bent and gave his grandmother a quick kiss on her cheek. She smelled of gardenias, a marked contrast to the scent of wildflowers that reminded him of Caelie. He breathed deeply and hoped it would help erase her from his thoughts.

It didn't.

"I will meet you at the Gardens, Grandmama."

"See that you do, my dear. Our time is running out. We must find Lady Caelie a husband and we must do it now."

The weight of their enterprise had never felt heavier than it did in that moment.

Caelie had only been to Vauxhall Gardens one other time. Her mother had disapproved of the place and considered any event that took place there far too aberrant for her daughter to attend. It had been Aunt Lorena who had brought her and Abigail the year her cousin had officially entered society. Mother had taken to her room for three days claiming a headache and Aunt Lorena had determined it best not to bother her with their social schedule. The night had been magical, the park even more so with its bevy of twinkling lights and beautiful patrons dressed in their finest.

Caelie had always wished to return to see it again, though this time, the heaviness in her heart somehow dimmed the twinkling lights, and the gardens did not seem half as enchanting as in her memories.

Lady Ellesmere had told her before they left the house that Spencer had made the decision to move to his bachelor apartments. Guilt filled her. She had driven him away from his own home. Was he ashamed at what they had shared? Or had her adamant rejection of his proposal embarrassed him?

She wished she could have spoken with him before he left, but he'd given no warning and what would she say after all?

Lady Ellesmere looped her arm through Caelie's and held her walking stick with the other. Like her husband, she used the accoutrement more for show than for actual use, but the marchioness claimed it came in handy when manoeuvring through crowds.

"Now my dear," she said as they made their way down the Grand Walk. "Huntsleigh will meet up with us inside the Pavilion. It is important that you appear a bit more interested in him than you have for the past fortnight. This will make Shaftsbury and Cranbrook take notice. We want them to think they need to make a move now, before another proposal is received and accepted."

"I will do my best." But she had already refused a proposal and the idea of pretending an interest made the guilt writhe inside of her like a serpent. Part of her hoped Spencer would not come at all. She wouldn't blame him if he didn't.

"Ah, I see Lady Franklyn and her daughter are here." Lady Ellesmere's observation intruded into Caelie's thoughts and she grasped the distraction with gratitude. "I find it exceedingly disturbing that the duchess continues to try and insert herself into Spencer's company when it is obvious that he—" Lady Ellesmere stopped abruptly.

"When he what?" What had she been about to say?

The marchioness shook her head. "Forgive me. I should not speak of such things."

"Think nothing of it. I am not as sheltered as you may think."

"No. I suspect you have seen far more than you had ever

wished to. I am sorry for what you have gone through. It must have been very difficult."

Caelie nodded. It had been difficult. But more than the censure from society, the loss of friends she thought more loyal, the public jilting of a man she had given her innocence to, the true pain came from watching her father deteriorate into a strange madness that left him unreachable. He had become lost inside that madness and she had failed to discover a way to find him and lead him back.

Is that how Spencer had felt about his own parents, watching their relationship deteriorate as it had? No wonder bearing witness to such bitterness had turned him sour on marriage.

"But let us think happy thoughts tonight, shall we?" Lady Ellesmere's voice brightened, though the cheerfulness felt as forced as the smile Caelie gave her in answer. Something bothered the older lady, Caelie could see it in her light blue eyes. Worry creased the corners and made the lines fan downward in deep grooves.

Caelie tried to bolster both of their spirits. Nothing would be accomplished if they walked through the party with dour looks on their faces. "Surrounded by such beauty, how could we not. This is not the place for sadness, is it?"

"It is not. Come," Lady Ellesmere nodded at the building up ahead and to their right. "Let's make our way inside. The air is a tad too chilly for these old bones."

The night developed much as the others before it, and with many of the same players. Lady Franklyn and Lady Susan held court with their crowd of admirers and attempted to give praise to Caelie though she laced it with more criticism than tribute.

Lord Shaftsbury and Lord Cranbrook were present and paid court, vying for her attentions and through it all, Spencer remained absent. Had he given up on her then? Had her pretense that their lovemaking had meant nothing injured his pride beyond forgiveness?

"You look absolutely exquisite, this evening, Lady Caelie," Lord Cranbrook said as he bent low over her offered hand. "I do not think I have ever seen a vision so lovely. You must promise me the waltz this evening. Do not break my heart and say you are spoken for. I could not bear it."

Caelie stared down at the earl's shiny head. He had attempted to comb the sides of his hair over to cover the large bald spot, but there had not been sufficient supply to do the job justice. She stuck a smile on her face as he straightened.

"I am distressed at the thought of bringing you such anguish, Lord Cranbrook, but I'm afraid I have already promised the dance to Lord Shaftsbury." The viscount had made a beeline for her the moment she had walked into the Pavilion and declared his interest in two of the dances on her card.

"More might appear unseemly," he declared, then leaned in and whispered. "Although you make a man want to forget himself in that regard."

Something sparked in his eye as he pulled away. Something that looked far more salacious than it should. She had wanted to pull her hand away from him but had not dared to make a scene. Then as quickly as it appeared, his expression altered and the glint disappeared leaving in its place the usual blandness she had come to associate with him. Had she only imagined it?

But no. Lord Cranbrook, too, stood much closer than was proper and the leering look he gave her made her skin crawl. "I understand you are acquainted with ways to alleviate a man's distress."

Cold invaded her insides and this time she did jerk her hand away. "I beg your pardon, my lord?"

She slid her glance from side to side. Had anyone else

heard his improper suggestion? No one gave them a second look, but over Lord Shaftsbury's shoulder, across the room, she saw Lord Billingsworth and Lady Franklyn. They stood staring at her and when Billingsworth smirked, she knew.

Deep in her bones, she knew.

He had broken his silence.

It was too late.

She was ruined.

"Would you excuse me, Lord Cranbrook?" She did not wait for his reply. She brushed past him and crossed the room. Billingsworth's smirk grew larger, more sinister as she drew closer. Anger emboldened her and she marched toward him. For too long she had stood silent while others cast aspersions on her. Whether true or not, Billingsworth did not have the right to ruin her life. She had done no more than he and at least she had gone into it with honest intentions and true beliefs.

Lady Franklyn whispered something in his ear then melted into the crowd. Likely to spread the gossip further. And for what? Because Spencer had appeared to have an attraction for her? What did it matter? True or not, Lady Franklyn had no claim to him. She was married, though that did not seem to matter to her.

"Lady Caelie." Her name slithered out of Billingsworth and made her stomach turn. "How do we find ourselves this evening? Fine and well, I hope."

His voice dripped of insincerity. How had she ever thought him worthy of her attentions? Now he only sickened her. The only good turn he had ever done her came when he refused to marry to her. She couldn't imagine a worse fate.

"What have you done?"

A broad smile lit his face. A face she'd once thought handsome, until she learned what true handsomeness was. It came from the heart, from character and honor and caring.

Billingsworth possessed none of these traits. He reminded her of an actor on a stage, playing whatever part served his purposes and exiting the moment he'd taken what he'd wanted.

"I said nothing but the truth. That you are not the innocent you portray yourself to be." His hand pressed against the space where his heart would beat, if he had one. "I cannot in good conscience allow Shaftsbury or Cranbrook to go forward with their plans to take you as wife when in truth, your behavior has revealed you are no better than a mistress."

Icy shards sliced through her body. She wanted to protest, to deny his words, but had her wanton behavior this afternoon not proven them to be true?

"Have you no response, my dear?" He chuckled. "But of course, you don't. You never really did, did you? Why I was able to break our engagement without so much as a whimper from you."

"Perhaps I did not feel I had lost anything of value where you were concerned." Her voice shook, but she stood her ground. She would not allow him to cow her.

"Ah, the kitten has found her claws. Such a shame. I would have enjoyed our time together much more, had you possessed such fire when we were together."

She kept her voice low to prevent anyone nearby from eavesdropping. "Had I possessed those claws when we were together, I would never have allowed you near me."

The truth of that hit home. She had become so accustomed to doing the right thing, abiding by Mother's dictates, that she had long forgotten how to think for herself. Only upon Mother's abandonment and Spencer's encouragement had she found her voice again, and with it, a desire to be her own person. Make her own decisions. Fight her own battles.

"Oh, I don't think—"

"Of course, you don't think, my lord. Thinking would

require a level of intelligence you do not possess. Acting on these thoughts would require a level of character you have never owned. You are little more than an empty shell with a well-cut jacket that you can ill-afford."

Billingsworth's eyes widened and his chest puffed out. "I beg your—"

Caelie kept a smile fixed on her face for the benefit of anyone watching their exchange. "You may beg all you want. In fact, perhaps you should get used to it, given your family's financial circumstances. It may be the only way you can continue to afford your fancy clothes."

Blotched color ravaged Billingsworth's pale face. "How dare you. As if you are in any position to speak. Your family was ruined by your father's scandalous affair with a whore and now you have proven you are no better. Tell me, did you spread your legs for Huntsleigh as well? Did he find you as lacking as I did?"

Before Caelie could find words to reply, Billingsworth spun around and in the blink of an eye lay prone on the floor staring up in shock.

In front of where he had once stood, Spencer flexed his hand and ignored the gaping stares of the crowd around them. "I believe I warned you once already, Billingsworth. I do hate having to repeat myself."

Blood trickled from her former fiancé's nose which appeared to have shifted to the left somewhat. Caelie should have been pleased by this, but all she could think at the moment was how everyone in the room and turned their attention toward them. Hitting Billingsworth had changed nothing. Her secret was out. She could see it in the knowing looks of the people surrounding them.

Spencer glanced at her and held her gaze for a brief moment before he turned to address their peers.

"It has been brought to my attention that Lord

Billingsworth has been spreading salacious lies about my dear friend, Lady Caelie. I'm sure many of you have heard them as he and Lady Franklyn seem to have made it their mission this evening to humiliate and ruin her."

Someone gasped but Caelie could not say who.

Spencer's voice carried throughout the room and the crowd drew closer. Caelie's face flamed until even the roots of her hair burned with heat. If only the floor would open up and swallow her whole, but it refused to cooperate.

"Please let me explain the reasoning for Billingsworth's behavior. You see," Spencer began to pace the small circle left open to them. "As you all know, Billingsworth has had a difficult time of late finding himself a bride after showing his fickle nature. It appears many of you with daughters, especially those with a sizable dowry of which he appears most interested, have shut your doors to him. A wise decision, I would think, given his current behavior."

"He lies!" Billingsworth attempted to rise, but Spencer planted a foot on his chest and shoved him back down, letting the toe of his boot slide downward until it hovered near the other man's throat.

"You'll want to be quiet," Spencer said, his voice quiet and deadly. "I've reached the end of my patience with you. If you rise again or breathe a word, I will kill you. Do you understand?"

Billingsworth did nothing more but blink up at Spencer, but Caelie saw the fear in his eyes. He was nothing more than a bully and a coward when it came down to it.

Caelie wanted to stop Spencer before he continued. Enough had been said. Enough to make her feel as if she had been stripped naked and left to stand there exposed to all. But she could not catch his eye as he stepped away from Billingsworth who heeded his warning and did not move.

Spencer's voice grew more emphatic with each step he took around the circle.

"Due to this shunning—and the fact his family is in a bit of a...financial bind, shall we say—Billingsworth decided the only way to justify his dishonorable jilting of Lady Caelie was to cast aspersions on her character. Aspersions that I can attest are nothing but lies."

"How do you know?"

Caelie's head whipped around to find the person who shouted the question, but the crowd had growth thick. It could have been anyone.

"I know because Billingsworth told me of his plan. I counseled him against it and warned him there would be consequences, but of course he is an idiot. And like an idiot, he did not heed my advice and so here we are. But I have come to know Lady Caelie and can attest to not only her virtue but her outstanding character. As can my grandparents, Lord and Lady Ellesmere. Do you think they are not sound judges of character?"

Spencer's gaze penetrated the lord and ladies as he waited for any response. A rumble swept through their ranks, but no one spoke out to deny his claim.

He smiled and turned to her, offering his hand. Caelie tried to read his expression, but she could not. The hardness she saw in his eyes frightened her. Still, she took a step toward him and slipped her hand into his.

"In fact," Spencer said, addressing his audience once more. "I am so certain of her good virtue I have asked her to be my wife."

Caelie froze. Her breath caught in her throat and blood pounded in her ears. Or was that the noise from the crowd? She tried to move, to speak, to do something, but shock had rendered her immobile.

Spencer held up his free hand to quiet the voices. "And she has graciously accepted."

Caelie remembered little after that. People approached her and offered congratulations. Lady Ellesmere reached her side and soon after that Lady Blackbourne and Lady Rebecca who she had not realized had even arrived. They flanked her and held her up and she plastered on a smile and nodded and said all the appropriate things.

She had no idea of what happened to Billingsworth, and Lady Franklyn and her daughter were nowhere to be found.

Somewhere nearby she heard Spencer's laughter as he accepted pats on the back from the gentlemen and the regretful congratulations of the ladies who now had to cross him off their prospective list. But his laughter sounded as hollow as her insides.

She did not look at him, though. She couldn't.

Every time she did, anger surged through her and stained any gratitude she should have felt.

How could he do this to her?

"Perhaps now would be a good time to take our leave," Lady Ellesmere whispered in her ear as the crowd began to disperse and people returned to their own business, though experience told her the whispers of tonight's events would last throughout the Season and beyond.

Caelie allowed the marchioness to lead her from the Pavilion. Their carriage awaited them and when she stepped inside, Spencer had already taken the seat across from her. She sat down and turned her attention to the window. Lady Ellesmere sat next to her and took her hand. Caelie was more grateful for the older woman's support than she could say.

"Lady Caelie—" Spencer said but she gave a sharp shake of her head to cut him off.

Her thoughts and emotions were too tossed and shaken to discuss what had happened.

"We will discuss this when we arrive home, my dear," Lady Ellesmere said. "She has been through a shock. Let her be."

Tense silence filled the carriage and followed them through the streets of London and into the welcoming warmth of the Kingsleys' stately home.

"Forgive me," she said, after giving Fenton her cape. "I believe I will retire for the evening."

Spencer stepped forward and reached for her. She managed to side-step him and reach the staircase. "Caelie, we need to talk."

"Later. Tomorrow." Never. She turned her back on him and walked up the stairs, not stopping until she had found refuge in her room.

———

"What else would you have had me do, Grandfather?"

It had been a long night and it had not ended yet. He had given Caelie the time she requested though he would have much preferred to explain his actions to her. Instead, he had searched out his grandfather, and hoped the man would understand he had done the only thing he could. He'd had no other choice. The moment he'd entered the Pavilion, two separate gentlemen he barely knew made veiled references about Caelie. It wasn't until he caught one of them by the throat and demanded he explain himself that Spence learned the truth. Billingsworth and Lady Franklyn had begun their campaign to ruin Caelie's reputation beyond repair.

He'd rushed inside in the hope of getting her out before word spread too far, but when he saw her standing toe to toe with Billingsworth, he knew he had failed.

That he did not kill Billingsworth on the spot was a

miracle in itself. Rage burned through him like an inferno. After hitting the coward and planting him on his arse for the second time, Spence's brain raced for a solution to repair the damage and came up with only one—denounce Billingsworth as a liar and a cad then reinforce Caelie's virtue by announcing their betrothal. As the future Marchioness of Ellesmere, no one would dare treat her with anything but respect.

A brilliant plan, really.

Unfortunately, Caelie did not appear to agree. Nor did Grandfather, based on his current expression. He sat in his chair in front of the fire with his fingers steepled beneath his chin, staring at Spence. "When did you make this proposal?"

"Ah..." Right. The only hitch in his scheme. "I haven't. Not exactly. I suggested it to her perhaps...earlier." He left out what had precipitated his asking. It would do nothing to warm Grandfather to the notion if he knew such details.

"And when you suggested it, what was her response?"

Spence picked at an imaginary piece of lint on his buff breeches. "She may have indicated it was a bad idea."

"It is good to see one of you had your senses about you then."

Spence glared at his grandfather. "That was before Billingsworth spread his lies, however. She is under our protection, Grandfather. Would you have had me leave such a thing unanswered? She would be forever ruined! You cannot tell me that is what you wished to see happen."

His grandfather turned his gaze to the fire, his aged hand rubbing against his chin. For a long moment, he said nothing, simply stared at the flames as they licked the back of the hearth. The wood crackled and popped, the only sound to permeate the silence in the room.

"Grandfather?"

"I know what it is like to protect the reputation of a lady you hold dear," he said, without looking at Spence. "But it is not always possible. We cannot always protect them against their own actions."

Spence shot to his feet. "What are you saying? Are you telling me you believe Billingsworth?"

His grandfather turned his attention back to him. "Do I have your word then that she has not been compromised?"

Spence dropped back into his chair. "She is a good person, Grandfather."

"Of that I have no doubt. Unfortunately, being a good person does not make you immune to mistakes."

"She has not made any mistakes." The mistakes had been all his.

A long breath escaped his grandfather and for the first time Spence noticed how deeply etched the lines of his face had become. Was it from age, or worry, that made them so? He couldn't say. Sometimes, it appeared Grandfather wore the weight of the world on his shoulders. He took to his responsibilities with a gravity most men would fear to attempt. Spence had done nothing to make the task easier for him.

He wished he could now, but it wasn't to be. "Grandfather, I have already announced our engagement."

"Yet she is not amenable to the marriage."

Spence stared at the fire. "No." But he could convince her, surely. Given the circumstances, her options were limited. It did not exactly bode well for a happy life, did it?

"Then she may still break it off?"

"You sound almost hopeful, Grandfather. I thought you would at least be pleased you will finally see me married off."

"To a reputable lady devoid of scandal, not one about to dive into it even further. It will not do, Spencer."

Spence stalked to the window. He understood his grandfather's concerns. He had concerns of his own about how they would navigate this marriage without sinking them both into a sea of despair. But what was done could not be undone.

. . .

Caelie knocked on Spence's bedroom door. He had indicated he would remain at the family home this evening. She waited on his reply, but it never came. Proof he did not want this marriage; that his proposal had been out of a sense of duty, a need to save her. It had nothing to do with love or wanting to create a life, a home and a family together.

She placed a hand over her mouth and held back the tears. She had gone in search of Lady Ellesmere. The older woman had said little during the ride home in the carriage, but her comforting hand on Caelie's had been the only lifeline that kept her from breaking down completely. She needed to explain, perhaps to even tell her the truth and seek her advice on what to do.

She hated that this family would pay the price for her mistakes.

But it had been Lord Ellesmere's voice she'd heard as she walked down the hallway. She should have moved on, but she didn't. She regretted that now.

Humiliation, shame and distress stormed through her like a tempest. Lord Ellesmere did not support their engagement. He did not want the marriage to take place. She did not blame him. She was damaged goods. A fallen woman.

They did not deserve this, and she would not see this family suffer for it.

She turned away from the door and hurried down the hallway. She burst through the door of her bedchamber, startling Elsie who had been in the process of preparing her.

"M'lady, I wondered where you got off—what is it?"

"Elsie, I need your help."

Chapter Twenty-One

"What do you mean she is gone?"

Spence had slept until well past noon, though perhaps sleep was too generous a term. Mostly he'd tossed and turned, Grandfather's final words echoing in his head. Grandfather was generally a more reasonable man, but no matter how Spence had tried to convince him marrying Caelie was the right thing to do, the man would not budge. Finally, he'd had to tell him no, much as it pained him to disappoint the man who had been more of a father to him than his own, he would not abandon her. He would marry her.

Not that the idea of marriage didn't terrify him. It did. For all the reasons it always had. Only now, it was worse. Now he understood just what he stood to lose when things went bad. Perhaps it wouldn't be so worrisome if he had even the smallest clue how to prevent it from happening, but he didn't. And his parents were certainly no help in that regard. Their example a cautionary tale of epic proportions.

But instead of finding Caelie in the breakfast room, or

anywhere else for that matter, to speak to her about what had happened last night, he'd found his grandmother instead.

Grandmama handed him the note that had awaited her when she came downstairs to the breakfast room. Spence took the folded sheet of vellum paper and flipped it open. Sun poured into the room through the window behind him and illuminated Caelie's precise handwriting where it flowed across the ivory paper.

He skimmed the words. She thanked his family for taking her in and treating her with such kindness and respect... expressed her deep regret for the suffering and embarrassment she had caused them...would not put them through any more distress on her behalf...appreciated Spencer's attempt to save her reputation....refused to hold him to his announcement of their betrothal...best for all concerned.

He dropped the letter onto the table. "Where has she gone?"

"She does not say."

"But this is madness! We are to be married."

Grandmama shook her head and the sadness he remembered from so long ago settled itself on her usually sunny expression. She sat down at the table and let out a long breath. "I had hoped this would end differently."

Spence glanced up from the letter sharply. "What do you mean? Did you...did you want us to marry?"

His grandmother smiled but it did not light her eyes. "How could I not? From the moment you arrived I could see the two of you had formed a strong attachment."

"We—I—How?"

"When we told you about Marcus, you leaned into her as if she was a safe haven. You have never done that before; did you know that? You are always the one providing support to others. Your parents when they fought their battles, Lord Blackbourne when he faced an unwanted marriage to Miss

Caldwell, Marcus when you knew he could not stand another sea voyage, and then Lady Caelie when her mother cast her aside and left her unprotected."

"I had no other choice."

"Yes, you did. But you had no choice when it came to falling in love with her, did you? I expect it took you quite unaware."

"I am not—"

She waved off his denial and just as well. He had no strength to put behind it. "You are and I know it terrifies you. But you are not your father or your mother. You have taken the best of them and you have left the worst where it belongs, buried in their graves. Do not use them as your example of what marriage can do. Use your grandfather and I. Use Lord Blackbourne and lovely Abigail."

Spence sat in the chair at the head of the table. "Those are only two examples, Grandmama. You are forgetting all the other unhappy ones I see every day. Ones I use to my advantage, if you must know."

"Do not think I am unaware of your...activities. Though I would point out, the marriages you insert yourself into have never been ones made by love. They were marriages brokered for money and titles and social advantage. Sometimes those marriages work, your grandfather and I certainly did. But many times, they do not. It is better to marry with your heart, Spencer."

"As my parents did? Yes, that worked well, didn't it?"

His grandmother reached across the table and took his hand. "Your parents loved each other, just at different times."

"What are you talking about? Father was the only one in love in that marriage."

"Your mother loved your father."

Spence scoffed. "So much so that she had a string of lovers. Including one she planned to run off with when she died, if you'll recall. Is that what you mean when you say she loved him?"

Grandmama lapsed into silence for several long moments. Spence opened his mouth to apologize for his churlish words, but she stopped him. "When your parents married, your father made his own choice, despite my misgivings. It was readily apparent that Margaret was besotted with your father. Much like you, Reginald had more charm and good looks than he knew what to do with. I counseled him against making an offer. I thought the imbalance of affections would cause difficulty."

"Yes, it is never a good thing to have someone love you, is it?" Spence could not keep the sarcasm from his words.

"Not when only one heart is engaged."

Spence scowled, the words hitting too close to home.

"Your father refused to listen. She was a beautiful woman from a good family. It was a feather in his cap, and your father had enough of an ego to think this was reason enough. I think he believed he could remain indifferent to Margaret, to do his duty without curbing his other behaviors. And so, he married your mother and kept to his parties and gaming tables and mistresses."

Spence shook his head. Grandmama had it wrong. "You are mistaken. Father doted on Mother. It was *she* who sought men outside of her marriage. *She* who took lovers and flaunted them in my father's face."

He still remembered the arguments. The shouting and accusations, the tears and misery. The constant push and pull with him caught in the middle like a pawn on a chess table. When his parents fought, nothing was safe. They attacked each other with a feral ferocity. Lamps, plates, clocks—anything that wasn't nailed down was fair game to be picked up and thrown. As a young boy, he often became trapped in the room with them. Though uncommon for children to be with their parents to such a degree, he had feared leaving them alone. Feared one day they would fight to the death.

It turned out he had been right. And he bore witness to that as well.

"Yes, in the end," his grandmother said. Sadness had crept into her voice. "But not always. Margaret came to the marriage with lofty, romantic dreams and she watched every one of them be dashed upon the rocks as your father treated her with casual indifference."

The tale Grandmama told was topsy-turvy. He remembered none of this. "When did it change?"

"Shortly after you were born. Your mother's sunny nature had dissipated by then. She transferred her love to you and cut your father out. It wasn't until he could no longer count on her full affections that he realized how much she had come to mean to him. He had done the unthinkable and fallen in love with his own wife, but he did it much too late. By then, your mother's heart had been scarred and jaded. She could not forget the hurts he had caused. She had turned bitter and wanted nothing more than to hurt him in return."

"I remember." The vivid recollections were never far from his mind.

"Your grandfather and I tried to counsel them to restrain their emotions, to behave with decorum. We feared if it went on, the results could only end in tragedy."

"And they did."

"Yes."

Spence spread his fingers and stared at them. He wished Grandmama had not brought it up. He did not like to remember that day. The long night, waiting next to his dead parents until someone found them, had been interminable. He'd cried at first, but then the tears ran dry. He had not cried since. Not when Grandfather arrived the next day with several tenants who had gone in search of them. Not at the funeral where they buried Mother and Father side by side. Not even when Grandmama tucked him in at night, tears in her own eyes, and promised everything would be fine. They would get through it together. That he was not alone.

But it had been a lie.

A part of Spence had always felt alone. Oh, he had his grandparents who loved him with everything they had. And he'd had the friendship of Nick and Bowen who were like brothers to him. But a hollowness remained in a part of his heart where his parents had once lived. Only when he'd found Caelie had that hole been filled. He hadn't noticed it at first, but now that she had left him the hollowness echoed inside of him once again. A staggering loss that mocked him once more.

Like his father, he had realized too late what he had and waited too long to act upon it.

And he had lost everything as a result.

"Why are you telling me this now?"

Grandmama shook her head. "I'm not certain, other than I think you deserve the truth. Perhaps we should have told you long ago. Maybe it would have dispelled this fear you have that marriage is nothing but misery. It isn't. Not if you treat each other right from the start. Not if you recognize the wonderful gift you can be to each other, and cherish that gift as if it is the most precious thing you own. Your parents didn't do that. If they had, maybe the outcome would have been much different. That is the mistake you should avoid making, Spencer. Not marriage itself."

Spencer lifted the letter he still held in his hand. "But I'm already too late, Grandmama. I have already missed my chance."

Caelie was gone. He had let her go. Right from the start, he had made it clear he had no interest in taking a wife, then he'd helped her find another husband so he could avoid marriage, when what he should have done was begged her to marry him. He'd been so caught up in his old beliefs he hadn't stopped long enough to realize his views had changed.

At least they had with respect to spending his life with her.

Now he had only the memory of what might have been to keep him company.

What a prize idiot he was.

———

The trip to Sheridan Park took two days, due to the condition of the roads. By the time she and Elsie arrived, Caelie was overcome with exhaustion. She had not sent word ahead. There had been no time. After overhearing the discussion between Lord Ellesmere and Spencer, Caelie had enlisted Elsie's help, who in turn had enlisted Mr. Garron's assistance, and between the three of them she had packed her things and had them loaded onto the awaiting carriage with all due haste. At the first inn they came to outside of London, they had sent the Ellesmere carriage back and hired one of their own, then set out again. Caelie hadn't wanted to stop, afraid if she did, she would turn around and go back.

But she couldn't. She had nothing to go back to.

She hated leaving without speaking to Lady Ellesmere personally, but she couldn't risk having the marchioness talk her out of it. Nor did she want to see Spencer, or hear him try to convince her not to go through with the engagement. She shouldn't have been surprised. He did not want to marry her. She'd known it all along.

He had an attraction for her, that she could not deny. But attractions waned when nothing deeper existed to hold them in place. And it did not appear Spencer thought of her as anything more than a duty. He would marry her because he had to, not because he wished to.

She was better rid of this place and its heartbreak. Better rid of London and its memories all together. She had come back and tried to recapture what she'd once had, but to no avail. It was not meant to be. In the end, she wasn't so certain she wanted it anyway.

After two years away from society, she no longer fit the mould of the proper young lady with starry eyes and an innocent heart, waiting for her Prince Charming to find her so her real life would begin.

Life, she discovered, did not play out like a fairy tale. Oh, real life had plenty of trolls and wicked witches to be certain, but the Prince Charmings were in very short supply. And her Prince Charming had no interest in a happily ever after with her.

No, best she leave it behind. She would stay with Abigail until her cousin's baby arrived, then she would go somewhere else, start fresh. Maybe she would change her name, create a new identity altogether. Bury Caelie Laytham in the past.

"Thank you for your help, Elsie. I know this likely isn't what you anticipated when you took the position of lady's maid."

Elsie smiled, her practical nature and positive outlook unhindered by the long hours in the carriage. "I have never been one to shy away from an adventure, m'lady."

"You're a braver soul than I."

"Oh, I'm not sure about that. Garron told me of your troubles with your mother. It takes a hearty sort to strike out on your own. We're not so different after all."

Caelie took a deep breath and tried to ignore the ache in her heart. Maybe Elsie was right. With no one to answer to, no one telling her what to do or how to do it, she could do as she pleased. The freedom left her a bit dizzy. And a little lost.

"Don't you find it lonely having adventures by yourself?"

Elsie's smile grew and a pretty pink colored her cheeks. "I suppose I'm not as alone as all that."

Caelie blinked and her brain clicked and whirled as she put the pieces together. "Mr. Garron?"

"He's a little rough around the edges to some, but he's a good man. Under all that gruffness is the heart of a gallant knight. And I cannot deny he makes me feel quite safe and pretty. Oh, but look at me talkin' such foolishness."

Caelie shook her head. "Not at all, Elsie. I'm very happy for you and Mr. Garron. Both of you have seen me through a very difficult time and I cannot wish you anything but happiness for your future."

"I thank you, m'lady. I wasn't sure I'd marry again after losin' my Rabbie, but I guess the heart heals after all, goin' about its business when we're not payin' attention."

"I hope so, Elsie. I truly hope so." Her heart could use some healing.

The carriage crested the final hill and relief flooded through her. She had not been to Sheridan Park since the annual house party the Sheridans threw every year. It had been her first public outing since her father's death. She'd been terrified no one would speak to her, let alone dance with her. But Spencer had been the first to approach her after she danced the first set with Nicholas. She knew Nicholas had had a hand in it. He'd wanted to make amends for what had happened to her father. She appreciated the gesture, appreciated even more not being left to stand against the wall like a potted plant, feeling like an eyesore everyone wished would leave.

The carriage stopped at the wide step and a moment later Garron opened the door and assisted her and Elsie out. She took a deep breath, prayed her arriving without notice would not be an imposition. The door swept open before they reached it and two footmen stepped outside to assist Garron with the trunks. The butler, whose name she could not recall, ushered them inside.

"I will alert Lady Blackbourne you are here, my lady," he said after he'd led her to the drawing room. Silence shrouded the house, save for the normal sounds of the soft tread of housemaids and footmen going about their duties. She took a seat and smiled at the housekeeper when she brought a pot of tea.

"Her ladyship will be right down, ma'am, and I've shown your Miss Brampton to her lodgings as well."

"Thank you—" She stopped. "I'm sorry, I don't know your name."

"Oh, Mrs. Hume, ma'am. Been here since the new lord was but a boy in short pants. Now you make sure you eat some of those biscuits. Her ladyship claims there is nothing that tastes quite like them."

Caelie nodded her thanks, but the turmoil in her stomach made it impossible to consider putting anything in it just yet.

"Caelie!" Her head jerked up at the sound of her cousin's voice. "I thought they must have been mistaken when they said you were here. Whatever has brought—" She stopped and a stricken look crossed her face. "Is it Marcus? Has he—"

"Oh no!" Caelie stood and rushed to her cousin who had yet to come further than the door. "Mr. Bowen is doing quite well. He is up and around, though Lady Ellesmere keeps chasing him back to bed insisting he needs his rest."

Abigail's hand patted her chest. "You scared me. But...why then are you here?"

Caelie hedged. "I...I thought I would come for a visit. Can I not come to visit my cousin?"

"You are welcome any time, you know that. But what of your husband hunt?" She clapped her hands together. "Have you settled on someone then? Are you betrothed? Oh Caelie, how wonderful! Who is it?"

Caelie should have known better than to think her cousin's curious nature would let her off the hook. "Come, sit down," she said and led Abigail to the sofa. The early afternoon light filtered through the window and created a halo around her cousin's blonde head. Marriage suited her. Marriage to Nicholas even more so. Gone was the anger and need for revenge that had once clouded her expression. In its place, she had recovered her quick smile and her cheeks glowed with health and happiness. Caelie envied her, but she did not resent her. Abigail had championed their family when she, broken and distraught, could not. She had earned her happiness the hard way and Caelie did not begrudge her a moment of it.

"You're making me sit down? Sitting down isn't good. Sitting down is what they make you do when they give you bad news. What is it Caelie? What has happened?"

She hated to dim the light that sparked in Abigail's blue eyes, but she did not want to lie to her cousin any longer. She had carried the burden of her secrets for as long as she could, but the weight had grown too heavy and she needed to set it down somewhere safe.

She waited until Abigail took a seat on the short sofa.

"I'm not sure where to begin." She had thought about this conversation from every angle. How much should she tell, what should she keep to herself? She still did not know.

"Begin at the beginning."

But where was that? Caelie stood and paced to the window to peer out into the gardens. In no time at all, it would be filled with color and scents, bumble bees and butterflies.

She let out a deep breath and returned to her seat on the sofa and took Abigail's hands in hers. She needed her cousin's strength right now. She turned to face her. "I am ruined."

Abigail blinked several times but said nothing for a long

moment. When she did, her voice pitched higher than her usual tone. "I beg your pardon?"

"Ruined."

The blinking continued for another moment. Caelie waited while Abigail processed the information. When she had, her eyes grew wide. "Huntsleigh?"

"No! Well..." She cleared her throat. "No. Not really."

"No, not really? Caelie, either he did or he didn't. Which is it?"

"Lady Caelie? Mrs. Hume said it was you but I did not believe her."

Caelie turned to see Nicholas stride into the room with all the confidence of a man who had found his place in the world. Quite the change from the disreputable rake he'd once been. Now he was the epitome of the respectable gentleman and happy husband, though if she looked close enough, Caelie could still see the hint of the devil he'd once been lurking beneath his silvery eyes.

Abigail jumped up from the sofa. "Huntsleigh has ruined Caelie!"

Nicholas stopped mid-step, his boot hitting the carpet with a dull thud. He echoed his wife's earlier question. "I beg your pardon?"

"Huntsleigh has ruined her." She pointed a finger at Caelie in case Nicholas was unclear as to which *her* Abigail referred to. Caelie's face flamed with heat.

"It isn't like that," she said, holding her hand out to ward off any further accusations before she could explain. It did no good.

Nicholas glared. "Then what *is* it like?"

"Don't ask her," Abigail said. "She's speaking in riddles. I can't get a single straight answer out of her."

"Perhaps if you sat down and let me speak that would help."

But Nicholas did not take the suggestion. "Answer me—has Huntsleigh ruined you?"

Caelie took a deep breath. So much for starting at the beginning. "Lord Huntsleigh has proposed, but—"

"Then where is he? And why are you here?"

"We are not going to marry. It's—"

"And why not? Has he reneged? He hasn't taken off again on one of those godforsaken ships again, has he?"

"No. If you would let me—"

Nicholas whirled about and shouted out the open door. "Gilmour! Have my horse saddled immediately!"

"Nicholas, please!"

Nicholas strode back into the room and wiggled a finger under Caelie's nose, close enough to make her eyes cross if she stared at it. "I will not have this! I cannot believe he would sink so low as to seduce my own family. This is beyond forgivable. I will kill him!"

"Please, you must listen to me!"

Caelie grabbed at Nicholas's sleeve as he turned once again and stalked from the room, the fumes of his explosion leaving the air around them polluted with his anger. But it did her no good. He moved too quickly to be caught and in a matter of minutes he was gone from the house and Caelie and Abigail were left behind to stare at the empty space left in his wake.

"He's a bit of a hothead, isn't he?" Abigail did not appear perturbed in the least at her husband's outburst and utterance of violence against one of his oldest and dearest friends.

"We have to stop him. It is not as it appears."

"It rarely is," Abigail said. "Sit down, tell me what has happened, and don't leave anything out. If I am to calm the beast and make him see reason, I will need the truth at my disposal."

Her cousin's calm nature surprised her. Usually, Caelie was the one who provided the voice of reason while Abigail went off half-cocked. When had the tables turned? "But he is on his way to London. We must stop him."

"Do not worry. Nick will not hurt Huntsleigh unless he deserves it. Does he?"

Caelie gave into her exhaustion and dropped onto the sofa next to Abigail. "No. He does not."

"Then he didn't ruin you?"

She shook her head and bit her lip. "My ruin came well before Lord Huntsleigh, Abigail. Perhaps I should pour some tea for us. This is a rather long and complicated tale. And once I finish, promise me you will send word fast on Nicholas's heels to ensure he doesn't do anything foolish."

"I promise. Now sit and tell me about this ruination of yours so I can send my husband after the correct perpetrator."

Caelie took a sip of the strong tea and began her tale, timidly at first, afraid Abigail may judge her or think less of her, but she should have known better. Her cousin had always been her staunchest ally and she continued to be so.

"Oh, Caelie, I wish I had known," Abigail said once Caelie had purged her soul and left it bare. "All the signs were there in retrospect. You seemed so broken after Billingsworth ended your engagement, more so than he deserved. And no wonder you counseled me to use caution when I was determined to throw my innocence to the wind with Nicholas. You knew only too well the consequences. I never liked Billingsworth. His behavior in this mess does not surprise me. But Huntsleigh—I am disappointed in him. I have half a mind to let Nicholas give him a proper thrashing. It would serve him right for letting Lord Ellesmere convince him not to marry you."

Caelie shook her head. "No, it is not like that. I am certain if Lord Ellesmere knew the full story, he would demand Spencer do the right thing, and I am equally as certain Spencer would comply."

"Then why do you not take that option!"

"Because he does not love me and he despises the idea of marriage. What kind of happiness would we have, entering into marriage under those conditions? I have spent the last two years being miserable and I will not consign my future to it as well—or his. He has done nothing to me I have not wished for. Shameful as it is, I wanted him, Abby. I desired him to such a degree I had no control over it. Nor did I want to. You don't understand—"

Abigail grabbed her hands. "Oh, but I do, Caelie. I promise you, I do. You are not the only one to be overcome by such feelings. But won't you at least consider that these feelings are strong enough to build upon together?"

Caelie stared down at their hands. "Only if we both shared them. But we do not." She looked up at her cousin. "Spencer proposed out of duty. If I allowed him to go through with this sham of a marriage, he would grow to resent me. I would be a burden to him. And I am so tired of being a burden, Abby. Don't ask it of me again."

Abigail sighed. "This whole disaster hurts my heart, Caelie. I had hoped this second chance would find you the happiness you deserved and now..."

Caelie smiled at her cousin, warmth spreading through her from the love she felt for her. "Do not feel sorry for me, Abby. I know you wish to fix this, but you cannot. The mistakes are my own and now I must live with them."

"Then I suppose I should send a man after Nicholas and ensure he does not beat his best friend within an inch of his life."

Chapter Twenty-Two

〜∂〜

"My lord, you have visitors."

Spence turned his head from where he sat and stared out the window at the Glenmor townhouse across the street. "Send them away, Alfred. I do not wish to see anyone." It had been his standard answer for the past several days and he saw no reason to change it now. Solitude suited him. Or rather it suited anyone who would have to bear his company given his current state of mind.

"It is Lord Ellesmere, sir. As well as Lord Blackbourne and Mr. Bowen." The graveness of Alfred's tone pulled Spence from his thoughts and he turned his gaze from the window to stare at the man. Bowen had come by once already and Alfred, upon his instruction, had said he was not in. He doubted Bowen had believed his butler but he hadn't pushed. Now it appeared he had brought reinforcements in Nick and his grandfather.

"Send them in." Bowen had been polite enough to leave without incident, but Nick was just as likely to pound down his door until it broke off its hinges. He lacked the refinement of Bowen. And even Spencer, his mood notwithstanding, knew better than to turn away his grandfather.

Unfortunately, Alfred did not get the chance to deliver the message. Nick barged into the room like a storm and grabbed Spencer by the lapels, pulling him out of his chair.

"You bastard!"

He shoved at Nick's broad chest and dislodged his hold then ducked quickly as his friend's deadly right hook swung toward his head. Nick had the advantage of greater height and weight, but Spence had always had better reflexes.

"Enough!"

Grandfather's voice echoed through the room with enough force to stop Nick's assault, at least for the moment, though Spence did not plan on taking his eyes off his friend.

"Would someone care to tell me to what I owe the pleasure of this visit?" He glared at Nick and pulled at his sleeves to set his jacket back to rights. It did little good. The garment had been set askew to start with, since he'd been living in it since his arrival three days ago. Or perhaps four. He'd lost track.

His grandfather leaned on his walking stick while Bowen entered quietly behind him, his gaze skimming the room before it came to rest on Spence.

"You look awful." Grandfather made this statement with the same matter-of-factness he would use had he been pointing out that the sky was blue. Except that it wasn't blue. The sky was, in fact, a dull, depressing gray. It fit his mood perfectly.

"Thank you." He had no quick quip at the ready. His thoughts had turned sluggish. Perhaps he should not have consumed quite so much brandy. He waved at a chair. "Please, sit."

His grandfather stepped further into the room. His walking stick echoed against the hardwood until the carpet muffled it. Unlike Nick's footsteps which resonated through the room like gunshots as he paced back and forth fuming over...over what? What had Caelie told him?

He had suspected, after a day of ruminating, that she had likely fled to Sheridan Park. He had considered writing her a letter, expressing his thoughts, but they were so jumbled every time he tried to put pen to paper, he ended up sounding like a royal ass. Balled up pieces of stationery from his failed attempts scattered the floor and table.

He was three times a fool to have let her escape, but he'd be an even bigger fool to chase her down and beg her to return when her actions made it clear she did not want him.

Grandfather stopped at the sofa without sitting down. Spence looked at the cushion and winced. Newspapers littered the surface. He'd thought to catch up on current events but found he had lost interest. Alfred had offered to take them away, along with the dirty dishes piled on the table, but Spence had brushed the suggestion off. He preferred the mess. The disorder matched the state of his mind much better than having everything neatly in its place.

Spence scooped the newspapers into his arms and looked around. He had nowhere to put them. Books on any number of subjects, none of which had caught his fancy, filled the other chair. The end table held his tray from breakfast which he had not touched, yet insisted to Alfred he would, thus it too was left behind. In fact, as he surveyed the room, he realized for the past several days he'd accumulated any number of piles of things that he had brought up, set down and then left.

"Perhaps we should sit at the table," Bowen suggested. It still had half its surface showing. "I asked Alfred to bring us some tea. Or perhaps you would prefer something stronger?"

He did not miss the wry tone of Bowen's voice. "Thank you, no. It is not yet even noon."

His grandfather sighed. "It is half past four, Spencer."

"Is it?" He looked out the window again as if the answers

were to be found in the thick cloud suppressing the city. What did it matter? Minutes and hours ran together until one was the same as the other.

His grandfather walked past him to the table and, with nowhere else to put them, Spence dropped the newspapers back onto the sofa.

"Blackbourne, sit down," Grandfather instructed. "You're pacing is most distracting."

Nick grunted and pulled out a seat at the table. He dropped into it with as much agitation as he'd paced the room with, his glare never leaving Spence. Those damn silvery eyes bored into him like a pair of bullets and if looks could kill, he would have been dead ten times over since his friend's arrival. Spence's stomach roiled.

Bowen took his seat, leaving the empty one across from Nick for Spence. By the time he seated himself, Alfred had arrived with a tea service and ginger biscuits.

Mrs. Faraday's ginger biscuits to be exact. He glanced up at his grandfather, then thought better of it and turned to Bowen as the likely culprit.

Bowen shrugged. "Mrs. Faraday was concerned you may starve to death if you did not have a steady supply and requested I convey them to you with all due haste."

Spence forced a smile at the thoughtful gesture. He would be sure to thank her, but in truth, he had no appetite. Not even for Mrs. Faraday's ginger biscuits.

His grandfather poured out four cups of tea and sat back in his chair. Spence stared at the cup with its swirly pattern of multi-colored wildflowers. Caelie had smelled of wildflowers. Pain stabbed deep in his chest and he took in a quick breath and closed his eyes.

"How long do you plan on continuing on in this manner?"

"This manner?" Spence looked around the room. "Oh.

Yes. Bit of a mess, isn't it?"

His grandfather inclined his head. "Your grandmother is concerned. I do not like to see her upset."

Guilt filled him. He had not meant to neglect her. But he could not step foot inside his grandparents' home without being assaulted by memories of Caelie. She had permeated every corner of the place, leaving him nowhere to turn to for escape. It was why he had left in the first place. That, and he preferred to lick his wounds in private.

"Blackbourne has revealed a rather disturbing bit of news."

Spence eyed his friend. "He has, has he? And what news might that be?"

"You have compromised, Caelie," Nick bit out, each word filled with anger and disgust.

The muscles around Spence's jaw tightened. "Ah."

Nick came out of his chair. His fists landed on the table and he leaned over breathing fire. "Is that all you have to say?"

Spence did not flinch from Nick's wrath. He could deny it, but to what end? It was the truth. He *had* compromised her. "If it makes you feel any better, I did propose to her."

"Did you? Because that's not quite the version of events I've heard. Ellesmere indicated you proposed after Billingsworth spread his lies. That same night, Caelie left London. Ergo, whatever happened between the two of you must have happened before that. Would you care to explain?"

The version of events Nick had received was accurate, yet full of holes. He did not know Spence had proposed before Billingsworth's attempt to ruin Caelie publicly. Nor did he seem aware of the fact Caelie had turned him down cold. Nor had Grandfather apparently informed Nick that, despite his objections, Spence had every intention of convincing her to marry him the very morning she had disappeared.

"I know you have no interest in marriage. Likely you celebrated when she left London and you did not have to go through with it," Nick said. "You have made it clear you do not wish to marry anyone."

His friend's estimation of his character hurt, but not enough to penetrate into the deep recesses where Caelie's rejection resided. Besides, he could not argue Nick's claim. He did not want to marry anyone.

He did, however, want to marry *someone*. He wanted to marry Caelie.

He had no idea how she had managed the grand feat of turning him around where the idea of marriage was concerned. He would not lie and claim the idea of marriage didn't still terrify him though. What if he couldn't make her happy? What if she fell out of love with him? Or worse, what if she never loved him in the first place?

Not that she had ever said she *was* in love with him. But he had thought, maybe...they had shared such an easy camaraderie after all. And she had kissed him, so she must have been attracted to him at some point. His attraction to her was absolute—not just to her outward beauty, though that did take his breath away on a regular basis. But the part that touched him the most was what he saw inside of her. Strength, caring, honor.

How could he not love her? Perhaps, if he did his best to emulate those qualities, she would love him too. And stay in love.

But he'd not been afforded that opportunity, had he? No. She had left without so much as a by your leave. As if he was forgettable. Inconsequential.

"Did you hear a word I said?" Nick had straightened and his fingers twitched at his sides as if he wanted to reach out and wrap them around Spence's neck.

"No." He couldn't deny it. Nick shouldn't look so put out. It wasn't personal. A cannon ball could have come careening through the window and likely he would not have heard that either. His thoughts overtook everything until the extraneous world barely existed to him.

"I said you have much to atone for and I plan on seeing that you do. I don't care if I have to drag you by the boots to the altar, you will marry Caelie. And do not look to your grandfather for help. After I made him aware of your transgression, he conceded marriage is the only option."

"I see." Spence rubbed at a spot on the tablecloth.

"Is that all you have to say?"

Spence forced himself to meet Nick's piercing gaze. "No. I suppose not. And I would be only too pleased to marry her, contrary to what you seem to think. There is just one problem."

"And that is?" Nick bit the words out.

"She does not wish to marry me. At all. A fact she has made abundantly clear when she turned down my original proposal and then again, most profoundly, when she ran off the morning after I announced our betrothal publicly."

The wind left Nick's sails and he'd eased back into his chair.

"And I suspect she made clear to you, as well, her wishes where I am concerned, did she not?"

Nick's mouth twisted to one side. "I didn't exactly wait around to hear her thoughts on the matter."

"Either way," Grandfather said, the gravity of his tone weighing into Spence. "She must be convinced."

Bowen reached over and squeezed Spence's shoulder in support. "You should go to her. Talk to her."

"She could be with child," Nick pointed out.

Spence's head shot up. "Is she?" Could they tell this early?

He threw his arms wide. "How would I know?"

"Of course," Spence said. "You didn't stick around to hear the whole story."

"Enough," his grandfather said. "Gentlemen, would you leave us? I wish to speak to my grandson alone."

Spence watched his two closest friends file out of the room. Bowen glanced back to give him an encouraging smile. Nick did not. Nick stalked from the room with the same purpose he had come into it with, anger keeping his shoulders stiff and his fists clenched. The idea he had let his friend down sickened Spence. This was not what he'd intended. He'd wanted only to escape London. To find a place to breathe. A place where he could be himself.

He had found that place. But it hadn't been a location. It had been a person.

It had been Caelie.

"What would you have me do," he asked.

"Bathing would be a good start."

It wasn't exactly what he'd expected. "I'll have you know I bathed just…" The words drifted off. In truth, he could not recall the last time he'd bathed. He looked down at his shirt and noted a dark stain against the white linen. He had spilled his tea the other day.

"This cannot go on."

This. Like it was a thing he could pack up and put away if he wished. "I don't know what you expect of me, Grandfather. I would think you'd be happy. You did not want me to marry her to begin with."

"Not to begin with, no. But soon after."

Spence's gaze shot to his grandfather. Obviously, he had heard wrong. "What?"

Grandfather cut his hand through the air. "I went about it all wrong, as your grandmother has spared no expense in telling me."

"You *wanted* me to marry her?" He vacillated between anger and disbelief. "Why didn't you just say so?"

"For heaven's sake, Spencer. Your whole life, when we have

told you that you cannot have something or you cannot do something, what did you do?" He did not wait for an answer. "You went after it as if your very life depended on it. I had hoped you would continue this behavior with Lady Caelie."

"But...when did you change your mind?"

"When it was obvious how you felt about her. My God, Spencer, you defended her so staunchly, you found fault with every candidate that showed an interest in her. Every time you spoke of her or to her your entire demeanor changed."

"Changed how?"

His grandfather smiled; a wistful, gentle smile Spence hadn't been expecting. "You were happy. *She* made you happy. But you seemed so blind to it at first, I worried you would let your views on marriage keep you from recognizing it. So, I decided to add an incentive. I thought if you fought me on it, it would prove my instincts correct, that you did love her, in which case I would not stand in your way."

"But what about the scandal—"

"Do you think I would keep you from the woman you loved because of that?"

"You were always so adamant about it in the past."

Grandfather shook his head. "Yes, so your grandmother pointed out as the grand flaw in my plan."

"Then you do not oppose our marrying?"

"I do not. If she is the woman you love, then she is the woman you should be with. Embrace happiness, Spencer. You deserve nothing less. I promise you, if you give it the respect it deserves, it will not desert you."

"Except that it has, Grandfather. She has deserted me. It is like my parents' relationship all over again. Someone is in love and the other one is indifferent."

"Are you so certain about that? Is Lady Caelie someone who would compromise herself and walk away from it as if it was nothing of consequence?"

Spence stood and walked to the window, staring out into the grey horizon. "I didn't think so."

"Then it is simple. You must marry her, Spencer."

Simple. As if he could just arrive at her door and propose once again and this time she would readily accept.

He turned around, frustration rushing through him. "I have tried to convince her, Grandfather. She will not have me. What do you suggest? I drag her kicking and screaming to the altar? Force the words 'I do' out of her mouth? Would that I could! It would certainly fix my problem."

"And what is your problem, Spencer?"

"She does not want me! That is my problem. She does not want me and she will not marry me and I can't force her because she has a bloody mind of her own!"

"What is it you want, Spencer?"

"What?"

"What do *you* want?"

The answer was simple. He wanted Caelie.

He wanted her here, now. He wanted to wake up in the morning and see the sun shining upon her face, turning her hair into waves of fiery bronze. He wanted to see their children running about underfoot and have a house filled with laughter and love, the way he wished his own early childhood had been. He wanted to spend his nights with her wrapped in his arms, curled against him, her skin warming his. He wanted to bury himself deep inside of her and know what it was to be lost and found all in the same instant.

"I want what I can't have."

"Nonsense."

"It is not nonsense," Spence said. Why did no one listen to him when he said Caelie did not want him, as if he could easily remedy the matter?

His grandfather rapped his knuckles on the table. "Of course, it is. Now go clean yourself up," he said, pushing himself to his feet with the aid of his walking stick. "It appears we are bound for Sheridan Park. There is a certain lady who needs to be convinced of the error of her ways."

"You need to do something big. Extravagant," Nick said from where he sat opposite Spence in the Blackbourne carriage. Nick had suggested Spence arrive under the Blackbourne crest, so as not to give advance warning he was coming and thereby allow Caelie an opportunity to hide or escape.

Spence didn't know where Nick thought she would go, but regardless, he was thankful the man had stopped glaring at him—at least for the time being. He had Bowen to thank for that, playing mediator as Spence explained he had tried to atone for his actions by proposing marriage but had been refused.

"Extravagant?"

Bowen cut Nick off before he could answer. "I think a more dignified approach would be suited. Subdued, but meaningful. Lady Caelie does not strike me as the type to go for overdone gestures."

The carriage bumped over a rut and Bowen winced. Spence had tried to talk him out of making the trip, but he refused to listen. He claimed someone had to be the voice of reason in all of this mess, and given as Bowen was far more suited to the role than either he or Nick, Spence had agreed. Still, he was concerned the constant jostling would do his friend more harm than good.

His grandparents would follow later in the Ellesmere carriage. Grandmother had insisted on coming, asserting Spence could use all the reinforcements he could get. It did not bode well for what they thought of his chances in convincing Caelie to agree to his marriage proposal.

"I thought I might simply explain the situation to her and make it clear that going through with the marriage is the best possible outcome for all concerned," Spence said.

Even Bowen looked less than impressed by this approach. "Good Lord, Spence. The woman may not want something over the top, but at least put a little effort into it. Woo her, at least."

"With a grand gesture," Nick added, spreading his arms as wide as he could without hitting Bowen.

Spence looked from one man to the other. As they stared back at him, both with their dark coloring and furrowed brows, he could not help but feel he was being taken to task by a pair of avenging angels. God help him if he made a muck of this. They would likely flay him within an inch of his life.

"I still can't believe it has come to this," Nick said. "What in the hell were you thinking, seducing Caelie of all people!"

Spence straightened. "I most certainly did not seduce her. It just...happened. One moment I was kissing her and then..." He waved a hand in the air. He did not bother to tell them she did not put up a protest when things escalated beyond a kiss. He did not want to cast her in an undesirable light. His behavior may have been suspect, but his intentions had been true. He had not seduced her. It had simply...happened.

"And then, what? Your clothes just fell off without your noticing?"

Spence scowled. Their clothes had remained in place, save for a few adjustments. A regret on his part. He would have loved to have felt her soft skin against his own, to let the warmth of her soak into him, envelope him. If he could convince her to marry him, he planned on remedying that situation repeatedly.

Bowen nudged Nick with his elbow. "Do not sit there like

a pious old vicar, Nick. Are you going to tell us you never found yourself in such a situation where your emotions overran your good sense?"

Nick sputtered and did his best to look indignant but everyone present knew better. "I—I married my wife!"

"And I am trying to marry Lady Caelie. I can hardly be blamed for her inability to see that this is the best course of action for the both of us."

Bowen winced again as they hit another rut. "I would suggest not leading with that reasoning when you propose to Lady Caelie."

Spence slumped against the cushioned seats. "I have a feeling any reasoning I use will fall on deaf ears."

"Hence the requirement of a grand gesture," Nick said. "Trust me on this one."

Chapter Twenty-Three

C aelie pushed the blankets aside and let her legs fall over the edge of the bed. Something had awakened her, but when she stopped to listen, only silence answered back. She sat still and waited. Something felt different. Out of place.

The sound came again. Muffled and outside. She rubbed at her eyes and stood. She crossed the cool floor to the window and pulled back the heavy drapes. In the gardens below, dark figures moved between the yard and the greenhouse but clouds hindered the moonlight and prevented sufficient light to see what they were about, or who they were. There appeared to be three of them...no, wait. There was a fourth. They would travel to the greenhouse, return with their arms full, drop their bounty on the ground, then gather together and...were they arguing?

Clouds scuttled above and the moonlight brightened enough to let Caelie see the men in question were dressed as gentlemen.

Why were there gentlemen in the gardens in the middle of the night and why were they raiding Abigail's greenhouse?

Caelie crossed the room to where her robe lay draped over the chair by the vanity. She shrugged into it and grabbed her shawl to ward off the cool night air, then she slipped her feet into a pair of thin slippers. She should wake Benedict, but he'd arrived weary from his long trip and she loathed to disturb him. Perhaps a footman was still about, or Mrs. Hume, though at this late hour she doubted it.

Her slippers tapped against the polished floors and the steps as she made her way down to the bottom floor. She turned to the right and headed toward the kitchen where a weak light still burned.

"Mr. Garron." Caelie breathed a sigh of relief. She really did not care to confront four strange men in the dead of night.

Garron set down a leg of mutton on the plate in front of him and stood. "M'lady, 'tis quite late. Are you well?"

"I am, Mr. Garron. Thank you. But there are strange men in the gardens beneath my window. Do you know anything about this?"

"Strange men, you say?"

"Yes. They appear to be gentlemen, but...they also appear to be stealing Abigail's flowers. I know how diligently my cousin has catered to her gardens and I would hate to see all that hard work destroyed over some strange shenanigans. Will you come with me while I look into the matter?"

"Are you sure you should be doin' that, ma'am?"

"Well, I can hardly ask Lady Blackbourne in her state and Lord Blackbourne is not expected back from London for several days yet. Lord Glenmor was so exhausted after his travels I would prefer not to disturb him. Please, Mr. Garron."

The burly man nodded and walked around the table and smiled. "A'right, m'lady. Let us go see what shenanigans these gentlemen are up to. Did you recognize any of 'em?"

"No, it was much too dark with the cloud."

"Oh, aye. Well enough." He did not seem the least bit

perturbed by the idea of strange men on the property. In fact, he looked amused if anything. Then again, it did not appear as if much perplexed Mr. Garron.

They slipped out the front door and around the stone walkway that led to the gardens. Caelie walked as quickly as her slippered feet would allow, worried the men would be gone by the time they reached them, but as they rounded the corner of the large estate, she could hear their muffled voices. They had stopped moving between the greenhouse and the gardens and were huddled together beneath the large oak, arguing. The closer she came to the group, the more she could make out snatches of conversation.

"...it should be in the shape of a heart... "

"No...does not convey the proper message..."

"...whole idea borders on ludicrous..."

"...not even awake to see..."

The closer Caelie came, the slower her steps and the clearer her vision of the garden thieves became until she stopped altogether and stared at them in disbelief. At her back, Mr. Garron chuckled and the sound silenced the four men who stood amongst a bevy of cut tulips.

They turned slowly to face her. Nicholas, Mr. Bowen, Benedict and...Spencer.

Spencer spoke first. "Ah. Well then. I guess we have eliminated the element of surprise."

Caelie pulled the shawl tighter around her shoulders as she drank in the sight of him in the dim moonlight. He had grown more handsome during their separation, she was certain of it, and her body warmed despite the chill in the air.

"What are you doing destroying Abigail's gardens?"

"Oh, that. Yes. Of course. Well...it is not so much a case of destroying exactly."

"Then what, pray tell, is it?"

Mr. Bowen stepped forward. "It is a rearranging, of sorts."

"A rearranging?"

"A grand gesture," Nicholas stated with a firm nod.

"I see. And what was this grand gesture to be?"

Benedict stepped away from the group as if to distance himself from their tomfoolery. "It appears, Lord Huntsleigh and his...cohorts...thought to woo you into accepting Huntsleigh's marriage proposal by decimating Abigail's tulips and spelling out some nonsense on the ground beneath your window."

"We were going to make a heart," Nicholas clarified.

"No," Spencer said. "I planned on spelling out my proposal."

"There are not enough flowers for that, clearly," Mr. Bowen stated, waving at the pile which, in Caelie's estimation, looked more than sufficient.

Abigail would have a fit when she awoke.

Benedict came closer and took her hands in his. They were warm and strong. "It appears much has been going on since my departure." His voice lacked any judgment or censure which relieved her to no end. It would grieve greatly to think she had added to his worries. "Perhaps we should all find our beds and we can talk about it at a more sensible hour."

"What of the flowers," Nicholas asked. "We should do something with them. Abigail will take a strip off me if we cut them for nothing. And I am not about to go down alone."

"Why not? It seems only fair. This was your idea after all," Mr. Bowen pointed out.

"Traitors. Fine then," Nicholas bent down and scooped a bunch of tulips up in his arms. "Help me get them inside and into vases. We can fill the breakfast room with them for her to see in the morning. Perhaps that will soften the blow when she realizes we have ravaged her greenhouse."

"I thought this was supposed to be my grand gesture, not

yours?" Spencer said as Nicholas shoved an armful of flowers at him.

"It was, but your arguing ruined that."

"Because I didn't agree with your idea of a heart? What does a heart say? Nothing. This required words. Specific words to convey what I meant to say."

"And what did you mean to say?" Caelie asked.

Spencer crossed the grass, stepping over a pile of crocuses to stand a few feet in front of her. "I meant to say I wish to marry you. That I think you the best choice for a wife and...I think you're quite pretty. Beautiful, really. That, I—I like your smile and the way you laugh. You are kind, as well. Very. And that I have been a complete ass at times, but despite this, I had hoped perhaps you would change your mind and agree to marry me after all."

Caelie's heart soared and plummeted, dipped and wheeled. There was so much good about what he said, but unfortunately it could not conceal the one thing he didn't claim. The one thing she needed from him most.

She glanced down at her feet and blinked back the tears where they pricked the corners of her eyes. She took a deep breath and forced a smile. "I do not believe you have enough flowers to say all of that," she whispered.

Spencer glanced over his shoulder at the piles accumulated. "No. I suppose you are right."

They stared at each other and she watched as the realization settled into the pale blue of his eyes. She knew the moment he understood what her answer would be. The light dimmed and his shoulders sagged.

"Caelie—"

She shook her head. "Please don't. I cannot marry you. I'm sorry, but it wouldn't be right." She looked at Benedict. "Would you escort me back to my room, Ben? I—I'm quite tired."

"Very well," her cousin said. He took her arm and looped it through his then turned to address Spencer. "You and I shall speak further in the morning."

She did not hear Spencer's answer or if he gave one at all.

"I hate to say, I told you so, but..." Spence shrugged, the tulips he still held in his arms rubbing against his wool jacket. He wanted to make light of her latest rejection but he couldn't quite find the energy to pretend. "She does not want me."

"You're a damn fool, Spence." The cruel words came from Bowen, surprising in itself as he usually chose his words more judiciously.

"He's right," Nick added, seconding the sentiment.

"Thank you both. Much appreciated."

Bowen turned and gave him a stern look. "While you rhymed off her countless virtues and physical attributes, what did you leave out?"

Spence shook his head. He had been quite thorough. "Nothing."

"Then you're not just a fool," Nick said. "You're an idiot."

"Sweet Judas! Do the two of you kick puppies in your spare time? I have been rejected for the third time by the woman I wish to marry and you have the gall to stand there and call me names? Have I not suffered enough for one night?"

"Why do you wish to marry her?" Bowen asked. "In a word."

Both his friends stared at him, their arms folded over their chests and slowly, far too slowly, he understood what he had done wrong. What he had left out.

"Oh."

"Precisely."

"Bloody hell."

Nick poked him in the chest through the tulips. "Fix this."

Spencer waited until Nick and Bowen had gone to their rooms before he climbed the stairs to his. Each step he took weighted with the mistakes he had made, the fears he wore like armor, and the new feelings and emotions he had not the experience with nor the context for.

Fix this.

Good advice. Unfortunately, Nick did not bother instructing him on how to accomplish such a feat, and given all that had gone on, Spence did not think saying those three little words would change anything. Could she not tell how he felt? Were his feelings toward her not transparent enough? He had championed her when she needed it, protected her whether she wished it or not, and did not hesitate to ask for her hand when there was no other choice.

He stopped. All of those things he did out of duty. Or so it must have appeared to her. In truth, it had begun that way. He left the ship to escort her home because honor and his friendship with Nick dictated that he not leave her unprotected. But quickly—far more quickly than he could have imagined—it had turned. It had stopped being about Nick or their friendship, or the right thing to do. He had protected her because she had become dear to him, because she mattered and he would have rather cut off his own arm than see her harmed or hurt in any way.

None of which he told her.

He'd thought conveying this with his body; what they had physically shared, would relay his message loud and clear, but she had not seen it as such. And why would she? For all she knew he was a practiced rake who took his pleasure where he could find it and then went on about his business unaffected by any of it.

He stopped and rubbed at his eyes. A headache had

formed behind them. Bowen and Nick were both right. He was a prize idiot and a damn fool.

He turned to the left and walked away from the direction of his room.

He knew what he had to do.

Chapter Twenty-Four

~~~

C aelie hadn't anticipated she would fall into such a
deep slumber so quickly after Benedict escorted
her back to her bedroom. With her mind racing,
her thoughts filled with doubts and fears, she expected sleep
would be hard to come by. But fatigue claimed her the
moment her head hit the pillow and it wasn't until something
thumped loudly in her room that she woke once again, unsure
of how much time had passed.

She opened her eyes. Darkness cast the room in shadows.
A sliver of moonlight slipped through the curtains where she
had pushed them open earlier to see what was going on
outside. The light spilled over the carpet at the end of her bed
and illuminated the two armchairs placed in on either side of
the hearth.

In front of the chairs someone...danced. Either that or
they were experiencing an apoplectic fit.

"Son of a...get off..."

She recognized the voice but was too stunned to say
anything. She watched a moment longer while the movements

continued. Caelie slipped out of bed and quietly padded across the floor.

"Do you require assistance, my lord?"

"Ah!" Spencer jumped back and stumbled against one of the chairs. "Sshh!"

She shot him a censured look though doubted he could see it in the dark. "I am not the one making all the noise. What, pray tell, are you doing in my bedchamber at this hour? Or any hour, for that matter."

He straightened and she realized he wore only one boot and appeared to be struggling to get out of his coat.

"I have come here to convince you to marry me."

"And this required you to undress?"

"I had planned on joining you in bed—" He held up his hands. "Not like that! I just thought...I thought we could talk and I'm bone-dead tired from a full day of traveling. I just wanted to lie down. Next to you. But my boots are covered in dirt from the garden, so I thought it best to take them off."

The half-smile he offered melted her heart. There were times when the image of the unrepentant rake fell away and she could see the sweet and caring man who resided beneath. The man who had stolen her heart, who had championed her and protected her. He had been the one to encourage her to come out of the safe little box she had existed in, to be her own person and to find her own voice. A voice that had been stymied and silenced for far too long.

Did he not deserve to be heard as well?

"Very well. Turn around." He did as she bade and she assisted him with his coat, yanking at the sleeves as he pulled his arms out. When she finished, he bent and tugged off his remaining boot then removed his waist coat, leaving him in just his shirt and breeches.

"Thank you," he said, standing in front of her.

She breathed him in. He smelled of the cool air and...

tulips. She smiled. The gesture had touched her and watching the four men argue like brothers made her long for family and friendship even beyond what she had with Abigail and Benedict. To be a part of the world of these friends, a full part of it, not just standing on the periphery.

A part of her had wanted desperately to say yes when he proposed. As he extolled her virtues she kept waiting, hoping to hear the words she needed to say yes with a clear conscience and a sense of optimism that they could be happy.

It never came.

Yet here he was. And here she was. And when he took her hand and pulled her to him, hope bloomed once more.

"Do you remember when you told me you thought a foundation of friendship to be the basis of a successful marriage?"

"I do." Although as his hand slid down her waist to rest on the curve of her hip, she found it hard to remember much of anything. Her attraction for this man went beyond anything she had ever experienced before. It made whatever feelings she'd once had for Billingsworth positively laughable.

"And are we not friends? After everything we have been through?" His words whispered against her skin.

"I—yes. Yes, we are." She could not deny it. She felt a kinship with him. A comfort that only came with friendship. Yes, she was attracted to him. Without question. But she also loved to sit and talk with him. To play cards. To laugh and be silly and know she could be herself without being judged harshly or told to change. Outside of Abigail, Benedict and Aunt Lorena, she had never experienced such acceptance before.

"Good." His lips brushed against her cheekbone and a deep pull made her press her hips into him. His breath caught and his hand moved to her lower back to hold her there. "And did you not also tell me you believed that from this friendship a great love could blossom?"

He let go of her hand and cupped her face, tilting her mouth to his. She expected him to kiss her, but he didn't. He lingered a hair's breath away and it drove her mad.

"I—I may have said something to that effect." When she spoke, her lips brushed against his until her head buzzed and her legs turned liquid.

"I thought perhaps I should inform you that you were correct." He dropped a soft kiss on her mouth, so brief it was gone before she could truly enjoy it. She longed for him to return with another but he did not.

"Correct?"

"Mm." He kissed her again, longer this time until not just her legs but her entire body threatened to give in. As if sensing this, he bent and scooped her into his arms and walked to the bed. He set her down gently and hovered over her.

"About which part?"

"All of it."

He reached for his shirt and pulled it over his head. His lean, muscular build reminded her of the marble statues placed throughout the gardens at Sheridan Park. She could not help herself and reached out a hand to touch the smooth skin where it stretched tautly over sinew and bone then down further where ridges formed against his abdomen. His breath hitched and he caught her hand when she reached the waist-band of his breeches.

"We should talk first," he said.

"First? And what shall we do second?" Her boldness shocked her and yet she felt no shame. Being with Spencer seemed the most natural thing in the world to her, as if it was meant to be. But was that enough?

"Second will be dependent on how the first goes."

He smiled and joined her on the bed, nestling in next to

her. He propped his head up with one hand to look at her. The other hand played with the ties of her nightdress where they dangled near her breasts. Every now and again, his knuckles would brush against them and pleasure flooded through her.

"Then talk," she said, before speech became lost in the desire his touch created.

"It was brought to my attention that during my latest proposal—and all the ones before that, for that matter—I was reticent in mentioning a certain aspect of my feelings toward you."

"Were you?" Her heart pounded and the ache between her legs became almost painful as his hand drifted away from her breasts, over her hip and down her leg. The thin linen of her nightdress did nothing to protect her from the riot of longing his fingertips created.

"Indeed. It appears I spent far too much time speaking of necessity and duty and even when I went beyond these things, I still neglected the most important issue."

His hand fisted around her nightdress and slowly drew it up over her thighs to leave her exposed. If he did not stop talking soon, she would expire on the spot from wanting him so desperately.

"My lord—"

"Spencer." His mouth kissed the tender spot beneath her ear.

"Spencer," she said as she tried to keep her thoughts focused. "I wondered if you might be agreeable to doing the second thing first."

"That would not be proper." His fingers lingered near her most private of places and teased her inner thigh.

"Nothing about this is proper and I fear I am finding it most difficult to concentrate on anything you have to say at the moment."

"That is most unfortunate." His fingers rose higher and she arched to meet them but the touch did not satisfy. It only intensified the deep ache.

"Spencer, please..." She could no longer hold the pretense of conversation or knowing or caring what he needed to tell her. The pent-up passion she had for this man consumed her body and demanded satisfaction before anything else.

"I suppose it would be ungentlemanly of me to ignore a lady's request."

But she didn't feel like a lady. She felt like a wanton. And it felt good.

He grabbed the hem of her nightdress and she lifted enough for him to pull it off completely, leaving her fully exposed. He gazed down at her with hungry eyes while he worked the front of his breeches open then wriggled out of them. The silly struggle caused a rash of giggles as one pant leg stuck on his foot and gave Caelie a moment to collect a few of her wits. Though once he returned to her, the skin on skin contact, as he nestled between her legs soon scattered those completely.

They stopped talking then, though continued to communicate with touches and kisses, sighs and whispers. He worshipped her body like a temple, leaving no aspect unattended. His mouth suckled her breasts and his hands traced her curves and his fingers...oh the things his fingers did to her. He made her bold and set her free and she gave in kind the best she could, until neither of them could stand another minute of the blissful torture. She opened to him and he entered her with reverence, stopping briefly to savor the moment before passion dictated he move, and so he did. The rhythm began slowly at first, a tease, a torment, but something drove Caelie on until she picked up the pace, racing toward something only her body could define. She reached the peak and Spencer's body stiffened in response and they fell over its edge tangled together, collapsed in mindless oblivion.

Spencer's head nestled next to hers buried in the feathered pillow. When he spoke, the words were muffled. "That was...I think..."

He stopped. His chest rose and fell with rapid breaths. Caelie did not prompt him to say more. She was too busy picking up the scattered remnants of her own thoughts. She had never experienced anything like this before. Their first encounter had been wonderful, but she'd been so torn, her thoughts and feelings too conflicted. But not tonight. Tonight, she had given over to the abandon of the scandalous passion they shared and it had been everything she could have dreamed of and more.

Spencer lifted his head and shifted his weight to rest at her side, his leg thrown over hers in a possessive fashion. He cleared his throat. "About that first thing..."

She had forgotten there had been a first thing and if his hand continued to massage her hip the way it was doing now, whatever he needed to discuss would soon be put on hold indefinitely unless he stated his business quickly.

"What of it?"

"I was attempting to impart to you that you have turned me over to your way of thinking."

"And what way of thinking is that?"

"About friendship and marriage."

"I see. So, you now believe good friends can make for a good marriage?"

"Yes." He nodded and his hand left her hip and drifted upward and cupped the underside of her breast. "Yes, I do. But..."

He stopped and dipped his head to draw her nipple into his mouth. Spirals of yearning shot through her. For all he had sated her desire a moment ago, he stoked it once again. She sunk her fingers into his thick hair and held him there as he taunted and teased.

"But what?" She gasped and arched into his mouth.

He chuckled and lifted his head to gaze down at her. A smile lightened his handsome features and did almost as much to flame the embers as his touch. "But it needs one other element to bind it all together."

"And what is that?"

"Love."

"Oh." She held her breath, afraid to move or breathe or blink.

"We have that now. At least on my part. That's what I forgot to tell you. That I love you."

The words washed over her like a dizzying array of starlight. They burst within her and embraced her heart and soul. "You do?"

He nodded. "Deeply, madly, and with no end in sight, God help me. But if this is to work, then I must know one thing."

"What?"

"Do you love me in return?"

She reached up and touched his face, outlining the sharp edges of his jaw, the full lips that had kissed her soundly, the brow that often furrowed or rose depending on what she had said or done. Did she love him in return? It seemed such a silly question. Of course, she did. She could not recall what it felt like not to love him and yet she could not pinpoint exactly when it had happened. Only that it had.

"With all my heart."

Spencer smiled then leaned down to kiss her with a gentleness that brought tears to her eyes. She had found the one thing she had searched her entire life for. Someone to belong to. Someone to hold her heart safe and love her back with all of his.

"Then we have but one recourse."

"Which is?"

"To marry. And to have babies. Plenty of babies with fiery red hair and green eyes that shine like emeralds." His grin turned wicked. "Perhaps we should begin tonight."

His body covered hers and his heart beat against her until her own matched the rhythm. Soon their bodies found their own rhythm, and love and friendship and marriage entwined together into an unbreakable bond.

Epilogue

Caelie looked up from the needlepoint pillow she was making for Abigail and Nicholas's new arrival, due the following month. Her breath caught as her handsome husband walked into the room, his hands filled with letters and a package tucked under his arm. They had been married a month and still she marveled at how her life had changed in that small amount of time.

Thankfully, Lord Ellesmere had arranged for a special license and their engagement had been very short and oh, so sweet. Soon she would be embroidering a pillow for their own addition, a secret she had hugged close to her until she was certain.

"What have you there?"

Spencer glanced up and smiled at her, a gesture that filled her heart and awoke every nerve in her body from tip to toe. "Invitations. The last flurry of parties before everyone comes to their senses and leaves for their country seat to escape this unbearable heat."

It had been unseasonably warm and while she enjoyed

being fully accepted back into society, she looked forward to retiring to Lakefield Abbey, the country manor Spence called home until such time as he took on the title of Marquess of Ellesmere. But this time, Caelie left with her head held high. Billingsworth's attempt to ruin her had failed and he had quietly left London in a cloud of shame. Good riddance, in her estimation.

"Do we wish to attend any of the parties?"

Spence made a face, giving her his opinion. "I would much rather stay at home with you."

"And what would you like to do?"

"I'm not sure exactly, but I'm quite certain it will involve a certain amount of nudity on both our parts."

"Oh dear." Her blood heated at the suggestion. She could live a thousand lifetimes and never tire of this man. "What is the package?"

He pulled the small package from beneath his arm. "It is for Bowen. From Cornwall."

"Is that not where his parents were from?"

"It is." Spencer gave the package a curious look. "But his parents have been dead for over two decades." He held the package closer to his ear and shook it.

"Spencer!"

"What? Do you not find it curious?"

"Whether I do or not, it is Marcus's business, not ours. Leave it be. I will have Fenton see he gets it. What else is there?"

Spence set the package on the low table and continued sifting through the letters then stopped, pulling one out for closer inspection. His expression changed. Darkened.

"What is it?"

He looked down at her. "A letter. It is from your mother. It was delivered from *The Swiftness*."

Her eyebrows lifted. Upon their engagement, she had written Mother to inform her of her impending marriage, sending it via one of Lord Ellesmere's fleet which was set to land in Italy for trade then return. Her letter would be delivered and any reply sent back. In truth, she hadn't expected a reply. She didn't expect anything where Mother was concerned.

"What does it say?"

Spencer opened the letter and scanned its contents. "It appears she and Mr. Beechum are unsuited and she wishes to return home."

"To stay with us?"

Spencer made a face. "One can only assume. What do you wish to do?"

Caelie took the letter from Spencer and read through the short missive. Nowhere within the written words did her mother apologize for what she had done or issue words of warmth or regret. Only that she disliked Italy, Mr. Beechum, and her current circumstances and expected Caelie to make arrangements to bring her back to London.

Caelie set the letter aside. "I think perhaps Mother has made her own bed and we should leave her there to lie in it. I know it sounds harsh, but I do not want her special brand of poison anywhere near our baby."

Spence's eyes grew wide. "Our what?"

Caelie smiled.

"Are you—?"

"I think so. I'm almost certain."

Spence whooped, tossed the remaining letters aside and scooped her up in his arms then whirled her around until they were both dizzy.

"Are you frightened?" She asked, when he finally stopped and sank into the chair with her across his lap.

"Terrified. You?"

"I will be fine if I know you are by my side."

He leaned down and kissed her long and hard until happiness and passion filled her.

"There is nowhere else I would rather be, my love. Nowhere else in the world."

A Sneak Peek

~~~

BOOK 3: A SINFUL TEMPTATION

A pox on the man's fickle heart.

It was the worst kind of luck to discover your intended's affections had drifted elsewhere.

Or rather your *intended* intended's. Lord Selward hadn't actually proposed as yet and, at the rate they were going, would not any time soon if drastic measures were not implemented. But what kind of drastic measures? Unfortunately subterfuge and machinations were not her strong suit.

Lady Rebecca Sheridan huffed out a breath and let her shoulders roll forward for only a moment before reinstating her posture. It would not do to be seen slumped over like a hunchback.

A proper lady comports herself in a dignified manner. Mrs. Dunbar's voice echoed in her mind even though her comportment instructor had passed on over two years ago. Likely she busied herself instructing the angels now, taking them to task for not holding their wings *just so.*

Not that anything Mrs. Dunbar taught her had proved useful this day. Did Lord Selward think she attended Lady Perth's annual tea to partake in the gossip about Rosalind

Caldwell's latest social gaffe—the third this week for those keeping count—or to nibble on overly sugared biscuits and sip tepid tea? No, she had come for the specific purpose of garnering his attention. Attention, he apparently preferred to lavish upon his gaggle of cronies rather than on her.

For Heaven's sake, must she jump onto her chair and wave her arms in the air to recapture his notice? If nothing else, it would give the gossips something new to titter about so they might leave poor Miss Caldwell alone, though Rebecca did not particularly care to take up the reins in that regard. Nor did she care to have her name mentioned in the scandal sheets.

Poor Father would roll over in his grave.

Rebecca pressed her gloved hands against the skirt of her new jade colored afternoon dress then kicked her feet out to stare at the pretty row of pink rosebuds embroidered into the hem. She'd had it made especially for this event, certain it would do the trick and catch Lord Selward's eye. The soft green made her silvery eyes stand out and gave her ivory skin a warm tone. Nancy had even styled her hair into a whimsical, yet intricate design—no easy feat given the length and thickness of her locks. Many of the other ladies had begun to shorten their hair, but Rebecca had often been told her inky black waves were her crowning glory and it seemed a little silly to rid herself of it for something as fleeting as fashion. Besides, Lord Selward had once complimented her on her hair and well...well.

She sighed again.

Hope. Such an irritating emotion. She had coasted on it for far too long.

At one and twenty, with her third Season on the verge of ending, the time to make good on Father's last wishes ran frighteningly short. Her next birthday loomed only a few months away. If Lord Selward didn't make good on his earlier attentions and propose, all would be lost.

Not that he had necessarily indicated he planned to make an offer, but a proposal had appeared promising based on his behavior, and surely that could be construed as almost the same thing. Could it not?

She had thought so, once upon a time.

Of course, once upon a time she had thought herself in love with him. Father's promotion of the pairing had been the icing on the cake. Perhaps that had something to do with the dictates of his will, though at the time she'd had no clue as to the late Lord Blackbourne's intentions. Father did not discuss such matters with her. It wasn't until after his death she'd become aware of his intentions as to whom she should marry. Father had always possessed a rather closed mind when it came to women and their capacity for understanding important matters. It had irritated her to no end, but she'd held her tongue in that regard. There had been enough strife in her family without adding more to the heap.

Regardless, because of the stipulations of Father's will, here she sat wishing for all the world that a man she no longer held an affection for would hurry up and propose. That she did not particularly want to marry him hardly mattered. The fact was, she *needed* to. Quickly.

"My dear, if you continue to sigh in such a manner, I am going to question whether or not you've sprung a leak."

Rebecca glanced up at her mother. "I simply don't understand why he will not come over. He has done nothing more than say hello since we arrived. Do you think he has truly passed me over for Lady Susan?"

The thought sickened her. After all, the only possible attribute Lady Susan possessed that one could consider even remotely positive was that her father was the Duke of Franklyn. Rumor had it, his coffers were richer than the King's. An exaggeration perhaps, though given that both Lady Susan and her mother, Lady Franklyn, were known to spend enough on fripperies alone to bankrupt Croesus, not much of one.

Mother reached over and patted Rebecca's clenched hands. "My dear, there is no reason we cannot take a turn about the garden and perhaps speak to some other gentlemen. There is any number waiting for you to show them some attention."

Rebecca gave her mother a sharp look. "I do not have time to encourage another gentleman, Mother. The Season is over in a few weeks!" She had not put all this work into capturing Lord Selward's attentions to simply give up now and start over with someone new. It was Lord Selward or...poverty.

"It is not as bad as all that," her mother said.

Rebecca gave her a dubious look. It was her mother who sighed this time. It *was* that bad, no matter how hard they tried to deny it.

The stipulations in Father's will were clear.

Also by Kelly Boyce

THE SINS & SCANDALS SERIES

Book 1: An Invitation to Scandal

Book 2: A Scandalous Passion

Book 3: A Sinful Temptation

Book 4: The Lady's Sinful Secret

Book 5: Surrender to Scandal

Book 6: A Sinner No More

Book 7: The Sweetest Sin

Book 8: A Most Scandalous Christmas

Book 9: A Hint of Scandal

THE BRIDES OF FATAL BLUFF

Book 1: The Outlaw Bride

SALVATION FALLS

Book 1: Salvation in the Rancher's Arms

Dear Reader,

Thanks so much for reading *A SCANDALOUS PASSION* – I hope you enjoyed Caelie's and Spencer's story. There is nothing quite so sexy as a redeemed rake. I enjoyed writing Spencer the minute he leapt onto the page in AN INVITATION TO SCANDAL, and rest assured, this is not the first time he'll pop up in the series! And Caelie proved a wonderful counterbalance to his wayward ways. Steady and lovely, but with a hidden strength not often noticed behind her quiet demeanour. Until one needs it, which, inevitably, Spencer will.

I do hope you will check out and enjoy the rest of *THE SINS & SCANDALS SERIES*.

Next up, is *A SINFUL TEMPTATION*, and what can be more tempting than falling deeply in love with someone you know you cannot have. Especially when there is a dark secret lurking in your past. A secret that could destroy everything.

To keep up to date on what's new, upcoming releases, sneak peeks on cover reveals, and to be entered into contests, please visit my website at www.kellyboyce.com and sign up for my newsletter.

If you enjoyed this book, please consider leaving an honest review at your favorite retailer. It is always appreciated!

All the best!
   Kelly

Acknowledgments

I think the biggest acknowledgement needs to go to my amazing husband. During the writing of this book, I was under several tight deadlines with nothing in the way of wiggle room. This meant early mornings wake-ups, weekends spent down in the dungeon (aka, my office), or taking off to the local coffee shop for the day, all in an effort to meet said deadlines. This left my husband to do the bulk of the dog-walking, supper cooking, housework, etc. Not once did he complain. Instead, when I was pulling out my hair because my characters were refusing to cooperate, he simply asked, 'Is there anything I can do?' So, to my real-life hero, thank you. You make my life, not only easier, but a complete joy. I can think of no one else I would want to walk through this life with.

To my Mom and Dad for all your support, not just now, but in the early years as well. Neither one of you ever batted an eye when I said I was going to be a writer when I grew up, instead you encouraged me and continue to do so. Best. Parents. Ever.

To my older brother, Craig – a natural born storyteller if there ever was one. Thanks for saying nice things about me to your friends. Yeah, they talk. You're busted.

To my younger sister, Alyson – if anyone is going to change the world, you will. Thanks for not letting me take myself too seriously (is that even possible in our family?). Keep the laugh-track coming.

And as always, to my sanity saving crew – Julianne MacLean, Cathryn Fox and Pamela Callow. You ladies are an amazing inspiration. I cherish our friendship and our regular dinners!

Anne MacFarlane and Annette Gallant – every second Sunday you gals kept me in line and on track. Thanks for sharing the journey. Here's to a long road ahead.

Nancy Cassidy – this one landed in your lap in kind of rough shape. Thanks for helping me mould it into something much more readable! I promise to keep working on those *was* statements.

To Michelle Helliwell – thanks for the links on travel times. You are a wealth of information. I plan on picking your brain more in the future. Fair warning.

To Kim Killion and Amy Atwell – my cover design and formatting gurus. Love you gals and your teams!

And to Cedar – comic relief is golden.

About the Author

Kelly Boyce started writing stories in Grade 2 when her favorite teacher, Mrs. Matheson, showed up with a box filled with plot ideas and she was immediately hooked. But it wasn't until she read Lisa Gregory's *Bitterleaf* that she fell in love with historical romance. Once she discovered Romance Writers of Atlantic Canada and learned how to turn those stories into books, it was full steam ahead.

A life-long Nova Scotian, Kelly lives near the Atlantic Ocean with her amazing husband and a clownish golden retriever with a stubborn streak a mile wide. She loves writing stories about relationships and creating a sense of community around the hero and heroine filled with secondary characters who take on a life of their own.

Along with *The Sins & Scandals Series*, she has also released several western historical romances . Check out the "Also By" for a full list!

Currently, she is hard at work developing a new three book series on the Lindwell Family, who were introduced in *The Sins & Scandals Series*.

Copyright

ISBN: 978-0-9936169-3-8

Cover design: Kim Killion
Editor: Nancy Cassidy